DARKENED DESIRES

Kings of Pointebreak Book 2

CARA WADE

Copyright © 2026 by Cara Wade

All rights reserved.

No part of this publication may be reproduced, distributed, or transmitted in any form or by any means, including photocopying, recording, or other electronic or mechanical methods including AI training, without the prior written permission of the publisher, except as permitted by U.S. copyright law. For permission requests, contact Cara Wade at cara@author carawade.com.

The story, all names, characters, and incidents portrayed in this production are fictitious. No identification with actual persons (living or deceased), places, buildings, and products is intended or should be inferred.

Morally gray? Sign me up.

ONE
ZANDER

"Wes," her quiet, breathy moan pulls me up short. Lucas is blocking the path. It looks like Wesley wanted some privacy, but also his exhibitionist side got the better of him. I know he gets off on being watched, just like I get off from watching. We're both a little fucked up in our own ways, but it seems to work. Even though we have similar tastes regarding kinks, we've never been in the same room while fucking someone. He's been doing me a solid and messing around with Riley in front of cameras where he knows I'm watching, or will review the footage later. I'm sure if the opportunity arose we would take it though. And what better night than tonight? Arousal courses through my veins as I hear her hushed pants of need. He's making her feel good, which means she'll be more willing to play if she sees me.

"How many people does he have around the perimeter?" I ask, standing directly in front of Lucas, taking in his dark clothes and bright white earbuds hanging from his lobes. He's not listening to Wesley and Riley, and a jolt of possessiveness courses through me. I hope the others stationed around are as smart as Lucas.

"Five," he answers without hesitation.

"How long?"

"For two hours or until one of us sees him."

I hear Wesley's groan, and I know it won't be much longer now. I nod to Lucas and walk past him. The guys know that if any of us hires them, all three of us may pass. Where one goes, we all go. That's the only way this works. Secrets among friends get people killed. And while we all carry secrets about our lives and our pasts, that doesn't extend to anything we do now.

"That's it, Riley. Fuck yourself on my cock. You're taking it like such a good fucking girl," Wes grits out. Mmm, I'm sure she does. Even from my few stolen kisses, I know she is absolutely perfect. I'm closer now, and while darkness cloaks them, it's difficult to miss two people fucking in the middle of the grassy area. She's on top of him, her hands resting on his chest as her hips move on him. She's still in school uniform, and she looks like a wet dream come true. Any man who doesn't admit to the schoolgirl fantasy is lying to himself.

She slows, casting a glance in my direction. I'm too far away for her to spot me in the dark; but I pause, wanting her to continue.

"Don't worry about them. It's dark now. They won't know it's us," he reassures her.

Wesley has to know it's me. It's the only reason I can think of why he hasn't stopped yet. I know he likes public displays, but it's different with Riley. He doesn't do PDA with her—the gym excluded. But he knows I'm the only one who has seen them. If I noticed anyone close by on the cameras, I'd warn him.

"God, you're beautiful. I can't wait to come deep inside you."

I bite my index finger knuckle to trap my groan of frustration. I've been turned on since I heard her moan Wes's name a few minutes ago, but hearing him talk about coming inside her makes me rock fucking hard. It's exactly what I want to do. I want to come deep inside her like he does. I still haven't figured out what it is about Riley that drives me insane, but she does. I want her more than I've ever wanted anyone.

I breathe deeply through my nose, and the scent of sex and the crisp night fills my senses. She looks breathtaking sitting on top of him. Her blouse is still on, but a few buttons have fallen open, and her skirt falls around Wesley's waist.

Stunning.

"Wes, I-I'm close," she pants, and a devilish smirk stretches across my face. God, I wish she were sitting on my cock. Tonight is the true test. Is she going to clam up, or is she going to accept it, accept me along with Wes? I continue closer and closer while they exchange a few more words, but I don't pay enough attention to their voices.

I push on my hardening cock. I came not too long ago, but jacking myself isn't the same as fucking a woman. Finding play partners here is easier than you'd think. I guess that's the perk of being a King of Pointebreak. Almost every girl jumps at the chance to be tied down and flogged, or played with like nothing more than a live doll. I found a kink partner, and that helps ease some of my needs, but I'm never fully satisfied. I may play with crazies, but I never fuck them.

The women around here aren't ones you mess with unless you're willing to put a ring on it or make a deal. Most marriages are for a business need, and an acquisition of sorts to unite families. True love surfaces occasionally, but that makes it more uncommon.

"That's it, baby. You're squeezing me so damn tight. I can't wait to come deep inside you," Wesley groans. I step into view, stopping at the top of Wesley's head, and stare down at them. She looks up, her big gray eyes full of questions, but darkened by a haze of lust. God, I want to watch her come in person. I've seen it enough times on video, and have heard it through the walls, but that's not the same. I fucking need her. Riley is mine after tonight. I don't give a shit. I can't keep denying myself the one person I want most of all.

"Come for him, Luna," I command, knowing she loves being told what to do. She can deny it all she wants, but I've watched too many god-damned hours of her to know better. I can read her like a book now. Her eyes travel down my body and stop at my dick. It's tempting to take it out and let her have a taste. But Wesley thrusts into her, and her body stiffens before she comes on a low moan, her body relaxing enough for him to flip them so she's on her back under him.

She reaches her hand out toward me, and I drop to my knees, sucking her finger into my mouth. She tastes sweet and slightly salty, probably a mix of the forgotten food amongst the blanket.

"Rub your pretty little clit and come again," I demand. She complies, her fingers snaking their way between their bodies as I watch, her gaze bouncing between the two of us. She doesn't know what to make of this. Hell, I'm not sure I do either. This is unfamiliar territory for us all.

"She's in her own head, Wes. Better change it up if you want her to come again." I can't help but give a little dig. What are friends for, after all?

"If you hadn't shown up, she would have come all over my dick again by now."

He pulls out, and I can't help but notice the shine of her juices on his hard cock as he pulls her panties down her legs and tosses them. Helping her flip onto her knees, he pulls her hips back to enter her again, then drags her up so her back is flush to his chest. My eyes travel to her panties, and the idea of taking yet another pair as a trophy makes my lips twitch in a barely there smile before focusing all my attention on her again. She looks gorgeous like this. Eyes heavy, swollen lips, and her mascara runs down her face just a touch. She must have sucked him off before I showed up.

"Kiss her, Zan. She needs you."

I hesitate, not wanting to break the spell we seem to be under. Her body moves with each of his thrusts, and I know the moment she decides she wants both of us. I grasp her chin between my thumb and forefinger, bringing my lips close to hers, barely brushing them.

"Daddy," falls from her pouty lips as her eyes close and her hands fall to my shoulders to steady herself.

It's the only invitation I need. I press my mouth against hers, my tongue exploring as I slide my large hand down the slender column of her throat. Her pulse drums steadily against my fingertips as she moans into me. My Luna likes it dirty. I've had a feeling. She really is perfect for me.

"I-I," she pants, and I squeeze her throat, cutting off some of her air as she bounces against Wesley, her body no longer under her control. He groans, and she matches him; their noises filling the space between us. Her head falls back, and Wesley whispers in her ear, prolonging her climax.

I stand and walk away, leaving the two of them to their private moment once again.

This is not how I expected the night to go. Riley is absolutely incredible. Not that I would have expected otherwise, but the way she responded to me tonight was more than I could have hoped for. She's been driving me crazy for weeks, parading around campus in the stupid skirt she has to wear that makes me want to rip it off every time I see her. Or how she works her way under my skin. I hate to admit how much I enjoy our tête-à-têtes.

But she chose Wesley, and I was willing to watch from a distance; but after tonight, I won't have to. I'm already planning how I'm going to corrupt my little Luna. I'm going to show her all the depraved things I know she'll crave. The fantasies run rampant in my head as I drive back home to watch them through the cameras once again. I've almost finished the code to upload everything to my phone so I can watch whenever I want. No more rushing home to catch glimpses of her, or secretly listening in on conversations through her phone.

Before running into them, I dropped some gauze and Vaseline off in her room, thanks to the key I had made from Wesley's copy, and then went to my meeting. Wesley told me her wrists got a bit ripped up today during her class, so I ran to the store to get them, along with a few other things—rope, duct tape, and lube. You know, the basics. I thought I had worked out a lot of my needs, but the moment I heard her breathy moans, my insatiable hunger for her flooded back. It's like the past hour locked in that room didn't exist.

I'm stuck in my head as I climb the stairs to my room. Julien's door is open, so I duck inside, but he's not there. The bathroom door is closed, so I leave and go back to my room. I'm not exactly sure what I would tell him anyway. Riley isn't who you think she is? She's fucking perfect for me and I want her as much as Wesley? We need her; I know that, and this entire plan is slippery at best. It's only going to work if she helps. Although Julien doesn't agree—the fewer who know, the better.

I'm sitting at my desk, staring at the camera feeds when Wesley comes up the stairs a few minutes later, and I want to ask him questions. He stops at my door, and I turn away from the screens I'm staring at to look at him. He smiles and winks, like the asshole he is.

"She didn't want you to leave, you know," he says. My heart leaps at those words. Did she say that? I blink at him, waiting for him to elaborate, my face void of all emotion. "She stayed pretty quiet on the walk back to the dorm. I'm sure it was a mixture of things."

"Hmm," I offer as I nod my head.

"I'm not telling you what to do, but she was into it tonight—the two of us." He gestures in the space between us. "She clamped down on my dick so hard when you showed up." He grins widely. "Plus, you know I love an audience. Maybe it could be fun to try something more. Just putting that out there."

He leaves, closing the door behind him. No doubt to take a shower after his time with Riley. I pick up my phone to text her, but put it back down. She needs some time to think about tonight, to decide if she really wants this. No matter what happens, she's stuck with us. So why not have a little fun along the way?

I lean back in my chair, memories of the night filling my head, and decide to take a shower so I can take care of my growing need and get my head screwed back on straight. She's like an addiction, consuming my every thought.

Riley Whittier, you'd better be prepared. I'm coming for you, and I always get what I want.

TWO

JULIEN

"We've got a problem," Zander yells from his room. Wes and I are in the kitchen and look at one another, then bolt up the stairs, taking them two at a time. I push Zan's door open with enough force that it bounces off the stop and comes back toward my face. Nothing riles Zander, and if he's yelling out for us, whatever he sees is huge. I look at his bright computer screens, and blackened squares I know should show a live stream from security cameras staring back at us.

"Someone cut the camera feeds by the dorms, and specifically the one in Riley's hall. She's not answering her phone."

"When did cameras go out?"

"Five minutes ago." Zander clicks some buttons and cycles through the cameras around campus. "I was in the shower and came back to this." The feeds around classroom buildings are still live, showing the dead campus. It's only the ones around Riley's dorm that are out.

Wesley immediately pulls his phone from his pocket, dials her number, and places it to his ear. He runs his fingers through his hair as he paces behind Zander, who is still furiously clicking through screens and typing away. I hear the faint ring on the other line before her voicemail picks up. He hangs up with a low growl and dials another number. I hear a female voice on the other end.

"Ava, where are you? Is Riley with you?"

"No. Wes, what's going on?" her muffled voice comes through the speaker placed to his ear.

"Where is she?" I grit out, annoyance lacing my words.

Wesley looks at me, then down at the ground before lowering his voice. "Are you with Nick?" He pauses and then says, "Stay where you are. Don't go anywhere alone and don't go back to your dorm." He forces out a deep breath. "I don't know. Zan will call you later. Stay put."

He hangs up and pockets his phone, running his hands through his hair as he paces the room. He bounces looks between the two of us. If anything happens to her, he will not be the same. Neither of them would be. I've been watching them with her and she's dug her way under their skin. Wesley is obvious; and also he's been fucking her. I'm going to ignore the twinge of jealousy that hits every time I think of them together. And Zander does what he does best…watches. As far as I know, nothing has happened between them, but I could be wrong. I haven't asked.

But he's been more obsessed lately. This is different. He's always watching for obvious signs of danger for us, now his sister, but his obsession with Riley is going to his head. He's more irritable, constantly glued to his monitors or sneaking out to let off some steam. Although right now, maybe that's a good thing. If he hadn't been watching the feeds or listening in, we wouldn't have known she was missing until it's too late. I hope it's not already too late. Five minutes doesn't seem like a long time, but that's long enough to hide a body and smuggle them off campus.

"I don't know where she is. She doesn't have her phone,

so I can't trace her location. And the little bit of conversation I could pick up from her cell phone speakers, she knows who came to her door but didn't say his name," Zander answers as he continues to type furiously on the keyboard.

"His?" I ask through clenched teeth. Who the fuck do I need to strangle? We've kept her away from almost everyone around here. I know from the terse conversation Wesley had with Ava that it wasn't Nick who came knocking on her door. Good thing too. Zander already wants to kick his ass for dating his little sister, but I'm not sure we could stop him if Nick did something to Riley. Zander's been after Nick's parents' money, and he won't get it if he harms their son.

Zander nods and pulls up the recording. The voices are low and muffled, barely audible, but I can make out her distinct voice, and my muscles tighten involuntarily. I clench my jaw and focus on breathing like normal. After listening for a minute, the male voice speaks louder, and the words are crystal clear. "...It will prove to you that they don't care..."

Don't care? I know without a doubt that whoever this asshole is, is talking about us. I may not care for her the same way Wesley does, or even the twisted way Zander wants her; but that doesn't mean I don't care. If only she knew the power she held over the three of us. How important she is to getting exactly what we've been working for over the past several years. The wheels are in motion now, with no one to stop them.

"Give me her room key." I hold my hand out, palm up, waiting for Wesley to comply. He's been training her for a few weeks and shows up every morning by letting himself into her room. I almost made my own, but thought better of it. I know Zander has one too. He made a copy from Wesley after he found out and ripped him a new asshole for making one. Not because it was for Riley's room, but because Ava lives with her and he would do damn near anything to protect his sister—even from his best friend.

Without hesitation, Wes hands me a small keychain with a silver key attached to the end. I snatch it out of his hand and I'm out the door before anyone can stop me. I run down the stairs and out the front door. It slams hard behind me with the force I pulled it closed. I run, knowing the path to her dorm like the back of my hand. This isn't the first time I've come this way. I've watched her outside her dorm like a fucking stalker. Not wanting her, but somehow not able to have her out of my sight. I don't care. Despite how much I hate that she's here, I can't stand the idea of something happening to her. Like tonight. She's ours.

How the fuck are we going to protect her? Trouble seems to find her and digs its claws in. Maybe Wesley needs to include more in his training—like how to stab a pen through someone's jugular. Faster and faster. My feet pound the uneven ground beneath me as the sound of crunching leaves infiltrates my senses. The trees blur past me as my heart pounds so hard in my chest that it feels like it will burst through at any moment. Even in the dark, I see the trees clearing straight ahead. I'm close to her dorm now. I'm not sure what I'm hoping to find—maybe a practical joke or something—but I need answers.

I push through the last branches as I slow to a walking pace. Breathing hard, my heart pounds in my chest, and my lungs ache. I look around for any signs of life, my discomfort pushed aside for the bigger issue. The building in front of me showcases lights on various levels, with students inside. I look up to her room, and the lights are on, but there is no movement. Jogging up the steps, I walk into the building and make my way up to her room. I get a few curious glances from people milling around in the halls, but no one stops me or comments. I guess it's even easier to take someone from these dorms than I thought. Looking the other way is all these people know. Not that I blame them. It's the life we live. Those who see things get killed. Even on a campus that isn't supposed to harbor those darker parts of our worlds, that doesn't mean other stuff hasn't happened.

Her door is ajar when I arrive, and I push it open, half expecting someone to be there waiting for me. It could have been a ploy to get one of us, or all three of us, here. It wouldn't be the first time in Pointebreak's history that students have attacked one another. Riley's phone sits on her bed and vibrates when I enter. Wesley's name flashes across the screen, and I swipe the answer button.

"She's not here. Her door was open when I arrived."

"Shit."

Yeah, shit. I look around her room. There's a lamp by the door lying on its side. Other than that, and a few random clothes tossed on the foot of her bed, nothing is amiss. Tilting my head to the side, I look down into the trash can and notice some gauze and Vaseline sitting on top. Why is that in the trash? I told her to put it on her wrists to help heal the raw marks. Wesley or Zander must have dropped it off for her tonight. A quick glance around shows me nothing else is out of place.

"No one's here. It doesn't even look like he came into her room; everything is in place. Cameras back on?"

"Yeah. They popped back on two minutes after you left, so either whoever turned them off turned them back on, or security fixed them," Wesley adds. "Julien, there's a plumbing van that left campus a few minutes ago. Zander found it as he was cycling through the feeds."

While a plumbing van isn't necessarily a cause for alarm, with Riley missing it raises the hair on the back of my neck. This looks more and more like a setup, and I don't like it.

"Make sure he finds out everything he can about that damn van. I'm gonna knock on some doors to see if anyone heard anything."

I pocket her phone, taking it with me. Those who answer their doors on her floor tell me they have seen nothing and heard nothing. I'm sure someone screaming would have set off a few alarm bells, so whoever took her kept her quiet. Smart. But when I find out who this fucker is, I'm going to murder him. No one takes what's mine without suffering.

My heart pounds as I take one more look at her building before making my way down the stairs and outside. Looking at the ground, I search for anything dropped or that may leave a clue, but the area is clean. I don't even know what to be looking for, or who to look for, so it's not like I actually expected to find anything.

A girl with dark hair steps outside and freezes when I turn my icy stare on her. I narrow my eyes in recognition. She's in our survival class. I've watched Riley talk with her before. I clench my jaw, my back teeth aching from the pressure.

"What?" I growl when she doesn't speak, causing her to jump in surprise. Timid thing. This school is going to eat her alive if she doesn't toughen up. Even in class she does fine, but it takes a lot of effort on her part. Riley is more of a natural in that department.

"There were four of them," she says, keeping her hands to her sides and her distance from me. Probably a good idea. I must look like a bull in a china shop—crazy eyes and ready to break everything in my path.

FOUR? There's no way she'd be able to fight off four men. She might have a chance with one from all the training Wesley's been putting her through, but not four. Even if they were students, which I highly doubt, that means they are men who are at least twice her size and strength. If they made it onto campus undetected, they know what they are doing. It would be easy to overpower her.

I slowly cross my arms, giving her the impression I'm not phased, when that couldn't be further from the truth. "Who took her out of her room?"

She shakes her head and looks at her feet, wrapping her arms around herself. "I don't know, but I heard her scream before they put her in a white van."

"How long ago was this?"

She shrugs her shoulders. "Thirty minutes ago?"

I want to scream at her for not going for help when she saw something was amiss, but stand down. It doesn't matter. All that matters right now is tracking down that van and figuring out who set this up.

I pull my phone from my pocket and dial Wes. He picks up almost immediately. "Four men took her. Get all the information you can about that van. I want to know who it belongs to and what the fuck they were doing here."

"On it." He disconnects the call, and I turn to face the girl once more.

"Thanks, Chloe."

Her eyes shoot up to mine, probably surprised I know her name. Survival is a small class. I know everyone, even if I choose to ignore them. She offers a kind, sad smile and nods her head before turning and giving me her back, walking inside again. No one else is around, so I walk through the woods back home. Hopefully, Zander has something he can give me.

Thirty minutes is too long. They could have her anywhere by now. I know Zander can review the footage and hopefully get a license plate or something; but this is bad. She's supposed to be safe here. Not from me, but from everyone else. And I sure as hell didn't put anyone up to this.

Riley's words from a few weeks ago come back to haunt me. *"Anyone ever tell you that you're an idiot, Julien? Or am I the first? You just gave every guy here a free pass to do what they want to me, to get to you!"* There are a lot of people here who would want to knock me down a few pegs. Hell, even someone involved in the underground fights; those betting or fighting. No easier way to beat someone than to fuck with them personally.

She's right, though. I didn't want to make this easy for her, and because of that, we're now in this situation. She should have stayed out of my way until I needed her. And as much as I want to blame her for it, I can't because she wanted to come here as much as I wanted her to.

I'm almost back at the house when my phone buzzes in my pocket. Scarboro's name flashes on the screen and I answer.

"Not a good time," I growl.

"There better be a damned good reason Riley Whittier is lying unconscious on my front doorstep."

My heart leaps into my throat as his words run through me and as a flood of relief washes over me. I pull up short, making sure I heard him correctly.

"Come again?"

"Alarms started going off around my property, and when I pulled up the cameras, I saw her stumbling through the woods. She all but landed on her face on my front porch. Looks like someone was chasing her. You wouldn't know anything about that now, would you?"

"We'll be there soon. Keep her there," I demand.

He snorts. "She isn't going anywhere for a while. Passed out hard. Must have taken something."

Or someone forced her to take something. "This isn't us. We'll be right there."

I open a text to the guys.

ME:

> She's at Scarboro's house, drugged, but alive. Get the car started; I'm on my way back now.

THREE

RILEY

Voices surround me, but my limbs feel like lead; I can barely move an inch. My mouth is drier than the Sahara desert, and my head throbs. Jesus, it feels like someone put me into a blender and spat me out again. The details of how I got here are a little foggy, but I know that will change soon. I'd kill for some aspirin or something right now. Anything to dull the pain lancing through my battered body.

I groan and manage to roll to my side, my arm falling off the side of the couch, brushing the floor. At least whoever found me took the handcuffs off. As my mind slowly wakes, the pain in every part of my body becomes more prominent. My wrists throb, along with my face and legs. What a hell of a night. I would rather succumb to the effects the drugs have on me, but I know I have to get up, eventually.

Wesley's gentle hands are on my back, rubbing soothing circles on it. "She's waking up," I hear him whisper. Thank God for small miracles, because if he had yelled, I think I might have killed him. Footsteps enter the room, and it's more than one set. If Wesley is here, that means Julien and

Zander are with him. They never do anything by themselves. Well, almost never. It seems fucking is something they don't share.

"Riles, can you hear me?" he asks as his hand brushes my cheek, tucking hair behind my ear. "Fuck, that looks bad," he says, and I know he's looking at my face and head. Even though I only remember a little of tonight, I can't forget being smacked upside the head with the butt of a gun. I can only imagine how it looks, because my face feels massively swollen. Fresh tears sting my eyes.

I attempt to swat at him, but I can't get my arm to move. It's still deadweight under me. It must be the aftereffects of the drugs they forced me to take. Why are the Kings here? Shouldn't my dad be here? Surely someone called him.

"Finally," another voice comes into the room, and I would recognize Julien's timbre anywhere. The fucking bastard set me up. My heart beats against my chest like a drum, as blood rushes through my ears, drowning out everything else around me. My stomach twists in knots, and I fight the urge to puke all over the floor.

"Go. Away," I manage to mumble through my dry lips. It's not as loud or confident as I'd like, but I'm proud of myself for even getting the words out. Tears fall from my eyes and land on the soft fabric beneath my head. Curling into a fetal position, I wrap my arms around myself, thankful for the blanket covering me. I stay as silent as possible, my body trembling with the effort. I know Wesley can feel it.

"You're safe, Riley. Can you sit up?"

"Fuck, that looks bad," Zander says, no doubt seeing my face.

As I become more alert, memories flood back. The four men, the woods, the chase; all of it. I begin dry heaving, and someone shoves a bucket under my face just in time for me to lean over the side of the couch and toss the contents of my stomach. Wesley pushes my hair back out of my face and helps me to a sitting position once I've got myself under control. My head swims, and dizziness takes hold of me, threatening to make me throw up once again.

He sits next to me and continues to rub my back. I don't have the energy to stop him, so I allow it, for now. I drop my head back against the cushion, closing my eyes, focusing on what happened and what almost happened. It was dumb luck that Mr. Scarboro had a house out this way and that I found it—barely. If I had passed out in the woods, those men would have raped me, and who knows what else. More drugs? Wounds? Who knows what those bastards would have done.

I was going to be sold. Used until I was of no use anymore. I would imagine the desperate, vile men who purchase another human also thrive off inflicting as much pain as they can. One can only hope they are shitting themselves for thinking they can play with me but ended up losing me instead. I stiffen as Wesley's hand lingers on my back. Even though his touch is reassuring, he's part of the reason I'm in this situation.

I turn my cold, hard stare on him. "Don't touch me," I whisper and shift to avoid his reach. Pain crosses his features before he pulls his arm back and away from me.

"What happened?" Julien demands.

I shift my steely gaze up to him and lock my jaw, forcing the need to cry down. He doesn't get my tears. Not anymore. I refuse to kneel to him, refuse to bend.

"What happened is you set me up, Julien!"

Zander and Wesley snap their heads in his direction in surprise. Almost as if they can't believe he would do something like this. It's the only thing that makes sense, though. Why else would anyone want to get rid of me? Julien hates me. He makes that apparent every chance he gets. I still have no clue what made him so angry, or what I did. So what better way to deal with a problem, then to get rid of it? He already has Wesley's dad as an easy contact, and I know Mr. Bastian is in the skin trade business. The only part of this whole thing I haven't figured out is why use Derek of all people?

He shakes his head. "This wasn't me."

I scoff, unable to believe him. "Yeah, right." I shake my head. "Go away. I know you were in my room last night." They all look at me like I'm crazy, and maybe I am. Nothing about this night is normal. Or early morning? I don't even know what time it is. "Leave me the hell alone." I stand and fall back down on the couch, my legs unable to hold my weight. Wesley's arms come around my waist, helping guide me to the sitting position again.

"Why did Mr. Scarboro call you and not my dad?" To be honest, I'm glad he didn't call my dad, considering how we ended our last conversation. But he is still my dad, and they kidnapped me from campus! Then a thought hits me—maybe Mr. Scarboro called, and he refused to come. That sinking feeling has me wrapping my arms around myself again.

"None of your concern; just be glad he did."

Just be glad he did? What a load of shit. My anger flares up once again. I can't control myself around Julien. He makes me want to punch the living shit out of him!

"Right. So, then what happened to me is also none of your concern. Great conversation. There's the door." I toss my hand out toward the front of the house, my eyes never leaving his. When he refuses to move, I yell, "Go!"

He narrows his eyes at me. "We're not leaving until you answer our questions," he retorts, the muscles in his jaw working overtime. He keeps balling his fists, the veins in his forearms popping with the strain. Good. I'm glad I make him as mad as he's making me. I hope he pops a filling with all that teeth-grinding. Anything to ugly up his perfect looks.

"Why, so you can have me kidnapped again and sold to Wesley's dad to be a sex slave? Make sure they do it right this time?" I seethe; the venom dripping from my lips.

"I told you I wanted nothing to do with that life, Hellcat," Wesley interjects, the sting of rejection echoing in his voice. Some of my bravado fades, and I slump my shoulders. I know he doesn't, and I know it was a cheap shot, but there's no way he doesn't see how twisted this whole situation is. Who the hell would try to get rid of me? The only enemies I've made here are Julien and Derek. And I wouldn't have an issue with Derek in the first place if it weren't for Julien. So it all circles back to him.

I turn my head slowly to look at Wes. "How much do you trust him?" I jerk my chin in Julien's direction, and he narrows his green eyes at me again in anger. His head is going to explode soon if I keep this up. "How much do you trust the words that come out of his mouth?"

"With my life," Wes says without missing a beat. My chest aches at his confession.

I look at Zander, who nods in agreement. "This isn't Julien, Wes, or me. Someone else set you up, and we need to figure out who and why," he adds, his dark eyes roaming my face. I assume he's assessing me for injuries, and I let the blanket slowly slide away, leaving my bare stomach and bra exposed beneath the torn sweatshirt. Every scrape and bruise from running blind through the woods suddenly feels loud under his gaze, my skin aching where his attention lingers.

My throat burns as I swallow hard. I point toward the door, my hand shaking. I drop it quickly, hoping none of them notice. "Those men were hunting me down like a fucking animal. They were going to rape me and then sell me. They called me merchandise." I grit out, attempting to get my point across.

Tears stream down my face as my chin trembles. "If I hadn't found my way here, I-I.." I cover my mouth and squeeze my eyes shut, letting the river of tears flow down my cheeks, not bothering to hide them any longer. If they see me as weak, so be it.

Gentle hands grab my shoulders, and I push out of his grasp, my face hardening in anger. "Don't fucking touch me," I scream at Wesley. Hurt flashes across his beautiful blue eyes, the eyes that held so much passion for me only hours ago. I want to take the words back; but I can't. I pull the ripped edges of my sweatshirt tight around me and run down the hall, thankful when I find the bathroom, slamming the door behind me and locking it as I slide down and land on my butt, my back pressing against the dark, cool wood.

My heart hammers against my ribs. My chest burns, a furious knot tightening with every shallow gasp, fueling the rage that threatens to consume me. Quick breaths are all I can manage as I fight the panic attack. Shouting comes from the living room, but I can't comprehend what anyone is saying. It all sounds like gibberish as I place my head on my knees and cover my ears, blocking out as much as I can. Tears fall freely as I rock, letting my attack pull me under. For the first time in my life since the panic attacks started, it's not so scary. It's numbing, and right now, I welcome that over the torturous thoughts my mind is conjuring up.

"Julien, now's not the time. Make some calls; I'll keep her safe. I have cameras around, so if anyone tries to get to her, they'll have to go through me. I'll come up with something to tell the school so she can lie low for a few days and no one should suspect anything," Mr. Scarboro says.

"Dorian," Julien warns.

His name breaks the haze, and I snort. I never would have pegged Mr. Scarboro as a Dorian. And since when does he take orders from Julien, anyway? I groan and drop my head back against the door. It shouldn't surprise me that they're working together. Who doesn't Julien have under his thumb here?

The rest of their conversation fades as they walk away from the door. The stress of the evening, along with the drugs, has me feeling strange, and I just want to go to sleep and pretend none of this ever happened. I turn on the faucet in the bathroom, take a long drink, and splash the cold water on my face. I peek into the mirror to assess the damage and cringe at the purple mark that's forming. My face is swollen, and it hurts like a bitch, even without touching it, but I don't think anything is broken. When I finally emerge a while later, Mr. Scarboro is standing there with a set of clothes and some towels. I look over his shoulder, expecting one of the guys to be there.

"They left. I told 'em to go home. Julien brought your cell for you." He hands the clothes, towels and phone to me, and I stare at them, unsure what he wants me to do.

"Shower and change. I have a spare room you can stay in for a few nights until we get everything figured out." I nod. "Wanna talk about it?" I shake my head, lowering my eyes to the ground in shame.

No, I don't want to talk about how I was going to be raped and sold. I don't want to talk about how easy it was for Derek to get me out of my room and into that fucking van. I'm angry at myself for not fighting harder, for not trying more. Sure, I kicked the guy in the leg, but what did that do? Nothing but piss him off. They still got me in the van and off campus easily enough. I wrap my arms around myself and swallow hard, shaking my head once more.

"Didn't think so."

I turn, planning on heading back into the bathroom when his words stop me.

"You know, you're gonna have to tell them everything, including who took you."

Looking at him, I narrow my eyes. "I don't need to tell them anything." I slam the door behind me and flinch at the noise.

Mr. Scarboro chuckles on the other side of the door. "Let's see how long you can hold out."

I'm not even sure what that means, or why he called them. I wish I had asked him why he didn't call my dad instead of slamming the door on him, but maybe it's for the best. There will be time tomorrow for answers. I pull the ripped pieces of material off my arms and toss them into the trash. Then, I undo my bra and pull my jeans down my legs and kick them off in a corner of the bathroom. I turn the water on hot and wait for it to heat before stepping under the spray. It's scalding, but I don't care. I let it wash away all traces of the evening as I let my mind go numb once again.

I wake to the sun streaming in through the open curtains and throw my arm over my eyes, protecting them from the light. A glance at my phone tells me it's already seven-thirty, and I'm starving. I slowly make my way into the kitchen, not sure what to expect, and Mr. Scarboro is sitting at the counter with a mug of coffee, scrolling through his phone. He looks up as I enter, giving me a quick assessment.

"Mornin'," he greets.

"Morning," I reply, offering a small wave. I feel so awkward standing in the middle of his kitchen wearing his clothes. "Um, thanks again for last night," I say awkwardly.

He nods. "You're lucky you found me."

"Yeah," I trail off. The silence between us is deafening.

The longer it stretches, the more awkward I feel. "Did you, um, did you call my dad?" I ask. It's the one question I had racing through my mind last night. I would have figured if he was called that he would have reached out to me by now to check in.

"No. You're eighteen. He doesn't need to know unless you call him."

I sit, slumping down into my seat. That answer shouldn't surprise me as much as it does. I figured if anything happened, the student's parents were called and informed. Not that it matters, I suppose. What's he going to do about it anyway? Nothing. He doesn't care. Tears fill my eyes, and I wipe them angrily.

"Riley—"

"Thanks for letting me stay here and for the change of clothes. I'd like to head back to my dorm and get to class. I don't want to be any later than I already am going to be. Can you give me a ride?"

He tilts his head, examining me. "No."

I jerk back at his response. "No?"

He shakes his head. "No. You're staying here for a few days. Someone will swing by with your personal items, and Zander is working on getting you and Ava a new room. You'll stay here until then."

"Mr. Scarboro—"

"Riley. It's not up for discussion. I'll figure something out with the school. Stay here. And for the love of God, don't go outside. Think of it as a mini-vacation."

He stands, puts his empty coffee mug in the dishwasher and slams it closed before leaving me alone once again.

What the hell is going on?

FOUR

ZANDER

"I don't give a shit," I growl into the phone. "My sister and her roommate aren't safe there. Someone broke in last night, so you *will* move them. You're lucky it wasn't more serious. Imagine if someone got wind of this story." The administration doesn't like that threat, especially because they walk a fine line between being in the town but pretending to be invisible.

"Mr. Fedorov, I'm telling you, we have nothing available for the first years."

I know how to read between the lines. "Then that means you have rooms meant for older students. Move them into one of those dorms. Hell, I don't care if they have to have separate ones. Make. It. Happen," I enunciate every word.

Fourth-year students don't have roommates, and they have en suite bathrooms in all the rooms. It's a nice setup, not better than the house of course, but it works. Even though the contract clearly states students must complete four years at the school, it doesn't mean there aren't some dropouts along the way. Often it's because of an arranged marriage, or someone taking over a family business after a death. Those spots then remain empty. No contract is ever truly binding if you know the loopholes.

She sighs, and I almost forgot she was still on the other line. "Zander," she whispers, "you know it doesn't work like that."

"Clarissa, you know I always get what I want. Are you really defying an order from your Sir?"

She squeaks on the other end of the line. "N-no, Sir." She sighs heavily again, and I know I'm putting her in a difficult situation. I saw her just hours before, and she let me tie her up and spank her until her ass was red and bruised. I hear her shift on the other side of the line, and I know it must be painful for her to sit down. She enjoyed it. I feel no remorse, even though I went harder on her than normal.

I found Clarissa in my second year here when I was going out of my mind with need. Not the need to fuck someone, but the need to own someone. To control every part of them. The internet is a wonderful thing. I found her through a play site, and it just so happened that she lived close by and applied for a job at Pointebreak.

Outsiders can only receive administrative positions. Few families want to work at a school as a secretary. There's a lot of vetting and paperwork, along with an NDA that needs to be signed, but there are still outsiders who want a job at Pointebreak regardless of the type of students who attend. Oh, there will always be those who apply for jobs because they are nosy little fucks, but they never get their chance.

I coached Clarissa on what to say, how to act, and how to dress so that she would get the job here. The work I put into her was purely for selfish reasons. I knew I would have easy access to her if she worked here, and I needed a fix. Playing with someone, pushing them to their limits and watching them fall over the edge because of my hand makes me instantly hard.

However, I've wanted to see her less and less since Riley arrived. Even when I had Clarissa hanging from the ceiling, all I could picture was Riley. She knew something was wrong because I've never sent her a text spur of the moment. Our sessions are always meticulously planned. I leave nothing to chance. She questioned me last night, and I gagged her instead, needing to work out some aggression on her instead of talking. I'm not a complete asshole though, and I stayed with her to bring her down from her high, along with giving her some snacks and cuddles. When she questioned me again, though, I told her I had to be somewhere. Then I ran into Riley and Wesley in the quad…

"Get them moved, even if they have to be in separate rooms. I know you can do it," I breathe. "Please, Clarissa. I don't know what I'd do if anything happened to my sister."

"And Riley?" she whispers.

My heart ticks up at the use of Riley's name. *Does she know?* Has she heard the rumors swirling around Pointebreak about Riley and the Kings? Does she even pay attention to that sort of thing?

"Riley too. She needs to remain safe."

She sucks in a shaky breath, and I know she's crying even without seeing her. "Clarissa," I warn in a sharp tone, not having time for her emotional outburst.

"Did I ever have a chance?"

No, she didn't. I never saw her as a permanent fixture in my life. She sure as hell wouldn't be able to handle the life I'm going to lead. She needs someone who can stay here and be the man she deserves. That's not me. Clarissa dreams of a three-bedroom house, a white fence, two kids, and the perfect husband who comes home to her every night. It just so happens that she enjoys more adventurous sex, but other than that, we have nothing in common. I can't commit to being what she needs.

"Get them moved. Today." I say, ignoring her question, and then hang up without allowing her another word. She'll do it. If not, I'll go up the chain of command until it happens.

This is one of the last conversations I'll have with her. I need to tell her we're through and her contact with me will cease, but she's not ready for that conversation yet. She has to get the girls moved into new rooms, and until she completes that, I'm keeping her close to me. She'll text as soon as it's done.

I walk into my class and sit down in my usual spot. Riley is still at Mr. Scarboro's house, hiding out. Mrs. Polnick walks into class, and when she notices the empty seat next to me, she shakes her head in disappointment.

"Let's pick up where we were yesterday," she begins, and I tune everything out. My phone burns a hole in my pocket. I want to text her and check in on her. She went through the wringer last night, and we will get to the bottom of it. Leaving Dorian's, I couldn't sleep—which isn't new for me, but it's never been this bad. I worked on coding all night and finished the damn app I had been slowly working on. Now, I'll have access to view her whenever and not have to worry that someone will hack into it.

Clarissa won't be able to get the girls together in a room, and it's going to break Ava's heart. She's really been enjoying having a roommate these past few weeks. But this is for the best. Which means as soon as I have her building and room number, I'll be installing cameras inside it to keep better tabs on her.

After we found Riley safe, I called Ava and made her come to the house to sleep for the night. Nick dropped her off, and as much as I hate her dating him, I'm glad he kept her safe. I'll play nice...for now. I'm watching him closer than he thinks to make sure he's treating her right. The first slip-up, and the guys and I will be on him instantly.

Who knows what would have happened to her if she had been in the room when the attacker came by. Would he have taken both of them? Killed Ava, so there were no witnesses? I clench my jaw and close my eyes, sucking in a deep breath through my nose to help calm me. Whoever the bastard is who did this is dead. I don't care about his fucking reason. No one goes after my sister or Riley.

Riley texted Ava this morning and told her not to worry. Relief washed over Ava's face when she got it, and the two of them went back and forth before she finally smiled over at me. I haven't told her what happened. I figure Riley can do that when she's ready to do it.

Way too many nefarious thoughts have been running through my mind, such as putting a tracker on Riley. It was dumb luck that she ended up where she did yesterday. And if she didn't…well, I don't even like thinking about that. Wes's dad sells girls. I've heard enough to know the type of situation she would have been in. Her only saving grace might be that someone would recognize her as Michael Whittier's daughter and use her for plain old blackmail.

I need to get out of my head. Casually, I place an AirPod in my ear and pull up the app that connects me to Riley's phone so I can listen in. I glance down at my screen and notice she's scrolling through social media. I look closer at the pictures that she's doom scrolling past and narrow my eyes, a familiar face looking back at me. What the hell is she doing looking at Derek's profile? Did he have something to do with her attack? I hear her growl and mutter something under her breath, but it's not clear enough to decipher. In frustration, she closes out of the app, swiping it completely closed.

She pulls up a new text thread to some girl named Leah

and starts typing that she wants to talk to her and deletes it. She does this three more times before sending nothing and closing it. I've heard her talk to another girl, and I assume it's a friend from high school.

I hear her opening cabinets and rummaging around, and I wish I had cameras on her to watch what she was doing. She's got to be bored out of her mind. I know Dorian told her to stay inside and not to leave the house. After last night, it would be a death wish if she disobeyed that order. There's no telling whether the four men are lurking around waiting for her or not.

Students pack their things and leave as class ends. Jesus, I'm really out of it today. I didn't even notice the time had gone by.

"Mr. Fedorov, a word," Mrs. Polnick calls out to me and cocks her finger in my direction.

I take my time packing up my laptop and meander to her desk. When the last student files out and the door closes behind him, she talks.

She points to Riley's usual seat. "Mr. Scarboro informed me Ms. Whittier had an accident last night." I nod, not elaborating. "I hope that's not of your doing."

I cock my head to the side, my eyes narrowing to slits. "Even if it were, why do you care?"

She sighs and shakes her head. "Be careful. Her father is more powerful than you think."

There's an interesting tidbit to store away for now. I figured Michael had been involved in some shady shit; how else would he have been able to get his daughter enrolled—last minute? I just hope he knows she will not go down without a fight, maybe to his disappointment.

"What do you know?" I ask, stepping closer to her desk. She stands, giving herself as much height as she can to match my own. I still tower over her, even in those three-inch heels of hers.

Students file in, and she gathers her things, acting as if the conversation is over. And I know it is, for now. We need some answers, and we need eyes on Michael. Walking out into the sunlight, I shield my eyes, looking for Wesley. I find him leaning against the wall, staring down at his phone. I know he's worried about Riley today. He's closer to her than any of us, and he's mentally kicking himself for what happened to her. It's not his fault. And I know he under-stands that, but he's not handling this well. My guess is it has something to do with what Riley said last night and bringing up his family. I know his isn't the only family who trades skin; hell, sex is a lucrative business. It's the fact that Riley tried to use it against him the first chance she got.

"Ready?" I ask. We are done with classes for now and are driving out to check on her. Wesley holds Dorian's key out for me to see, and I nod at him. Julien got a copy of it today, and we are planning on bringing a few personal items over. See if she'll open up and tell us a little more. If she tries to hide it, the truth will come out; it always does. Even if I have to tie her up and spank it out of her. And trust me, being able to play with her like that would be no skin off my back. For the first time today, a smile tugs at the corners of my lips. Riley's going to play, even if it's by force.

FIVE
WESLEY

Zander's quiet on the ride over to her dorm, not that I'm surprised. Unless he has something to share, he isn't one for small talk. I get it, but I also need an outlet for this pent-up energy. Normally I'd use the hanging bags we have in the basement, or get one of them to spar with me, but we don't have the time today. I don't want Riley to be alone longer than she has to be, even if she doesn't want us there.

We pull into a spot and get out, walking up to her dorm room. "Any luck in getting them moved?"

"Still working on it, but I'm sure I'll hear something soon. They might not be rooming together after this, though." I turn to look at Zander, confused. He waits until I get her room unlocked before continuing. "My connection is trying to get them into the upperclassmen dorms, and those are all singles. They are the only open rooms on campus."

I nod, understanding. Although I know him, cameras are going into that room without her knowledge so he can watch her. Julien already wanted them for her current room, but wouldn't ask Zander because of Ava. If they aren't sharing a room though, all bets are off. I look around the space, and nothing seems out of place. She made her bed, and everything is neat except for her uniform, which she threw haphazardly on top.

Opening her drawers, I pull clothes out of them. I don't love that she's been in Scarboro's clothes all day, and I'm sure she would rather wear something of her own. I almost drove back last night to drop off some of my clothes, but thought better of it. She needed some time to sort through what was going on in her head last night.

Jesus, I don't even know what happened. I walked her to her door, and within an hour Zander was telling us someone had cut the video feeds and she wouldn't answer her phone. The entire night came crashing down on me. Not only did I tell her about my brother and father's business, but she has it in her head that Julien went behind my back to her father. I know she doesn't understand our world, or how Julien operates, but he would never do that.

Julien is loyal. Maybe to a fault. I trust him with my life, and I know he would never go to her father of all people. Plus, her being taken and sold is the last thing any of us want. She's a means to an end, and I know Julien's not messing that up. Their problem is pure sexual tension, and if given the chance to fuck her, I'm sure his tune would change quickly.

Zander bends and picks up some stuff from her trash—gauze and some Vaseline. "I put this in her room yesterday after you told me her wrists needed some attention from the zip ties."

I scoff and run my hand over the top of my head. "Well, that explains why she thought Julien was in her room. I walked in on them after her class, and he was examining her wrists. Told me she needed to take care of them."

He nods and continues to search. If I had to guess, he's looking for some sort of camera or listening device because he picks up random items and examines them as if they hold a secret.

I shove the last of her personal items into a duffel bag I brought with me, and we lock the door as we leave. Zander pulls his phone from his pocket and looks at it before putting it away again.

"Done," he says. Looks like his contact moves quickly.

I sigh and nod. At least that's one less thing to worry about. "I'll drive." I know he's going to want to order whatever electronics he needs to get them set up before she moves in. We'll come back and pack her up. Normally we hire guys to do this kind of grunt work, but she doesn't have a lot of belongings with her. Plus, I don't want anyone else invading her privacy. The last thing she needs or would want is someone going through her things.

Dorian isn't there when we arrive, and I unlock the door, both of us stepping into the quiet space. It's too quiet, so I put the bag down as softly as I can. Both of us look at one another and then scan the room. He points down the hall toward the kitchen, and I nod, pointing at the stairs. I toe off my shoes, opting for as little noise as possible. I don't think anyone would be stupid enough to break into this house, but you never know. And since we don't know who took her, they could still be lurking around somewhere.

I grasp the brass doorknob and turn it slowly as I push the door open. Light bathes the room, but the furniture and decor are dark. It smells masculine in here, and I'd bet this is Dorian's room. I close it quietly behind me and find my way to the next closed door. I turn the knob just as slowly until I can peer into the room. The curtains are closed, and I see her lithe form resting in the middle of the bed with the covers down around her waist. Her blonde hair is sprawled around her head on the pillow, reminding me of a halo. She is fucking perfect. She shifts and turns to her side, unaware I'm even standing here.

I pull my phone from my pocket, sending a quick text to Zander that I've found her, and then put it away before taking a few steps closer. I know the moment she realizes she's not alone. Her breathing stops as she holds her breath and her body goes stiff.

"It's just me, Hellcat," I say in a hushed tone.

She blinks at me and sits up straight, pushing her hair out of her face. We stare at each other until Zander comes up behind me, and her eyes shift to him over my shoulder.

"W-what are you doing here?" Her voice wavers as she tries to keep control of it.

"We brought you some clothes and wanted to check on you," I say, taking a step closer. She scurries off the bed, keeping the piece of furniture as a barrier between us, and I can't help the ache in my chest that pulses. Just yesterday I was balls deep inside her, and she couldn't get enough of me. I don't like this scared version of her.

She licks her lips as her eyes dart around the darkened room. "Great. Thanks."

"We aren't gonna hurt you, Riley. We want to find out who is responsible for last night just as much as you do."

She nods vigorously and wraps her arms around herself. "Okay."

Zander steps in behind me and places his hand on my shoulder, stopping me from going to her. I know she doesn't want me in here, but I'm having a hell of a time leaving. She doesn't have to do any of this on her own. If she lets us in, we can help her. I need to help her. I was going out of my mind with worry last night. It felt like a cruel joke the universe was playing on me for all the shit my father's done. What a fucked-up twist of fate that someone was kidnapping her to sell her.

When she tossed her theory out there last night, it gutted me. She thinks so little of Julien that she believes he would go behind my back to my father, of all people, to get rid of her. My father hates that I'm friends with Julien. He's half the reason I won't be taking over the family business when I graduate from Pointebreak. Julien, Zander and I have our own plans, and they sure as hell don't involve selling women.

"Come downstairs when you're ready. We have a bag for you there. We need to talk," Zander says.

She shifts her eyes to him. Starting at his feet, and works her way until she's looking into his face. I glance behind me, his arms crossed in front of his chest. She nods once, and he turns, leaving us alone.

"Hellcat," I try once again to take a step toward her. She takes one step back, pressing her body into the wall behind her. I sigh and shake my head. "I wouldn't do that to you. Wouldn't allow anyone to do that to you. Believe me." I place my hands, palms up, in front of me. "If I had known something was going to happen, you never would have been left alone."

"I don't know what to believe, Wesley," she says in a whisper. "But Julien—"

"This isn't Julien's doing," I cut her off, and she jumps with the irritation lacing my words. "I know you think he hates you, but there is more to it than that."

She narrows her pretty eyes at me and licks her lips. She holds her body rigidly. "If you know so damn much, why don't you tell me, huh? What makes that man tick? Is he bipolar? Is that why he seems to have so many personalities?" She doesn't yell, but I know it takes a lot of effort for her not to. When I don't reply, she sighs, knowing I won't tell her anything. "I'll be down in a minute."

I leave, closing the door behind me, and meet Zander in the living room. He's looking at his phone and replies to a message before tossing it on the table and leaning forward, his elbows resting on his knees. Running his hands over his face and head, I know he's fighting exhaustion. He was up almost all night working on his computer. I saw him sitting in the kitchen at four this morning.

He sent us the app he created to watch Riley. I'm sure he's going to have to sync the new cameras up to it, but after that it will be good to monitor her whenever.

Riley stands at the bottom of the stairs, and we turn to face her. Zander points to the chair next to him. "Sit." She scoffs and rolls her eyes, but does as she's told, sliding into the seat. "What do you remember? Any detail can be important; try not to leave anything out."

"No." She lifts her chin.

I cock a brow and lick my lips, pulling the bottom one between my teeth before popping it back out. "No? Are you sure that's the answer you're going with?" I challenge.

Her face flushes, and she looks from Zander to me. I know what Zander's already thinking, and I'd love to be part of it. Spanking is his thing. I know he has someone he plays with from time to time. I've seen him leave the house with a duffel bag, and I know it's not gym clothes in there.

She shakes her head. "Please don't make me." A tear falls from her eyelashes and travels down her cheek before landing on her leg. She wipes her eyes with the hem of the shirt she's wearing and flinches when she knocks over the gruesome bruise that covers the upper part of her face.

"Riles, please," I soften. "We can't help if we don't know. This isn't us."

"You and Ava are being moved into new rooms with extra locks. If this were us, why would I go through the trouble of making sure you're both safe?" Zander reasons.

She bites her bottom lip and tips her head to the side, looking at him. Riley watches Zander like he's an anomaly.

When she still doesn't respond, he says, "Why were you looking at Derek's socials this morning?"

I glance at him, and even I want to know the answer to that question. She shouldn't have anything to do with that asshole. I thought Julien scared her enough that she wouldn't go near him again. I know she tried after everything in the woods went down, but he refused to talk to her, and as far as I know, that was the end.

Her jaw drops open, and she snaps it shut again, red staining her cheeks as she looks around the ceiling for cameras. "How the hell do you know that?" she demands.

"Doesn't matter. Is he the one who came to your room? Someone cut the camera feeds last night, but I still heard you on audio when you opened the door. I knew you recognized the person."

She stands, her body shaking. "How did you have audio if you didn't have video?" He opens his mouth, but she says, "And so help me, Zander, if you say it doesn't matter, I'm going to kick you."

A laugh bubbles out of me so loud that she stares at me. After seeing her so meek last night, this is a welcome change. This is my Hellcat. The one who won't go down without a fight.

"Yeah, Zan. Why is that?" I turn my attention to him, playing dumb just to see how he's going to handle this. A wide, teasing grin tugs at my lips, enjoying his moment of discomfort.

SIX

RILEY

Zander looks up at the ceiling, clearly annoyed at having to admit this, and blows out a breath. "Your phone."

My heart pounds in my chest, and the blood rushes through my ears. "My phone?" I echo his response. He nods once and doesn't elaborate. Not that he has to. It doesn't take a genius to figure out what he means. How long has he been listening? I've had private conversations with my dad and Leah. Conversations no one else should be privy to. It's such an act of deceit that I stand there dumbfounded, staring at them.

"When?" I spit out, standing from my seat to stare down at him.

"First weekend of school." He keeps his face neutral, and I want to smack him for it. I hate that he's so composed. Almost as much as I hate the invasion of my privacy.

I turn my glare to Wesley, and he looks like a kid in a candy shop, having a grand old time listening to this conversation. "You knew?" I scold.

He nods and gives me a big smile, wiggling his eyebrows.

He rests his ankle on top of his other knee and leans back in the chair, his hands behind his head as he relaxes. "I knew, Hellcat."

"And you didn't think that's something *I* should know? And why the hell are you smiling?" I stomp my foot, unable to contain my anger any longer.

"Not our fault you left your phone lying around one day to be picked up. Remember, I told you to always keep your phone with you."

My eyes widen, and I cover my mouth with my hands as my stomach drops. A wave of nausea churns in my stomach. "What else have you heard?"

"Zander's been having a hell of a time listening in on our training sessions. Right Zan?"

My face pales. *Please don't let him know anything about what I'm doing with Leah.* I've had very few conversations on the phone with her. Most information I've sent through email. However, if he has access to my phone, he has access to my email. I need to log out of it and respond to her only on my laptop.

I swallow. "Just my phone?"

Zander narrows his eyes at me and leans forward. "Why Luna? Got secrets you're trying to hide?" I shake my head furiously. "Smart girl. We'll always find out. Remember that. There's nowhere you can hide and nothing you can hide from us. Understood?"

I feel like a kid someone caught with her hand in the cookie jar. My head lowers to look at my toes and nod, understanding. "I don't like my privacy being invaded. Get rid of it."

"No."

I didn't think it would be that easy. It never is with these three. As soon as I give them an inch, they take a mile and demand more. Nothing should surprise me at this point. There's got to be someone on campus who can take the spyware off for me. I haven't gotten close to anyone at the school well enough to know yet. I bet Ava or Nick can find someone for me, though.

"Okay," I answer. I'll get a new phone. They don't need to know. I'll log out of my email and reach out to James or my dad, telling them my other one broke and I need a new one. They can't know what I'm working on with Leah. I don't know how they would react, but I know it's not something I want to find out. My eyes immediately land on Zander, and heat pools in my belly. I have a very good understanding of what *he* would do to me if he found out. I've caught glimpses of his true personality and tastes from how he's acted around me and the things he's said. Feeling heat rise to my cheeks, I press my chilly hands to my face to cool them down, being careful of the side of my head.

"A new phone won't stop me," Zander says, reading my thoughts. "Tell us what happened."

Flopping down into the seat, I let out a heavy sigh. My head throbs, and I want to sleep in my bed for a week. I don't want to stay here longer than I have to. But I know I won't be able to leave unless I give them something.

"Then can I leave?" It's the only thing I care about right now.

"We can get your stuff. We have guys that'll move it all, but you can pack it so no one else is touching anything. You'll move into your new room early next week."

"And Ava?"

"She's moving too, but you two won't be roommates anymore."

My chin trembles as I deflate instantly. I've put Ava in danger by rooming with her. I should have expected Zander would separate us at some point, but I didn't think it would be this early in the school year.

"The only rooms they have available are for fourth-year students, and they're single dorms. I wouldn't take you from her if it weren't the only option."

I don't know how he does it. It's almost as if he can read my every thought without ever asking a question. It makes me wonder if he's always been like this, or if I'm special. My stomach flips when the special thought hits, and deep down I hope that's the real reason; even though I doubt it. "Oh," I answer quietly. Wesley is sitting closest to me, and he reaches over, grasping my hand in his, giving it a gentle squeeze. He offers an encouraging smile, and I nod as he releases me. "After Wesley dropped me off at my dorm, I went up and someone had destroyed it. My stuff was thrown all over the place, but Ava's side wasn't touched at all. I saw gauze and Vaseline on the table and figured it was Julien trying to mess with me." I give a humorless laugh. "He was being so nice to me after class when he saw my wrists were red and a little raw. He told me to put it on my wrists to help." Images of that tender moment flash briefly before disappearing once again. "Then Wesley walked in to get me after class, and he was his cold asshole self again as he stalked off."

"I brought that to your room," Zander states. "He told me you had a rough class and needed it. I went to town and picked it up."

"Oh." I bite my bottom lip. I hadn't expected that answer. It's surprisingly sweet, and it makes me wonder why Julien would ask him to do that for me, given how much he keeps me at arm's length. "Thanks." He nods, and I continue. "It took me almost an hour to get everything put away. I was going to run to your house and give him a piece of my mind, but then someone knocked on my door."

"Who?" Wesley asks, leaning forward, his arms now resting on his knees as he listens with rapt interest.

I swallow, my throat bobbing as it works overtime to swallow what little spit I have. My mouth is so dry, it feels like I've been chewing on cotton balls. I know the moment they figure out who took me out of my room that he's a dead man. Julien broke Derek's finger and roughed him up over a little kiss. There's no way he's going to let him live knowing he kidnapped me. But I need to know who he was working with, and they might help me with that part of the problem.

"Derek," Zander states, putting the pieces together of why I was looking at his socials. It doesn't surprise me that he figures it out before Wesley. His brain works through puzzles instantly.

I nod, keeping my eyes trained on the ground as shame floods my system. My cheeks burn hot. If I hadn't dragged Derek into my stupid plan to piss off the Kings, none of this might have happened.

Wesley jumps to his feet and drags his fingers through his short blonde hair. "That son of a bitch," he says while pulling his phone out of his pocket.

"Who are you texting?" I ask, panicking, jumping up out of my seat once more. My heart speeds up, and I reach to take the phone out of his hand. He holds it high above his head and glares at me. "Don't, Wes. Please," I beg.

He narrows his eyes, and for once, I'm terrified of who's looking back at me. This isn't the fun-loving Wesley; this is the cruel King who doesn't take shit from anyone. "Why are you protecting him?" He demands. His jaw clenches, and the muscles in his face and neck bulge with each breath.

I shake my head, hoping they will just…get it. It's not about protecting him. I want answers, and I know if he's dead I'll never get them. "I'm not." Tears sting my eyes as I fight to find the words to explain how I'm feeling. My brain still feels foggy from the hell I've been through, and words escape me.

"Can't get answers out of a dead man," Zander chimes in.

We both look at him, and I nod frantically. I knew he'd get it. "Yes," I breathe. "He was working with someone," I rush out, remembering him on the phone. "When they were forcing me into the van, he called someone and said, it's done." I lick my dry lips, forcing the words out. "I-I don't know who he called, but he's working for someone. I don't want him to disappear or hide out before I have time to get answers."

Wes slumps back into the seat, and I close my eyes, inhaling on a shaky breath before continuing. "Derek came to the door and told me I was in danger because of you three and that I shouldn't trust you." *I guess he was right about the danger part.* If they weren't trying to control my life, I never would have been the center of all this attention. I probably could have flown under the radar…for a little while at least. "Then he said he wanted to show me something and asked if I trusted him."

Wesley snorts and shakes his head. "I hope you told him to fuck off," he mumbles.

I shrug and rub my arms. "I tried. H-he pulled a knife on me and forced me to leave."

"Motherfucker," Wes spits, then rubs his hands down his face.

Risking a glance at Zander, he sits calmly, but his jaw tightens, tendons standing out beneath his skin. "I assume you're the one who called me?" I ask. He gives a slight nod, confirming my suspicions.

"You never said his name. I knew he was familiar to you because you asked him what he was doing there. It was hard to hear, and Julien said he found your phone on your bed when he went to the room."

I nibble at my bottom lip, worrying a rough patch of skin between my teeth. "Why him?" I ask. The guys exchange looks, a silent conversation passing between them, as if they're deciding who's going to draw the short straw and answer me. "And don't you dare say he needs me," I add, my voice tight with frustration. "He's a controlling bastard. If he really needed me, you'd think he'd tell me why."

"No, Princess." Julien's voice comes from behind me. I spin in my seat, a sharp breath tearing from my lungs as my heart stutters. My gaze snaps upward, colliding with his hard, green eyes, the air between us suddenly thick and charged. I didn't even hear him come in. Goosebumps cover my arms, and I rub them, willing them to go away. His eyes track the movement, so I drop them to my side. I wish I had something to hide under. Julien makes me uneasy. I can't get a read on him, and because of that, he's dangerous. I never know what to expect when he's around, and it keeps me on edge. Not that I'll tell him that. I'm sure he'd have a field day with that information.

Wesley must have texted him after all, and I glare at him. "Thanks for nothing," I mumble under my breath.

Julien turns his attention to Zander, pretending I don't exist once again. "What did you find out?"

My nostrils flare, and I clench my hands into fists, trying to hide my frustration at being cast aside once again. God, I want to punch this man. Memories of last night fill my mind when I had these same thoughts, and my anger is back tenfold. "I'm standing right here." I wave my hand in annoyance, and he barely offers me a cursory glance. "I don't need this shit," I say more to myself than them, and I turn toward the staircase. My foot hits the first step when Wesley wraps his arm around my waist and lifts me off my feet, dragging me back into the room.

"Hold on, Hellcat. We haven't finished yet."

My body warms in his embrace, and my stomach does a few flips. Well, I guess that answers that question. My body knows what's good for it, and Wesley Bastian is it.

He puts me on my feet, my back to his front, and drapes his arms over my shoulders. He presses a kiss to my head before resting his chin on it and looking at the other two once again. A contented sigh leaves my lips, and I can't help but snuggle back into him. He had nothing to do with last night. I knew it when it was happening, but I freaked out when I saw them last night. It was more of a fight-or-flight reaction than anything.

Julien though… I'm still not convinced.

"Why?" I ask, meeting Julien's steely gaze once more. "Why did you come looking for me? Why not Wesley or Zander?"

"Zander was busy trying to get the cameras back on, and I wanted Wesley to stay close in case you reached out."

I shake my head. It's such a cop-out; a bullshit answer. "Or were you close by because you set the whole thing up? Wanted to make sure it went off without a hitch?" I feel Wesley stiffen behind me, and I know that was the wrong thing to say.

"You really think I did this to you? Why the hell would I go behind my brothers' backs like that? You think I'd take their plaything away from them?" Shame burns through me at being called that. Coming from his lips, it's such a derogatory statement. "I need you alive, and I wouldn't fuck with them like that."

I've seen the three of them in action, and they are as close as they can be without being blood-related. There are no secrets between them. And having me kidnapped would be akin to treason between them. I know it without a shadow of a doubt. Julien may hate me for reasons I still haven't figured out, but he wouldn't do that to Wes and Zan.

"This wasn't me," he slices into my thoughts. My eyes lock on his, and a smile—cold, merciless—curves his lips. "When I want you gone, I'll make sure there's nothing left to find."

SEVEN

RILEY

As Julien finishes, I instinctively step back, pressing closer to Wesley. A low, possessive growl rumbles from his chest as his arms wrap around me, pulling me in protectively. My stare doesn't waver from Julien's, despite the fact that I want to crawl into a hole and hide. That was more than a threat; that was a promise. If I step out of line, or do anything he doesn't want me to do, he's telling me straight up he will dispose of me like yesterday's trash.

"I wasn't close by. I ran from the house to your dorm when the cameras were down and you didn't answer your phone. This. Wasn't. *Me*," he clips. "Who took you out of your room?"

I inhale a shaky breath, and Wesley loosens his grip, feeling the threat dissipate around us. I risk a glance at Zander, who is sitting straight but keeps a neutral face. Not that I'd expect otherwise. "I'm surprised Wes didn't tell you that information when he texted you," I snap. Twisting my shoulders, Wesley removes his hold on me. I don't know why Julien gets me so riled up, but he does. He crosses his arms but doesn't answer me, waiting for me to tell him instead.

I roll my eyes and shake my head. Focusing on him, waiting for his reaction. "Derek paid me a visit. He told me he wanted to show me something that would prove why I shouldn't trust you. When I tried to hit him with a lamp, he pulled a knife on me and made me leave with him."

"And no one was in the hallway? You couldn't scream for help?" he accuses.

"Oh, gee, thanks so much for that helpful advice. I'm so glad I didn't think of it as I was actively being kidnapped," I snap back.

He steps closer to me, and I square my shoulders, waiting for the fight. I feel the heat of Wesley behind me, and when Julien steps directly into my space, my breath hitches. I have to tilt my head back, resting it on Wes's chest to maintain eye contact with Julien. I hate how much height he has over me. He reaches out, collaring my throat with his rough hands. My pulse thrums against his fingertips, my mouth opening with the minute pressure he applies. The air around us swims with unspoken anger, mixed with pure sexual tension. Why does this turn me on so much? Are they feeling it too? I want to risk a look at Zander to gauge his reaction, but I can't peel my eyes from Julien. No matter how much he tells me he hates me, I know it's not true. His lust simmers just below the surface, just like mine. Every argument feels like foreplay, and one day one of us is going to snap.

"You know, I can stuff your mouth with something else if you keep the attitude up."

"No guarantees I won't bite this time, Cupcake," I taunt, remembering the chase with him in the woods.

His lips turn up at the corners into a barely-there smile, and butterflies race through my belly before he squeezes, cutting off my air. My hands fly up to his wrist, instinctively tugging on them to free myself.

"Enough," Zander's deep voice booms, and Julien takes a

step away. I suck in a deep breath and cough, turning into Wesley, who rubs my back and kisses the top of my head.

"No one was in the halls; he dragged her by knifepoint outside." Zander turns toward me. "What happened after that?"

"He tossed me to the guys—there were four of them," I add before anyone asks. "I kicked one of them in the knee and he went down pretty hard, but I couldn't fight them all off. When they dragged me into the van, Derek called someone and said, it's done." I lick my lips, wishing for a glass of water. The burn of acid claws up my throat as I force the tears back. Somehow, I've managed not to make a complete fool of myself with one of my stupid panic attacks, so I'll take that as a win. "I tried to yell for help when we stopped at what I assume was the front gate, but one guy smacked the butt of his gun across my face." I gesture to the bruise. "Then they forced me to swallow something and told me they were going to chase me, and…and…" Tears sting the corners of my eyes. "Rape me," I finish in a whisper. "It's dumb luck I ended up here at all."

"Hey, you're okay. You're safe," Wesley says as he draws me in. I don't stop the tears. I let them mix with the anger curling in my chest. Whatever Julien is hiding, Wesley has nothing to do with it.

"I need to have a conversation with Arthur Adkins," Julien states, pulling his cell from his pocket and begins typing away on it.

"Who's that?" I ask, confused.

"Derek's uncle. Current headmaster," Wesley explains.

"How do you plan on figuring out who he's working with?"

Julien turns to me, and the smile he gives me sends chills down my spine. "Start with him and follow the trail."

I felt bad for Derek after he got hurt because of my

stupid plan, but now? I don't feel bad for him for one second. He brought this hell upon himself when he tried to have me kidnapped. In a sick way, it's a relief that I have the guys in my corner.

"Are you gonna kill him?" I ask, unsure whether or not I want to know the answer.

"I'm going to make him wish he was already dead," Julien says, looking up from his phone. "No one touches what's mine and gets away with it."

What's his? He can barely be in the same room as me without snarling. How in the world he assumes I'm his is beyond me.

He walks out of the front door, slamming it shut behind him before I can say anything else.

"Come on, Riles. We've got to pack your room. You're moving."

Ava pushes past her brother and pulls me into a tight embrace as soon as she enters our dorm room. She squeezes me so hard I have to tap her back to get her to loosen her grip so I can breathe.

"Oh my God, Riley! What the hell did they do to your face?" she asks, holding me out by my upper arms, examining the bruise.

"Great to see you too, Ava," I say, trying not to squirm under her gaze.

"Sorry," she lowers her voice. "I was so scared when Wes called me. I'm glad you're safe," she says, pulling me in for another hug. Nick stands in the doorway watching us but makes no move to come closer. He turns his attention to Zander, who glares daggers at him.

"Hey Nick." I wave.

"Hey Riley." He waves back, and I push Zander out of the way to pull him down into a hug. Nick is my friend as much as Ava is, and I was terrified I'd never see him again either. He has the good grace not to mention the bruise on my face, and I'm thankful for that. I don't think I have enough makeup in the world to cover it when I go back to classes.

"I hate that we won't be roomies anymore," she says, looking at my packed bags and empty side of the room. Zan and Wes helped me pack up my stuff, and they said their guys should be by soon to take my things. Ava can move in tonight, but Zan told me my room won't be ready until Tuesday. Something about repairs in the room. Wesley has graciously offered his room for the next few days.

"I know. Me too. But it will be so nice not to have to listen to your snoring." I smile wide and laugh when her mouth drops open in shock and her face reddens. Probably because Nick is standing right there and less with what I said.

"I do not!" she exclaims.

My laughter dies down. "I'm teasing, Ava. I'm gonna miss you."

"You realize your rooms are next to each other, right?" Zander chimes in.

"So?" Ava replies, putting her hand on her popped hip.

He shakes his head and sighs. As much as he doesn't want to admit it, he loves his sister and all her crazy antics. Maybe not so much her dating life, but that's a problem for another day. I look at the pictures I had taken off my wall and placed on her bed. She turns to see what I'm focused on and shakes her head.

"Hang 'em up in your room. I can make more."

A knock on the open door draws our attention, and Wesley stands there with a few men behind him. "Time to go," he says, and I move out of the way for them to grab my stuff.

I'm dying to be in my own space again. Don't get me wrong, the past few nights in Wesley's bed have been wonderful, but all we've done is sleep. Even when I try to instigate anything, he stops it. If anything, I need him to stitch the jagged pieces back together. I'm aching for the connection between us that feels like it's come undone. Plus, living with Julien is not my idea of a cup of tea. He avoided me whenever we were in the same room together.

I push open the door and gasp. My new room is nice… really nice. The outside of the building looks the same as Belknap Hall, but Grafton Hall puts that place to shame. I spin, looking around my new living space. The room is massive, complete with an en suite bathroom and high ceilings. There is a small walk-in closet to my right, and a queen-size bed in the middle of the room. A large desk sits in front of two large windows with dark blackout curtains hanging on either side. The walls are cream-white, and because I'm on the top floor, I know the room will get a lot of light.

The guys delivered all of my things to the room, but I need new bedding because my old bed was a twin. Wesley volunteered to run out and get me some things while Zander helps me get settled in. I haven't seen or heard anything from Julien since he rushed out of the house this morning. Not that I care. I'd much rather not see him if I didn't have to.

Zander sits in the chair at the desk, watching me. The silence stretches between us until I'm wound so tight I feel like I'm going to explode. I don't do well in silence with others around, unlike Zander.

He still hasn't answered my question about the spyware on my phone and why he put it there, but my head is pounding, and I don't want to start another fight. Like Julien, he spent most of the weekend in his room—alone. That seems to be a trend with him, and I wonder why. Ava is so outgoing and loves to be around people. Zander is the complete opposite.

I have another question that I've thought about a lot lately. My face burns as I work through the way I want to phrase it in my head. I know the moment he realizes something is up because he tilts his head to the side, waiting for me. He notices my reddened cheeks, and I duck my head to avoid his gaze. *I can't believe I'm about to do this.*

"Do you, um, enjoy listening to Wes and me?" I don't need to elaborate; he's smart enough to figure out what I mean.

"Yes."

That one word in his smooth and deep voice makes my heart skip a beat and my body warm. "Do you enjoy watching us?"

He smirks, his dark eyes brightening. "Do you enjoy the thought of me watching you?" he asks, ignoring my question.

My face burns as I turn away from him, pretending to be occupied with unpacking. I can't even focus on the items I pull from my bags, and I still when his hands grip my upper arms.

"Luna," he says, his voice holding a warning to answer him.

"Yes," I whisper, my back still turned to him. My pulse spikes the second the word leaves my mouth. I've replayed this moment endlessly. From the instant I learned Zan was watching us on the cameras during training, the thought took root. It wasn't just the fantasy that soaked my panties; it was the knowledge that he was watching, and the hope that it unraveled him the same way it did me.

"Yes. I love watching you. You're addicting and it's infuriating."

My eyes snap to his in surprise, as my belly does a little flip. I lick my lips, my breathing harder than it should be.

"Why did you leave that night on campus?" I ask, no longer afraid. He's already answered some of my questions; why not pour more fuel on the fire.

"Because I'm no good for you."

I shake my head, stepping between his legs, and he leans back in his chair to stare up at me, making no move to touch me. "That's not true." Why do these men think they are no good for me? Wesley all but told me the same thing. I think I can decide for myself. I may have my own issues with Julien, but Wesley and Zander are different. In their own unique ways, they elicit the same feelings.

Lust.

Fear.

Protection.

It's strange to feel this kaleidoscope of emotions.

"You're too innocent for me, Luna. I'd ruin you for everyone else, make you second-guess every decision you've ever made, all because I can."

My breathing picks up, and I'm not exactly sure what that means, but I want to find out. There's been a constant pull between us. "I'm not that innocent," I counter.

His hands run down the backs of my thighs and, when he gets to my knees, pull them forward so I straddle him on the chair.

"I play dirty, Luna," he whispers, searching my face for something. I don't know what.

"I like being dirty," I whisper back. My skin tingles all over. I'm hot and cold at the same time. I lick my dry lips, and a small whimper escapes when his hand wraps around my neck and he squeezes. My body tenses, and my hands fly to his wrist, holding him. He hasn't cut off all my air, and I can still breathe, but it's labored. That, along with how hard my heart is beating, and I'm lightheaded.

"If you agree, there's no turning back. I'll use you. Claim you. Is that what you want, Luna? To be my little fuck toy?" His tone turns cutting, meant to wound. But I hear what he isn't saying. This is him trying to scare me off. Pushing me away before whatever's building between us can do actual damage. He's terrified of it, of me, because he can't control how he feels.

Rocking my hips, I feel his hard length beneath me. I want him. I want the Zander the world forgot about. If I agree to this—to him—I know there's no going back. Zander plays for keeps, and unless he's done with me, I can never be done with him. A thrill runs down my spine at the thought.

"Yes, Daddy."

EIGHT

ZANDER

I remove my hand from her throat and wrap my arms under her legs, standing up with her. She gasps and wraps her arms around my neck, pressing her breasts against my chest. I can't wait to play with them. My little Luna has no idea what she's agreed to. I'm going to keep her dripping with need. She's going to become addicted to me. I know she's with Wesley, and with the amount of shit he's dealt with in his life, I would never take her from him. I've seen them together. He needs her the same way I do. I still can't figure out what draws me to her, but my body has figured out something my brain can't comprehend.

This is new. I don't know how to navigate these murky waters, but I'm willing to dive headfirst into them with her. She feels so small, so breakable in my grasp, but I know she's anything but. This past week proved just how much she can take and still come out standing on the other side. I wasn't sure at first if Julien picked the right girl, but now I know without a doubt she's the one we need. She's the key to everything.

I toss her onto the bed. She shrieks as she lands and

bounces once on the soft mattress. I love that she's standing strong even after everything. She could have shut down, but she didn't. And I know she's pulling me close for now, but I wonder how long until that stops.

I place one knee on the bed to steady myself and pull her ankle until her ass is at the edge of the bed, exactly where I want her. I admire her for a moment, taking it all in. She's wearing a pair of black leggings and a fitted Bon Jovi t-shirt that rides up, showing off her creamy stomach. There are a few superficial scratches along her skin, and I frown as I continue looking her over. I land on the bruise on her face, and my hands instinctively close into a fist as I think about what could have happened to her.

Everything could have ended. All because of Derek. I clench my teeth and push a harsh breath through my nose, my anger getting the better of me. I don't want to hurt her, and I know if I let myself crawl into the dark spaces of my mind, I will.

Riley notices the change, points to her face, and jokingly says, "You should see the other guy." She forces a smile onto her face, and when I don't return it, she sits up and places her small, warm hand on my cheek, bringing my attention to her eyes. "Zander, I'm fine."

"You're not fine, Riley. I couldn't protect you. This is my fault." Anger courses through my entire body. I need to get some of this pent-up energy out, otherwise I'm going to explode. I flex my right hand and ball it again and again. She glances down, watching the motion, and sucks her bottom lip between her teeth, making the skin around it turn white.

"How can I help?" she finally asks.

"Take off your pants and underwear." I command without giving it a second thought. Spanking Riley has been a fantasy of mine since the bonfire, and I will not turn down the opportunity to do it because I don't think she's ready. I know she can handle it. She's already told me she wants me. She's going to play in the shadows with me, and will learn to love my darkened desires. I'm not stupid; I know she's never done this kind of thing before. But she will learn to love everything I do to her and to find pleasure in pain.

She lets out a shaky breath and stands on wobbly legs to do as I ask. She pulls the stretchy material over her hips and ass and bends at the waist, pushing them down her slender legs. At least she doesn't appear to have cuts or bruises on her lower half, and the ones that adorn her abdomen and chest are superficial and will fade within a week. The bruising will take a little longer, but she'll heal.

She keeps her head down, looking at her feet, and I sit on the edge of the bed. My dick strains against the zipper on my jeans at what's about to happen. I tap my thigh. "Lay over my leg, ass in the air."

She visibly swallows, her throat bobbing, and hesitantly she moves closer to me before resting her upper body over my thighs. My inner monster is champing at the bit to lay into her, but I know I have to be controlled or I'll scare her. Just like the other night. I was fucking terrified. I couldn't save her; couldn't do anything but stare at blank screens and rewind audio to listen to over and over. Without control, I have nothing. Riley has been spinning out of my control since the moment I met her, but not anymore. She's going to become my obedient Luna.

Running my hand over her bare ass cheeks, she jolts the moment my rough hand meets her soft skin. I know it's instinctive. I rub my hand in calming circles as her breathing turns rapid in anticipation. By the time this is over, my pants are going to bear evidence of both of us.

"There are rules, Luna. Are you familiar with them?"

I look down at her, and she shakes her head. "No,

Daddy," she replies. My dick jumps, and she shifts her weight trying to find a comfortable position.

"We'll use a stoplight. Green means you're good. Yellow means slow down. And red—"

"Stop," she finishes for me. "I understand."

"Good girl," I praise, dragging the words out, giving her ass a light slap. She jumps and whimpers as I continue to rub her skin, warming it up under my rough hand. I love spanking a pretty girl's ass until it's sore and red. It's my way to own and control that person. I need to have control, otherwise it all falls to shit. Thoughts flash through my brain, and I close my eyes, shutting them down before I do something I know I'll regret. Deep down, I know this isn't Riley's fault. But it doesn't change the fact that I need to spank her for it. My inner beast needs this control to assure myself that she's fine.

"Count, Luna," I command, and then my hand comes down on her left cheek, hard.

She rears her head up, her entire body jerking with the motion, but I keep my left arm over her lower back, holding her in place. "O-one," she whispers. I do it again, this time on her right cheek. Her creamy skin is turning a pretty shade of pink, and I can see the outline of my handprint. "Two," she says, this time without a waver in her voice.

I slide my fingers down her slit and press two of them into her pussy. She's soaked for me. She tries to spread her legs to give me better access, and I tut at her.

"Don't be greedy, Luna." I bring my hand down once more, this time adding more force behind it. Her juice glistens in the light on her ass from my fingers. It's beautiful. She's doing so well. I can't wait until I can string her up and do this. To fuck her dripping cunt after abusing her ass, knowing she's going to be soaked for me.

She cries out, "Three." It's louder than I think she

intends. Anyone outside her room could hear her, but maybe deep down that's what she wants. I love pulling these moans and whimpers from her pretty lips.

"Shhh, Luna. Unless you want the building to hear your needy cries." I smile to myself, my body reacting to hers. "Although I bet you do, don't you? You want everyone around to know what a needy slut you are, huh?"

She moans deeply at my words. I slap her upper thigh, and she bites back a cry. I know that one stung like a bitch; my hand throbs with the force of it.

"Four," she whispers. I plunge my fingers deep inside her once more, pumping them in and out. She rocks against my hand, gasping for air. "P-please, Zander," she moans.

"Please what, my little slut?"

She groans and continues to rock her hips against my hand. Wetness drips out of her and onto my pants. I'm hard as fucking granite, and I know I'm not walking out of this room without getting off. The final shred of control I was gripping onto slipped when she opened her mouth to beg. Thoughts of pulling my dick free and slamming it into her dripping cunt consume me. I pull my fingers out of her, and she sags against my legs, whining at the loss. I bring them to my mouth and suck her off me.

"The best fucking dessert I've had in a long time. Do you want to come?" I ask. She nods her head frantically, a sob ripping through her as I bring my hand down on her red ass for the final blow.

"Five."

Her body shivers as I steady her on her feet. She sways, eyes heavy with dark, simmering with desire. She's breathtaking like this—wanton and desperate for me.

"On the bed, on your back," I say.

She sits at the edge and lies back, her hand falling over her chest. I look down at her, admiring her sexy body, and my hand falls to my dick. I press on it and groan. Her eyes travel down my body until they rest on my hand. Licking her lips, she sits up, the perfect height to reach out and touch me. She brushes my hand away, and I allow it, needing her fingers on me. She tugs at the belt to undo it, and then pops the button and pulls down the zipper. Her hand slips beneath my boxers and pulls me free. The tip is an angry-looking red, and is leaking. She rubs her thumb over the tip and swipes the bead of precum up, sucking it off her thumb. I hiss in a breath, my abs constricting as she wraps her hand around me and pumps up and down.

"Jesus, Luna," I groan.

She smiles, and I choke on air as she takes me into her warm mouth. She keeps her hand firmly at the base, controlling how much of me she takes in. I'm going to train her to take all of me. I want to use her mouth, pussy, and ass as often as I want. If I could tie her down and leave her there to use as I see fit, I would. Make her learn to love the roughness of it all. Maybe get Wesley in on the action.

I wrap her hair around my fingers and thrust my hips forward. She gags and tries to pull back. I allow her a small amount of space as I test how deep she can take me.

"Hands behind your back," I order. Riley looks up at me through glassy eyes, worry lines creasing her forehead. "Slap my leg once for yellow, and twice for red. Do you understand?"

She swirls her tongue around the tip, and I pull my hips back, my cock popping out from between her lips. "Yes, Daddy."

I want to roll my eyes. She's such a good girl like this. She's going to be the perfect replacement for Clarissa.

"Good girl, now take this dick like the good little slut I know you want to be."

Riley shifts on the floor, her wetness sliding down her

inner thighs. I want to taste her just as badly as I want to come inside her. She opens her mouth wide, sticking her tongue out, and I pop it into her mouth once again. I hold her head in place and thrust my hips back and forth, pushing in a little further with each move. She continues to swirl her tongue around my length as drool drips from her red, swollen lips. Tears fall from her eyelashes, and I have never seen her look more beautiful than she is right now, choking on my cock. She gags, and I pull back, resting the tip inside, giving her a moment to calm her body. When she sucks harder, I know she's recovered.

All the worry, pain, and anger rush through me, and before long my orgasm sits at the base of my spine. I'm marking her. I want my come all over her pussy lips. Pulling out of her, I push her back onto the bed. I pull her ass off the edge, drop to my knees, and toss her legs over my shoulders.

"Zan," she whimpers, but I shut her up, licking her soaked pussy from ass to clit. I've wanted to do this for so fucking long. It's like a dream come true at this point. I pump two fingers into her, massaging her g-spot each time I pull out. She's bucking her hips, riding my face as I suck her clit between my teeth and bite. Her back bows off the bed, and I know it won't be much longer. Her inner muscles pulse and flutter around my fingers. I reach out for my aching cock and stroke myself, faster and faster. I need more. She needs more. We are both so close and I can't take it anymore. I stand, pulling her hips off the bed in a bruising grip, and plunge my cock deep inside her.

I see fucking stars as she screams my name and comes all over my dick. I pound into her, wanting to extend her orgasm and keep mine at bay for as long as I possibly can.

Can't.

Stop.

Her body grips mine like a vise. I think I'm going to pass

out. No one has ever felt so damn perfect before. Riley Whittier is made for me.

"Zan," she whimpers, "please." Her eyes fall closed, and her back bows off the bed. I think she's going to come again, and I know I can't hold it this time. Right as her second orgasm hits, I pull out, my hand slick with her come as I fist myself and release all over her pretty little pussy. My heart pounds in my chest, and I give a final shake before squeezing the tip, coating my fingers.

She's still on the bed, her chest heaving and her arm slung over her eyes. I bend over her, pushing her legs up higher, and say, "Open." She does so without hesitation and sucks my fingers clean. Then I run my fingers through the come coating her body and slowly finger-fuck it into her. I may have wanted to mark her today, but that doesn't mean I don't want my come deep inside of her, too.

"Damn," his voice startles us, and I snap my head in his direction as she pulls her legs from my arms and tries to tug her shirt down to cover her half-naked body. I was so wrapped up in the moment that I missed the door opening entirely. It's happening more and more, and I resent myself for it as I pull myself together and turn to leave.

He grabs my arm, stopping me in my tracks. "Don't you dare fucking leave her again, Zan," Wesley whispers so only I can hear. "She's not like your plaything. You can't leave her if you expect to keep her."

And Wes's words hit me like a gut punch.

NINE

RILEY

Wesley and Zander stare at one another; a silent conversation plays out between them. The only word I heard from their hushed conversation was plaything, and now I have questions. Does he have a girlfriend? Why would he have sex with me if he did? I've felt this push and pull between us, and if tonight was any indication, he feels it too. I know he does. Every time we are in the room together, the sexual tension is off the charts.

Wes turns his attention on me and smiles warmly. "Not going to lie, Hellcat, I'm jealous."

My face flames with embarrassment as I scramble off the bed and reach for my panties and leggings; but Zan is quicker. He snags them before I can.

"You know, I'm going to start thinking you enjoy wearing women's underwear. You're gaining quite a collection." I yank my pants from him and pull them up over my come-soaked thighs. I'll take a shower after they leave.

"They're trophies, Luna. And I plan on taking every damn pair you own." He spins them around his finger,

66

mocking me. I reach to grab them, but he shoves them deep into his pocket before I can.

My body heats and I look to the ground, unsure what to say to that. I want him to take them. I would love for him to order me not to wear anything under my uniform, just for him. Would he drag me into an empty classroom, pin me against the wall and fuck me? Just the thought of that sends a bolt of lust straight to my clit, and it throbs. I cross my legs, trying to ease some of the feeling, and I know Zan's caught on to me. He rubs his hand down the front of his pants and gives himself a small squeeze.

Damn him to hell!

Then I look at Wesley, who is standing at the door with a shit-eating grin on his face. I have a feeling he also knows what I'm thinking. "What do you mean, jealous?"

He raises an eyebrow and rubs his hand over his stubbled jaw, casting his eyes up and down my body. "He got you to come, and I didn't get to watch the entire show, only the finale."

My eyes nearly bug out of my head, and I choke on a cough as I try to swallow my gasp. Heat floods my face, my entire body going up in flames. My mouth opens, closes… completely useless.

"Maybe next time." He bends down and picks up a bag at his feet that I hadn't even noticed. "Let's get your bed made, get into the shower, and then go to bed. Classes start again tomorrow, and we have training."

I groan at the mention of training. "Could we take a week off? At least give me some time to heal?" I point to the side of my face, and he frowns when he looks at the bruise. I know it looks horrible. I've seen it enough times in the mirror. It will fade eventually, and all this will become a distant memory. The biggest obstacle will be facing Derek after what happened.

A smirk crosses my face at the thought of that. He's going to shit his pants when he sees me standing there in the cafeteria tomorrow morning. I was supposed to be long gone. I'm sure he's going to deny any involvement. And I actually wonder if it would be better to take a few more days off from classes. Give him time to really think he's gotten away with it. Maybe the guys to tail him to see who set him up. But he has to know I got away.

"Actually, I was thinking about this…" I trail off.

"What?" they ask in unison.

"What if we set up a tail on Derek? Maybe it can lead us to whoever he's working with. You can start tapping his phone," I say to Zander. "Watch how he reacts and who he talks to." My request may be for more selfish reasons too. I'm scared to face the rest of the student body. I don't know how I'll react to the whispers and looks. Will people think this is from the Kings? Does anyone know about Derek?

"Julien's already set up the tail," Zan tells me.

I scrunch my face in confusion and sit down on the edge of the bed, my hands tucked under my thighs. "Why would he set that up?" Wes or Zan make sense, not Julien. Maybe I need to stop thinking the worst of him. I know I don't have the best judgement in people, Derek, point in case, but I feel I have a decent read on Julien. Every chance he gets to push me away from him. *Except for those few times when he's been sweet or worried about you.* I shake my head, ridding those thoughts from my mind. Regardless, he's using me for something, and once he gets what he wants, I'm of no use to him.

"We'll figure this out, Luna," Zander reassures.

"Now, here's all your stuff." Wesley places the bag on my bed and takes the new set of sheets and comforter out for me to look at. It's a pretty pastel pink with sheets that match.

It's not what I would have picked out, per se, but I'm sure he figured it was my favorite color because it's what my other bedding was. I didn't get to choose that either. It was nice of him to get me anything at all, and I won't complain about it.

"Thanks. This was sweet of you." I stand on my tiptoes, placing my hand on his chest, and kiss his cheek. When I attempt to pull away, he firmly places his hand on the back of my head and holds me to him, deepening the kiss. I cling to his shirt, allowing him to control it. He feels like safety and comfort, and I want to melt into him. My nipples peek under my shirt and bra, and I moan into his mouth, rubbing myself against him.

He smiles and drops his forehead to mine. "Needy slut," he whispers, and I pull my lower lip between my teeth, nodding my head. I should be upset he's using derogatory names, but I can't help the way it turns me on instead.

"Zan, you're gonna have fun playing with this one," he says louder, not taking his eyes off me.

"Already have been," he replies, and I turn my head to look at him straight on. "I'm gonna get some dinner for us. We can eat here and figure out the next few days."

I nod, but there's a pang of sadness in my chest. He's leaving…again. I can't be that clingy girl. These aren't the type of men who go for that. I stand a little taller, trying my damndest not to sulk or appear upset. "Okay."

He's standing in front of me in two long strides, tipping my face up to look directly into his dark brown ones. "I'm not leaving you, Luna. I'm taking care of you. Do you understand?" I nod, and he lifts his brow, waiting for a verbal response.

"Yes," I reply quietly.

He kisses the top of my head, and my heart skips a beat. "Lock the door behind me." He holds his hand out, palm up, and Wes tosses him my room key. He catches it and pockets it before turning and leaving.

I don't know where this is headed, and I'm not delusional

enough to think it's forever; but I'd be lying if I said I didn't want to see how it plays out. I'm not naive enough to think whatever is happening between us will be a long-term thing, but right now, it feels good—right. They both fill a gap I didn't realize I had.

Wesley shakes out the sheets and starts making my bed, not even waiting for me to snap out of whatever daze I'm in. I stand on the other side, and when he tosses the comforter over, I help him straighten it out. When it's done and the pillows are casually tossed on top, I exhale slowly.

"Come here," Wes commands, holding his hand out to me. I walk around the bed and place my hand in his. He pulls me close and wraps his arms around me, kissing the top of my head in the same place Zander did moments ago. "I was so scared, Riley," he admits. "I'm not sure what I would have done if they had taken you from me."

"Good thing they wanted to chase me through the woods instead," I joke, a poor attempt at lightening the mood. He draws back, stepping away and turns my face to get a better look at the damage they inflicted.

"I swear, if I ever find out who did this to you, I'll kill them."

I place my hands over his. "No. Let the cops handle it." He snorts, and I realize my mistake and smile. "Fine, maybe let someone else do it. You're a King after all. Don't you have peasants to take care of that for you?"

His bright smile is contagious, and I mirror his expression. "Come on, let's get you cleaned up."

He leads me to the shower and turns it on before helping me pull my t-shirt over my head and pushing my leggings down my legs. I reach to cover my breasts, and he shakes his head. I let them fall to my sides, exposing myself to him and lick my lips when he pulls his t-shirt over his head and throws it onto the pile with my clothes. It's seriously not fair how fit these three are. I haven't seen all of Zander or Julien yet, because Zan decided to fuck me with his clothes still on, but I've felt each of them. Julien might have a bigger build than Zan and maybe Wes, but that doesn't mean they are small men.

"Like somethin' you see, Hellcat?" he asks when I won't stop staring at him.

I swear all the water in the world couldn't help the case of dry mouth I have. "Y-yeah," I say. And when he drops his pants, his hard length bobs up, a tiny bead of precum present, and saliva floods my mouth. I want to taste him. I want to compare how he tastes and feels to Zander. A whine escapes, and I try to cover it by clearing my throat.

He knows what I'm thinking, but he helps me step into the spray of the water.

"Turn around, let me wash your hair."

I turn and tilt my head back, letting the warm water cascade over my hair and body, soaking me. He squirts some shampoo into his hand and washes the strands, massaging my head as he goes. I groan; it feels amazing. Wes kisses my shoulder before he puts some conditioner in, making my hair feel silky smooth.

"I could get used to this," I say, relaxing a little more as the water slides down over us.

He hums in response and picks up the soap, rubbing it between his hands, and takes his time washing every inch of my body. When I'm cleaned to his satisfaction, he washes himself with my soap and turns off the water. He offers me a fluffy towel, and I'm a little disappointed to see he's still hard and he tried nothing again. I turn, giving him my back as I dry droplets of water from my skin. He knows I just had my brains fucked by his best friend, yet he still thinks I'm too fragile.

"Did you like him fucking you?" he asks, and I meet his

gaze in the mirror. I bite my lip, not sure if I'm going to make things better or worse with my reply. But liars never come out on top.

I straighten my spine and raise my chin. "Yes." I say, keeping my eyes locked on his. "But I also enjoy fucking you. You both make me feel good in different ways."

He smiles, and my heart kicks up a notch. "Good girl. Hear that, Zan?" he says louder, and I jerk my head to the door, noticing Zander standing there, arms crossed over his enormous chest. I didn't hear him come back, but it doesn't surprise me Wesley did. He always seems to know where his best friends are.

"I hope you know what you're signing up for, Luna."

I give myself a second to breathe, to accept what I'm about to do; because once I cross this line, there's no going back. Running isn't an option; it never has been. The second those three set their sights on me, I understood the game was rigged. But I'm not the fragile thing they think I am. They'll soon learn just how dangerous I can be.

"Yes."

TEN

RILEY

"I hope you understand what you're saying, Hellcat. I'm not letting you go. Especially not after the other day."

He looks at Zander, who nods. "You're ours, Luna. And I plan on using your body the way it was intended. I'm going to wring every bit of pleasure from you, and then demand more."

Why does my pussy clench at their words? Why do I have the urge to bend over and let them do whatever the hell they want to me? I don't have a lot of experience with sex, but with multiple partners? I don't even know how this is going to work. But it has to. I can't picture my life without either of them. And even if Julien and I never make it to friendly terms, I know he's part of the deal. Wherever they go, he goes. And if I want to keep Wesley and Zander, I need to find common ground with Julien.

"I do."

Wesley hums. It's low, dark, and insanely sexy. "Drop the towel. Zander's turn to watch as I come deep inside of you."

I squeak. Holy shit, this is really happening. I take a deep breath, trying to calm my racing heart and wipe my clammy hands on my towel before lifting my arms and letting it drop to the floor, pooling at my feet.

I look at Zander, who is sitting on my bed. He lifts a brow and then crooks his finger, motioning for me to stand in front of him. I do as he asks. With him on the bed, he's at the perfect height to reach my breasts. He cups his right hand around my left one and pulls it up to his mouth, sucking on my taut nipple.

"Zan," I gasp and drop my head back on Wesley's shoulder as he brings his arms around my waist and slides them down to my opening. He finds my clit, and I jerk in his grasp.

"Wes," I moan as I dig my fingers through Zander's silky locks. I know Wesley told him to watch, but I don't want him to. I want him to know I need him as much as Wesley.

"Sit on his lap, facing me, and open that pretty mouth of yours, Hellcat. I want you to suck my dick as you rub your ass over Zander."

I suck in a shuddering breath and turn around, perching on Zander's lap. His calloused hands dig into my hips as he pulls me down firmly on top of him. His jeans grate against my heated flesh like sandpaper. He pushes his hips up, and I moan when his hard length digs into my ass. Wesley drops his towel, still hard from our shower, and steps closer to me. I open my mouth wide and stick my tongue out, breathing deeply through my nose as I wait in anticipation.

Zan's hands come up to my breasts, and Wes slides his cock past my lips at the same moment Zander squeezes. I moan around his length as he hisses in a breath. He wraps his hands around the back of my head and tangles his fingers through my hair, fisting the strands.

"That's it, baby. You're taking my cock so fucking well." He groans and tilts his head back, looking up at the ceiling.

"Luna, open your throat, really let him in there." Zander

rubs his fingers up and down my throat, on either side of where Wesley's dick slides in. I roll my hips on top of him. Sharing this moment with both of them fills me with intense longing. I want to sit on Zan's cock and suck Wesley, or the other way around; I couldn't care less. I want to feel both of them together. I need both of them right now.

Wesley thrusts his hips forward, and my stomach seizes as I gag on it, tears spilling down my eyes and drool pooling from the side of my lips, falling on my breasts. Zander uses his finger to wipe it up before spreading my legs wide with his own and touching my sensitive clit. I jerk on his lap, and he tightens his grip on me at the same time Wesley tightens the hold on my head.

"You're fucking perfect, Riley. So sensitive. So damn needy." I nod the best I can and moan once again around Wes's cock in my mouth. "You didn't even need to prep her, Wes. She's fucking soaked."

"Good," he growls. "I want her to suck your cock. Our good slut needs her holes filled. Isn't that right, Hellcat?" He clenches his jaw and pushes a deep breath through his nose as his abs contract. Is it possible he's close already? My pussy clamps down when Zander pushes two fingers inside me.

"Up," he says. Pulling his fingers from me, he slaps the side of my hip, and I yelp. Instead of standing, I slide down to my knees, not wanting to lose the feel of Wesley. I'm too far gone, too high on whatever this is.

Lust.

Desire.

Need.

I hear Zander undoing his belt buckle. Then, the agonizingly slow pull of his zipper. The teeth open one at a time, and I swear all it does is make more liquid flood between my thighs. Wesley pulls my head back, pulling himself out from my swollen lips, and bends down to kiss me hard on them. I push my tongue into his, needing more of him. I want to wrap myself around him and never let go. When did this happen? When did I become this girl who can't control her primal urges?

"Fucking beautiful," he growls.

I blink up at him, at a loss for words when his gaze shifts behind me. I follow his line of sight as Zander scoots up the bed, resting against the headboard. His t-shirt is gone, and his pants are open, his large cock standing at attention. I scan his body, taking in all the tattoos. His upper body is littered with them—each more intricate than the last. There's writing across his chest, Russian maybe? The characters aren't in the English language. Then there's the full sleeve adorning his chiseled arms. Flowers, crosses, skulls, and black ink adorn his olive skin. I want to touch them all. But the most troubling are the scars that line his body. Circle burns in various sizes, welts that have long since healed. I look into his dark eyes. Who would do something like this to him?

His eyes soften, if only for a moment. He knows what I see. "Put my cock between your pretty little lips and let me fuck your mouth."

I look over my shoulder at Wesley, who nods. His bright blue eyes are dark as he watches me kneel on the bed and crawl over to Zander. Sexy isn't even the right word to describe how I feel, despite my bashed face. I have never felt more seen or wanted in my life. There is only one other person who has made me feel this way, and he disappeared ages ago. These men don't care about some bruises. All they see is me. I crawl between Zander's legs and look into his eyes. His jaw tightens as he works himself up and down, and releases a slow, steady breath. I lick my bottom lip between my teeth and hold it, helpless to look away.

"You're going to suck my cock, Luna, while Wesley fucks

you from behind. I want your cunt and belly full of our come. You're going to swallow it all, do you understand?"

I nod. He raises his brow in question, and that's when I realize he wants a verbal answer. "Yes, Sir."

"Such a good little slut, aren't you? Remember your colors?"

My cheeks flush. I'm not sure I'm going to get used to being called that. "Yes."

"Tell me," he demands.

"Green is good, yellow means slow down, and red means stop."

"Good girl," he draws the words out, and a new bit of wetness pools between my thighs. Oh yeah, I am so screwed. I want this, want them. "Tap my leg once for yellow, and twice for red. Understood?"

I nod and add, "Yes, Sir."

"Daddy," he corrects. "You'll call me Sir when it's punishment, but Daddy when I'm fucking your pretty little holes."

Oh God. If my panties were on, they'd be ruined. I've never heard anything so sexy in my entire life. I want to know what he means by punishment. If it's more spanking, I could get behind that. I wasn't sure how I would handle it, but it was like a switch was flipped when he started. Something that seemed so scary before I knew it is something now I wouldn't mind experiencing again. Maybe not right now, but soon.

I lean down and push my damp hair over my shoulder when it falls into my face. Wesley gathers it into a ponytail in his hand as he comes up behind me. He presses my shoulders down, forcing me to pop my butt in the air, giving him better access. His warm body is against mine, and I feel his hard dick pressing at my entrance. I know I'm wet, and it will be easy for him to fill me. Is this really happening? Am I really going to suck a man's dick while someone else screws me from behind? My head spins. I can't believe this is really happening. I mean, I've thought about this since I first met them, but I never thought it would actually happen. No one shares the Kings. That's what that girl said. So what makes me so different?

I spread my legs wider and dip my head, taking Zander to the back of my throat. My body tenses as I gag, and Wes takes that exact moment to push into me. He's so big, and I stretch around him, feeling so full with a satisfying pressure. I sag and moan around Zan, who puts his hands on the back of my head and pushes me down as he thrusts his hips up. I gag again, and Wes groans behind me.

"Fuck, man, every time you choke her, she tightens around my cock. Feels so fucking good," he says on another groan. There is nothing gentle in the way he uses my body. Nothing like how he's been acting with me these past few days. He pounds into me, my whole body jerking toward Zander, yet the hold he has on my hair keeps my head in place. I want to come so badly; want them to come in me. I feel like the needy slut they keep saying I am, and I whine when Wes slows down right as my body is on the verge of release. He slaps my ass and I jerk forward, Zander's dick sliding down my throat. My whole body reacts, and I slap his leg once. He pulls my face free from him, and I stare into his beautiful brown eyes through my water-filled ones.

He runs his hand down the side of my face, wiping away some tears that have fallen. "Good girl," he praises.

I moan, "Wes, please. I need to come." Wes slides his thumb through my wetness and brings it back to my puckered hole, rubbing the pad over it. "N-no," I try to pull away, but Zander holds me in place. I've never thought about anal before. I know if whatever between us continues, it's going to happen, but the thought of it terrifies me.

"Shhh, Luna. Not tonight, but we will fuck your ass. You're ours. Relax, let him play with you."

"Rock against me," Wes tells me, and I do, as he slowly works his finger into my tight hole.

I gasp when it sinks in, and he thrusts his hips forward once again. It feels odd, but not as uncomfortable as I thought. There's pressure there, but it only enhances the feel of his dick in me.

"I want to come, please," I beg, keeping my eyes locked on Zander. His hand moves absentmindedly up and down his length.

"Suck it deep, baby." Zan presses his cock forward enough for me to pull it back into my mouth and lick around the head and shaft.

"If you make her gag again, I'm going to come in her, Zan," Wesley announces. The muscles in my pussy clench at that thought, and I moan around Zan, silently begging him to do it. I'm too close. My body is warm and tingly all over, and I want the release. I need to feel the two of them come inside me.

I pull off Zander, look him dead in the eyes and with as much gumption as I can muster say, "Please fuck my mouth, Daddy. I want you both to come in me."

"Jesus Christ," Wes groans as he picks up the pace. I know he's close. His dick gets harder as his balls slap my pussy, and his movements are more erratic. He's holding off as long as he can. Zander pushes my head down over his cock and thrusts hard and fast into me. Tears pour down my face from the harsh throat fucking, and my body convulses from the intrusion; but I don't care. I hold back the churning in my stomach to allow Zander to use me like I begged him to. Being here with them, like this, I feel safer than I've ever felt before. My orgasm hits me so hard I can't even breathe. Between Wes's finger in my ass, his dick in my pussy, and

Zander's cock down my throat, I'm floating. This must be what an out-of-body experience feels like. I'm vaguely aware of hearing Wes groan behind me before slapping my ass, keeping his dick stuffed in me when I hear Zander's harsh breathing and he says, "I'm coming. Fucking swallow it, Luna."

Most of it spills down the back of my throat, and I cough, trying to keep it all inside and swallow it. I want to be his good girl, and that's what he told me he wanted me to do. I moan over him and lap at his dick, getting the last bit of come off him. When Wes pulls out, I wince. Zander gathers me in his arms, and I lay my head on his chest, listening to the erratic beat of his heart. He kisses the top of my head, and I snuggle into his warmth.

Wow. Holy shit. What exactly just happened? I don't even know what to think. Wes comes back with a wet face-cloth and helps clean me up. He pulls his clothes on and sits on the edge of the bed, where Zander is still holding me, his fingers dancing up and down my side.

"Food is probably cold," he says. I pull my head away and look up at him and smile. The smile quickly turns into a laugh. I can't help it—I'm tired, and blissed-out, and possibly have a concussion from the gun butt to the head. I never got that checked out. If something serious were going to happen, it would have by now. I think so, anyway. Plus, no one else seemed terribly concerned.

"Come on, Hellcat. Let's get you some food, and then off to bed." He tosses my t-shirt at me. I pull it down over my head, knowing damn well I'm still naked from the waist down. Wes eventually tosses me some clean panties and leggings from my drawer. Zander puts himself back together and pulls out bags of food. He didn't go to the cafeteria like I thought he would. This looks like it's from a restaurant. We make ourselves comfortable. Me on the bed with Zander, and Wesley sitting at the desk.

The lid pops open to display a large burger and fries. I briefly wonder if it's from the diner I went to with Leah, where I saw Zander for the first time.

"Your first meal in Barrington. Thought you might enjoy it again," Zander offers.

"Did you know who I was?"

He nods and takes a bite of his burger.

For how long? Why were you looking into me? Why me? All these questions jump around in my mind, but I settle for silence instead. Eventually, I'll get my answers. I put my food down after a few bites and glance between the two of them. I don't want to be alone tonight. I've had the security of Wesley and the house for a few days. Staying in a dorm again is scary.

I look down at the ground, hating that I feel so vulnerable. "Will one of you stay here tonight?" I ask. They exchange glances, and I rush out, "I mean, only if you want to. Don't feel you have to. I know you've got things to do—"

"Riley. Riley, stop," Wesley says, stopping my ramble. I blink at him, closing my mouth and tightening my jaw as I wait. "I'll stay. Let me get my stuff for classes, and we can go to breakfast together tomorrow."

Relief washes over me, and I nod. "Thank you."

ELEVEN

RILEY

The alarm goes off, but I've already been lying here awake for what feels like hours. I fell asleep for a while after dinner last night. Zander stayed with me until Wesley returned with his things. Then I woke around midnight feeling like I was being suffocated. Wesley's arm was slung over my body, and I had to wriggle my way out of his hold to get up and use the bathroom. He startled awake, and I had to tell him I was just going pee. He settled back and waited for me to return before going to sleep again.

I will say that not having to leave my room in the middle of the night is a nice luxury. Staying at the house, I got used to the en suite, so it's a bonus that it can continue. I'm not looking forward to next year when I have to walk down the hallway again. *Maybe things will work out with the Kings and me, and I can spend more nights at their house.* I know I'm getting ahead of myself by thinking things like that. One has to survive this school year before thinking of the next one.

Wesley stirs next to me and pulls me in, burying his face in my chest and groans when I playfully push him away from me.

"Rise and shine, Sugar Plum. Big day ahead of us, after all." I push the covers off me and stand, stretching my arms above my head.

He rolls to his side and props his head on his hand, staring up at me. "Oh, yeah, and what is that?"

"Seeing the look on Derek's face when I'm magically back at Pointebreak," I grin, but I know it looks as devious as I feel. He raises his brow, and the smile grows wider across my face. "I had a lot of time to think last night. You snore, by the way." He chortles and shakes his head as I continue. "You see, I thought it would be great to act like nothing had happened. Mess with him. Play the dumb girl he thinks I am."

"You've got a dark side under there, don't you, Hellcat?" he asks, scooting to the end of the bed. I stand at the edge, my legs hitting the side.

He pulls my thighs against his face and kisses them. "I'm pissed," I admit.

Having had time to process it all, I'm not scared anymore. Now I'm furious and demand answers. Going in there, guns blazing, isn't how I'm going to get any information, though, and I know that. I need to play the game. Zan told me Julien has a tail on Derek. I'm not sure how long until they get anything useful, but I'm not sitting on the side to watch everything unfold around me. I want to be part of the action.

"I don't want to be scared, and I don't want him to get away with this."

His face softens as he gives me a sympathetic smile. "He's not going to. We'll make sure of it."

"But I want to help. Use me, make me part of the plan." I plead.

He shakes his head. "No. We know nothing yet, and until we do, we can't involve you."

I snort and cross my arms over my chest. "That's bullshit, Wes." I want to stomp my foot, but I know that won't get me anywhere. So, I square my shoulders instead and try to look more confident than I feel. I'd be lying if I said the thought of being used as bait didn't scare me, but this is non-negotiable. I won't be pushed aside.

He sits up in the bed, tossing his legs over the side and then stands, towering over me. Placing his fingers under my chin, he lifts it so I'm looking up at him. "We're not putting you in more danger. The only reason you're in this mess is because of us, and we will make damned sure no one has the chance again." I open my mouth to protest, and he places his finger over my lips, silencing me. "When new information comes in, you'll be the first to know. I promise." I nod. It's not the answer I wanted, but it's better than it could have been. "Come on, training first, and then we don't wanna be late for breakfast."

It's only been a few days, but with my already sore body, the training today seemed unnecessarily harsh. Wesley didn't try to fuck me into the mat, but he did take it easy on me; and for that I'm thankful. I kept looking up at the camera, hoping Zander was watching. And when he met us outside my dorm this morning, I could tell from the gleam in his eye that he had been.

Zander keeps pace on one side of me, Wesley on the other, boxing me in. My personal bodyguards. As we pass other students on the quad, they stare at us; but look away as soon as one of them glares. My makeup isn't thick enough to cover the bruising entirely, so I know some people are looking at that. Or maybe because Wesley has his arm around my waist, while Zander holds my hand—the three of us walking through campus as a unit.

Internally I smile, but I keep my face stone-cold on the outside. Two of this school's hottest men are attracted to me. I'm not sure where Zander and I fall in terms of relationship status, but Wesley and I discussed it this morning while getting dressed, and he called me his girlfriend. It was difficult to leave my room after that. I already thought of him as my boyfriend, but I hadn't said it out loud yet.

Nick grabbed Ava this morning, or maybe he never left her room. I'm not one-hundred percent sure because Zander was scowling and staring at the two of them as they left the building. Good on Nick for not being intimidated. Zander is a whole different level of scary sometimes. His poor daughter, if he has one. She'll have to wait until she's thirty before she can date; and even then he might arrange it instead.

Wesley opens the door to the cafeteria, and I enter with Zander right behind me, never letting go of my hand. The noise diminishes as we enter, but doesn't stop entirely as students turn their attention toward us. They are looking at me. I'm sure people have gossiped since they haven't seen me for a few days. I pull Wesley closer, and he tosses his arm over my shoulder, offering his silent protection.

We get in line and load up our plates with food before finding a spot to sit. Julien sits alone at a round table in the center of the room, the surrounding seats conspicuously empty—like he's Moses, effortlessly parting the student body without so much as a raised brow. His gaze flicks up to mine, jaw tightening for half a second before his expression smooths out again. Then he points at the seat, the faintest smirk curving his mouth, a silent *sit* wrapped in plausible deniability.

I put my tray down with a little more force than necessary, catching the attention of a few students nearby. I arch a brow, theatrically wipe away a speck of nonexistent dirt, and slide into the seat anyway, smoothing my skirt beneath me. His gaze follows the movement, too steady to be accidental. If he's going to act like royalty, then fine, I'll play along. I might as well remind him that I don't kneel without a fight.

"Thought you didn't eat here?" I ask, placing my napkin in my lap as Wesley and Zander settle in on either side of me with their own trays.

He drums his fingers on the top of the table; the pace keeping beat with my heart. Almost as if he's syncing himself to me. "Do you see food in front of me, Princess?" He finally answers, raising his brow, and I clench my jaw. I roll my eyes and shake my head, ignoring the incessant nickname. I hate the way he says it—like it's dirty. He leans forward, and all of us do the same. "I have news, but we can't talk here."

Zander nods. "Contend after classes." He glances at me. "I'll come find you, and we'll go together."

"Okay," I agree.

I scan the room, spotting plenty of familiar faces; but not the one I'm looking for. I want to see the shock on Derek's face when he realizes I'm here, seated with the Kings, free. Not locked away somewhere, like he planned. Maybe he knows about his goons' fuck-up and is lying low, hoping this all blows over. It would probably be smart, but he can't hide forever.

"Julien's walking you to class this morning. Zan and I have something to take care of," Wes says, kissing the top of my head, pulling me out of my thoughts. I've eaten maybe half of the food on my plate, but my stomach is now in knots.

I look to Zander for help, but he nods once and stands to leave. He brushes his fingertips over my upper arm, and goosebumps prickle my skin. Thoughts of the two of them last night flood my mind, and I can't help it when my cheeks flame.

I stand, not actually done with breakfast, but not wanting to sit alone with Julien either. He takes the tray out of my hand and deposits it on top of the trash can before stepping behind me, forcing me in the direction he wants.

"I'm not an idiot. I know where my class is."

"Never thought you were."

I slow my steps and blink a few times. I turn to him when we get into an open area and stare. Was he just *being nice* to me?

"What?" he asks when I stay frozen in place

"Why did you ask Zander to get those items for me?" I rub my itchy wrists, and his eyes follow the motion before I drop them to my sides again. They've healed, but I still rub them. It must be a mental thing now.

"Zip ties hurt like a bitch."

I nod. That's the truth. "Yeah, but still." There was no reason for him to suggest getting me stuff to help, none except that he was trying to be nice. And I know Julien Azarian would never admit to being nice to anyone, especially me. But he's not going to tell me anything unless he wants to.

"You said you were going to talk with Derek's uncle. Did you find anything out?"

He scoffs. "Not anything that's substantial. You're not missing, which to him means no harm, no foul."

"No harm, no foul? Are you kidding me?" I yell a little too loudly. Julien shoves his hand over my mouth and forces me to walk backwards, pressing me against the side of the building. The cool, rough stone digs into my back as he crowds me. He's pinned me here once before. The same day I arrived at this stupid place. I narrow my eyes at him and pull his hand from my face.

"Don't touch me."

The familiar cruelty curls his mouth into a smile. "You like when I touch you, Princess. And I'm sure, given the chance, I can make you come better than Wes or Zan could."

I suck in a shocked breath. "How…"

"How'd I know they're fucking you?" He chortles a humorless laugh. "I know them, and there are no secrets among us. You're really doing a number on them." He glares down at me. "You're a pawn, Riley. And once you're not useful, you're gone. I've already told them to have their fun." He presses his hips against mine, pinning me in place, and drops his lips to the shell of my ear. "Did you think they liked you?"

I swallow past the lump forming in my throat as tears fill my eyes. I blink them back and inhale a shaky breath. He's lying. I know he is. There's no way either of them could fake their connection to me. Zander operates at a constant ten. Feelings like what he's shown me don't come with an off switch. And Wesley, he's too kind-hearted under it all to fake something like this with me. He knows it would break me. But that would be a cruel twist of fate, wouldn't it?

I shake my head, refusing to believe it. "You're lying. I don't know what you gain from it, but I know."

He shrugs. "Am I?"

Then he grabs my arm and pulls me with him to get to class, where he leaves me alone with my thoughts.

Just as I'm about to dive into the water for swim class, the door to the pool opens, and a woman walks in. She stops to talk to Mr. Evans, who blows the whistle to stop me. "Whittier, go change. You have a visitor."

A visitor? I scrunch my face in confusion and look at the woman. She's a little older than I am, probably in her mid-twenties, with brown hair she has pulled into a high ponytail and a nice skirt and top on. Her eyes land on me, and she looks me up and down. I might as well be an insect under a microscope with the look of intrigue she sends my way. I grab my towel and turn away from her.

I change fast and touch up my makeup quickly before rushing out of the locker room to meet the woman, and I follow her.

Who the hell would visit me? My dad hates me. He dropped me off in this hellhole and doesn't even want to talk to me. There's no way Leah could get on campus, and James would have no reason to come visit. That ends the list of those closest to me who aren't already on campus.

I shoot a quick text to the group chat I started with the Kings to tell them I'm headed to the office because I have a visitor, and my phone blows up. I ignore Zander's calls and then I remember he has access to the microphone; and send another message to the group.

ME:

I'll be fine. Listen in on my phone and come if it sounds bad.

ZANDER:

We're on our way to you now. Who are you with?

"What's your name?" I ask the woman who walks a few paces in front of me.

"Clarissa," she says, turning her head to look back at me. She offers no form of warmth, and I shiver under her gaze.

I muster up the friendliest smile I can. "I'm Riley, but you already know that ."

"Yes. I do."

My haunches go up reading the words. There's something about this woman he doesn't think is safe. My heart beats harder, and my legs shake the closer we get to the administration building. The only time I've been here is the day of arrival when I checked in and got my room key. Other than that, I haven't had a reason to be here. She hurries up the steps and opens the door, holding it with her back as she waits for me to join her.

I'm barely inside when I flinch at his familiar booming voice. "You should have called me the moment you knew she was missing! What would you have done if you had found her dead? Buried her without my permission?"

Michael Whittier. What the hell is he doing here? I look at Clarissa, my eyes wide with panic, but she offers no consolation. He's my problem, and the way the other staff members look at me when I enter tells me everything I need to know. I'm the only one here who will make him stop his tyrannical speech.

"Dad?" I ask, coming to a stop behind him.

He spins on his heel and glares at me. The pure rage on his face forces me to take a step back. When he sees me, his face softens, and he pulls me into a tight embrace.

"Jesus, Riley. What the hell did they do to you?" He turns my face to the side and inspects my bruise. "I heard what happened, and I came straightaway to see you. Why didn't you call me? It's been almost a week, and you didn't think to tell me?" He chastises. "You need a doctor to look at that and make sure there are no other serious injuries."

He grabs my upper arm as if he's going to drag me through the building door, but I snatch it out of his grasp. "No," I all but shout as he narrows his eyes at me in question. "I-I'm fine." I look at the terrified girl sitting behind the desk and mouth "sorry" to her. "Is there a room we can talk privately in?" I ask.

She points down the hall. "Second door on the left."

"Thanks." I turn to look at him and jerk my head in the direction she said. "Come on. Let's talk."

He follows closely behind until we reach the room. I close the door behind us and turn to face him as he paces around the space. "I throw so much support at this sorry excuse for a college, and this is how they repay me? You were nearly kidnapped. And who knows what else would have happened!"

He rambles on as I tune him out and push a heavy sigh past my lips. I've learned through experience that allowing Dad to go until he exhausts himself is the most effective approach. Sometimes it's quick, and sometimes it feels like it takes an eternity. But who told him about my kidnapping? Mr. Scarboro told me he wouldn't call him and that it was my responsibility if I wanted him to know. Did Julien somehow slip the information to him? Wesley? Zander? None of it makes any sense.

"Who told you?" I blurt out mid-sentence. He stares at me as if I've grown ten heads. Apparently, he didn't think that part of his rant was important.

He sighs. "Arthur Adkins." Now, that's an answer I didn't expect. Why would he call my father? "What's more surprising is *you* not telling me," he chastises.

My eyes bug out, and I scoff. "Why would I? You already

made it clear you didn't care about me. Lying to the press about having conversations with me, and then the other night on the phone…"

"I'm still your father," he shouts, making me jump. His face looks more like a tomato than it did moments ago. My heart pounds in my chest, and I feel my airways constrict as I fight to maintain control of myself. Deep breaths, Riley. In and out. Focus on grounding yourself.

"What did Mr. Adkins say?"

He sighs again, heavy and drawn out, as if the conversation is wearing on him. "He said a plumbing company came to fix a leak, and you were taken in their vehicle."

"Did he tell you how I got away?"

"No," he says through clenched teeth.

"Okay." For once in my life, I don't want to tell him. Something tells me not to trust him, and listening to that instinct feels like a small death. I never imagined Michael Whittier would be a man I couldn't depend on. But this doesn't seem right. Even if my dad found out from Arthur, why doesn't he seem more concerned? Wouldn't most parents get in touch with the cops or something? Try to catch the men involved, not pretend it didn't happen.

I take a step back and reach for the handle behind me. He notices my movement and sighs, dropping his head and rubbing his forehead. "I'm sorry, Riles."

"I'm fine. You should go. I doubt it looks good for your campaign to spend any time here. They may suspect something is wrong."

He opens his mouth to reply, but nods, knowing I'm right. And I can't help the sinking feeling that forms in my gut. Once again, he's putting his career before me. I wish my mom were still alive. She would never have let this happen. I would be at Dartmouth right now if she were still alive. Then again, I wouldn't have met the Kings or Ava. And the closer

I get to them, the more I realize how empty my life would feel without them. Even if what we have is for a moment in time, and not forever, it's what I need right now.

He pulls me into a hug. His heart drums a steady beat, and tears prick my eyes as I squeeze back. This almost feels like a last goodbye. He presses his lips to the top of my head and pulls away. Then he opens the door, leaving me alone and confused. I sink to the floor and let the tears fall down my cheeks, my heart shattering in my chest.

TWELVE

ZANDER

The three of us arrive at the administration building in time for Michael to push through the doors and stride down the steps. He has his cell phone in his hand, texting someone, not paying us any attention. Julien glares at him, and as if he can sense it, Michael pauses and looks over his shoulder at us. Julien's rage surrounds him like a live wire. Though he appears calm on the outside, he's fighting the urge to put his fist through Michael's face; and it's taking everything he has not to do it. Michael turns and continues walking without another thought. The asshole really is full of himself. He thinks he's untouchable. I'd love to be the one to teach him a lesson. The thought of sending him a video or pictures of the depraved things I'm going to do to his daughter flits through my mind, but I quash it. I don't trust him not to sell them.

Wes pulls open the door and stops at the desk, where Clarissa and her co-worker Stacy sit. I know Stacy suspects something between Clarissa and me, but has never asked questions. Even without an NDA, it's best not to question things around here. He glances at them and smiles brightly. His typical charming self shining once again.

"Hi ladies. We're looking for our friend, Riley Whittier. Have you seen her?"

"No," Clarissa gives a clipped answer, her eyes glued to mine.

Wes raises an eyebrow in surprise. "You sure? About five-three, blonde hair, great tits." His smile widens like he has a secret he's hiding. She does have great tits though, no lie there.

"Where is she?" I growl, not in the mood to play these games. Clarissa's mad at me, not Riley. When I got the text that Clarissa was the one who came to get her, I ran through thousands of scenarios. I thought maybe she'd tell Riley about our connection, or worse. Clarissa can be submissive, but she hasn't survived working at Pointebreak this long without having some balls. The only person she has a hard time standing up to is me. And I know this. Which is why I've been exploiting it. "Can I speak with you in private?" I stand in front of her desk, demanding her attention.

She looks down at her hands resting on her keyboard and nods before pushing her chair back and standing.

"We'll keep—" Wes turns to the other woman, "what's your name, sweetheart?"

"Stacy," she answers, a blush creeping up her face.

"Stacy, company. Won't we, Julien?"

He grunts in reply, and I'm surprised he offered that much. There's another fight this weekend, Julien put his name in the same night Riley went missing. He's been training twice as hard. I almost feel sorry for whoever steps into the ring with him. It won't be a fair fight. Julien is running on adrenaline and fury.

Clarissa leads me down the hall, and she pulls me into

the open kitchen area. Not exactly the private spot I'd hoped to have this conversation in, but it will work.

"Why her?" She asks, crossing her arms while her foot taps. Tap. Tap. Tap. Each beat scrapes my nerves raw, feeding the tension coiling tight in my chest.

"I don't know what you're talking about." I keep my face neutral, refusing to give anything away.

She scoffs. Then, dropping her voice to a whisper, replies, "You must think I'm an idiot, Zan. I'm not. Why else would you ask me to move her and get it done immediately? Are you fucking her?"

Yes. She was the best sex I've ever had. I plan on ruining her for anyone else. I focus on Clarissa's question again. She's not an idiot. This might be easier if she was. She knows something has been different between us. I've tried to keep it hidden from her, but apparently I wasn't discreet enough. And if I want anything with Riley, I know I have to end things with her. "She's my sister's friend, and someone broke into their dorm." I tell her the same thing I told her last week when I demanded she move them both into a new room.

"I thought I meant something to you." She takes a shuddering breath and closes her eyes, tears falling down her cheeks. I never meant for it to be this way, but she knew we weren't dating, and it was mutual play. Feelings were never supposed to be involved. I made that very clear from the beginning. And I know that makes me sound like an asshole, but so be it.

I place my finger under her chin and force her to look up at me. "Meet me tonight." I say, already knowing she's going to hate me more than she does now. She needs to hate me to let me go. Hearing footsteps, I glance over her shoulder, and Riley is watching the two of us.

"Yes, Sir," she says. Riley tears her gaze from us and walks out of view. A smile brightens Clarissa's face. She knows Riley saw that and heard that. And I'm sure she expects Riley to run for the hills. I drop my hands from her face and leave her there as I find my way back to the guys. The three of them are standing on the stone steps outside the front door. Wes has his arm slung around Riley's shoulder, and she leans her head on him.

Her big gray eyes catch mine as soon as I shove through the glass door and jog down the few steps.

"Come on, let's get over to Contend," Julien says, walking away expecting us to follow.

We walk to Julien's nearby car, and he slides into the driver's seat. Wesley tries to get into the back with Riley, but I shake my head and point to the front next to Julien.

"Oh, come on," Wes says with a grin. "I figured we'd give you both a little show on the way. Might help Julien finally pull the stick out of his ass."

"Front," I demand. Riley slides over, and I get in next to her, pulling the door closed. She looks out the window, ignoring me as Julien pulls out of the spot.

"It's not what it looks like, Luna," I murmur.

"Ironic that she's the one who came to fetch me today." She crosses her arms tightly over her chest. And bounces her leg in aggravation.

"Clarissa and I have only ever been friends with benefits. Nothing more. She's an easy fuck, not my girlfriend." Even as the words leave my mouth, I know that's not entirely true. Clarissa developed feelings for me. She did shortly after our arrangement started, and I pretended not to notice. As much as I hated to admit it, I needed her. I needed her submission. I needed her comfort. But that all changed the moment Riley agreed to be mine.

Mine to use.

Mine to break.

Mine.

There's no doubt she's exactly what I need. I know in time she's going to crave every sinful thing I can imagine. I may have spent too much time and money on some special items specific for Riley. Plugs, restraints, nipple clamps—I bought a little of everything.

Riley gives me a cursory glance, appraising me before looking at the window once more. "She didn't get the memo, Zan. She wants you. I can't believe I let you fuck me." She says the last part quietly, the words meant more for her than for me.

"Riley," I bite out, the warning clear in my tone. "You want to know what we did?" She doesn't answer, but I take it as a yes. "Don't say I didn't warn you."

Julien pulls up to Contend. Before the car fully stops, Riley opens the door and slams it behind her. Julien glares at her through the windshield as she walks around the front to stand close to Wesley, who types in the code for the door, and it opens. We both step out and join them.

"How do you know the code?" she asks.

He grins. "Contend was our idea. I'm the bookie. Julien fights, and Zander handles the operations along with security. It's a nice steady stream of income, among other ventures."

"Don't look so surprised, Princess." Julien adds gruffly. "We're not all good looks. There are working brains there, too." He taps the side of his head.

"I never thought you were stupid." She pauses before adding the insult, "Well, not Wes or Zan anyway."

He steps into her space, towering over her, anger rolling off him in waves. There's no way she doesn't feel it. He narrows his eyes, a true hunter on the prowl. "Remember my promise of stuffing your mouth if you can't keep it shut?"

She cocks a brow and crosses her arms over her chest. I don't think she realizes when she's trying to be tough, or pretend something doesn't affect her, she holds her muscles tight. "Yes. Remember mine about biting?" The sly smile she offers him almost makes me laugh. Almost. She thinks she has the upper hand here, but Julien is chock-full of surprises.

"I've got an open-mouth gag with your name on it. Why don't you come over and we can try it out? Your cock-sucking skills could use a little work."

She grinds her teeth as her face flames. I step between them and put my hands on Julien's chest as he looks over my shoulder at her, his teeth bared. She needs to be better at reading him and know when to tease and when to shut the hell up. And I know he's not joking about the gag, except it's mine, not his.

"What info did you get?" I ask, bringing us back to the reason we're here.

He backs up, putting some distance between himself and Riley, runs his fingers through his short hair, then leans against the wall, his arms crossed over his chest. "Derek's been M.I.A. since last week. The guys have been on the lookout for him with no sightings. I paid a visit to his dorm, and his roommate said he hasn't seen him in two days. When I asked Arthur about it, he denied knowing anything about it. Said he must be sick. But I'm not buying that bullshit."

"You think Arthur's involved?" Wesley asks.

Julien nods. "I think Derek is hiding out at his house, waiting for this to blow over. No doubt news has gotten back to him that you're back on campus." He looks at Riley, who nods. "I asked him how the plumbing van got on campus, and he said there was a report of a water leak in one of the dorms."

"How convenient," Wes pulls a chair over and plops down into it, stretching his long legs out in front of him. "Come here, Hellcat." He locks eyes with Riley and pats his thigh for her to sit down. She barely shakes her head before he grabs her wrist and pulls her down onto his lap, nuzzling her throat. Images of her rubbing herself on his thigh pop into my mind, and suddenly I want to see that. I want her to soak a spot on my lap as she comes all over me.

"What happened today?" Julien's words snap me out of my daydream.

Wesley sits back, allowing Riley a moment to breathe. "Oh. Um, my dad said Arthur's the one who called him to tell him about me. That's the reason he came by." She squirms under our gaze. "Maybe he's not involved. We know Arthur knows about the kidnapping from Julien. Maybe it starts and ends there?"

No, nothing is ever that cut and dry. Even if he didn't know about the kidnapping until Julien said something. Arthur knew Derek was involved. Julien tipping Arthur off may actually hurt us in the long run, but only time will tell. Someone wants her out of Pointebreak, so we need to find out who. Although I find it odd that he was yelling at the staff and not Arthur directly. Why put on a spectacle if you aren't even speaking to the person who could help?

There's no way they would have known she would be with Wes and me that night. That factor is impossible to determine. Riley is a creature of habit, though, so it wouldn't be hard to find her in the library. The only thing I can come up with is that Derek knew she would be at the library and figured he had some time to mess up her room to keep her there. Was he watching the building so that he knew when she came back? But then why wait so long? I don't have enough answers for the number of questions, and I don't like that. There's something we are missing, and unlike Riley, I'm not ruling her father out on anything.

"Who else wants you gone?" Julien asks Riley.

She bites her lower lip and frowns. "It could be anyone. If you haven't noticed, I haven't made a ton of friends around here. Most of the students hate me or won't talk to me." She pauses and closes her eyes like she's trying to remember something. "There was a girl in the library who told me to…" she pauses again, "stay away from him, *bitch*." She opens her eyes, her soft ones falling on me first and then traveling between us. "I'm not sure which one of you she was referring to, but obviously she thought you were hers. Originally, I thought she might have been talking about Wes, because I've been getting closer with him." She takes a deep breath, and she locks eyes with Julien. "But I think she was talking about you."

"What did she look like?" he asks. The only sign of his ire is a slight twitch in his fingers.

"Blonde, pretty." She shrugs. "She didn't stick around long. I haven't seen her in any of my classes, so most likely not a first-year."

"Stella," I say. I know there is a possibility of it being someone else, but where Julien has already told her to get lost, it makes the most sense. She's been trying to sink her teeth into Julien for the past three years. He throws her a bone now and again, but always keeps her at arm's length. She wants the title and the protection that comes with being in our inner circle; but she has ulterior motives. She's a terrible gossip, and I've heard she planned on trying to get pregnant with his kid. Julien stopped having sex with her after that.

His jaw clenches and his nostrils flare. I don't know exactly what he's thinking, but I wouldn't want to be Stella right now. "I'll talk to her. Find out what she knows. Who else?"

Riley shakes her head and shrugs. "I don't know. Besides you three and Ava, I only talk to Nick, Julie, and Darcy. And Julie and Darcy only talk to me when I'm with Ava. I've tried striking up a conversation with others in class, but…" she trails off with another shrug of her shoulders.

I hate that we're the ones who have made it impossible for her to make friends here. Riley has such a light about her, and if we aren't careful, Pointebreak will snuff it out. It's what they do best. Kill any goodness left in someone and leave behind something hollow. I understand the school's methods, but I don't have to like them. It was my fear with Ava. She's like Riley—pure. She has seen so much shit in her life, yet she is constantly a ray of sunshine. I don't want to see her soul turn black like the rest of us. Which is why I'm keeping a close eye on her too. I don't trust anyone around her.

"J-Julien," Riley says softly. He glares down at her, lifting a brow, waiting for her to continue. "Thanks for telling Zan to get the stuff for my wrists."

And he does the damndest thing of all.

"You're welcome."

THIRTEEN

ZANDER

Checking my watch, I groan in frustration. I swear time is moving backward. It's the fifth time I've looked in just as many minutes. She's late. Which is unlike her. Usually, she's early to a session, always desperate for any bit of attention I'm willing to toss her way. But we both know tonight won't be for pleasure.

I've felt this shift between us. Even over the summer, when I was in New York and she was texting, asking if she could come down for a visit. No. She knew that was going to be the answer, but she asked anyway. Life in New York and life at Pointebreak are very different, and the two can't mix. I made it very clear in the contract she signed before we started anything. She's a plaything. Nothing more.

Clarissa was never long term. She was merely a stepping stone—a pleasure release. We enjoy the same kinks, and I needed to work my aggression out on someone in a controlled environment. What separates us from animals isn't intelligence; it's control. And Clarissa fit the bill. Someone who didn't require more than sexual favors. But she's been asking for more lately. More aftercare, more dates, more phone calls. Each time I've reminded her of the contract she signed, she has backed down. But she's been asking too much and pushing matters that don't concern her.

Riley showing up at Pointebreak has changed my relationship with Clarissa. The last time we were together, she did nothing to ease my stress. Sure, I got off, but I was just as tense as when we started. But with Riley, it's different. As soon as I sank deep inside her, I knew there was no one else. I swear her pussy was magical; it made me see stars. And if she's as open to certain kinks as I think she might be, this is going to be the start of a beautiful relationship. I'm going to do every dirty, depraved thing to her, and she will thank me when I'm done.

The door opens a crack, and Clarissa steps through, closing it tight behind her. I cross my arms over my chest, and she drops to her knees, crawling toward me, her eyes focused on the ground. It's how I've trained her to come to me. Nothing more than a fuck toy, something to use. She stops in front of me and sits back on her heels, her hands resting on the tops of her thighs. I take a deep, steadying breath and pat the top of her head.

"You're late," I announce.

"Sorry, Sir." Her breath hitches. "I got stuck on a phone call. It won't happen again."

I take a deep breath into my lungs, holding it until they burn before releasing it slowly. The smell of fear and arousal fills the open space. She tied her hair back into a braid just as I like it, and if I guessed, she ditched her panties before she stepped foot in here. My body doesn't even react to that knowledge. She's not who I want. Riley is. In a strange way, I find relief in that. Riley is our future, and Clarissa is just standing in the way.

"No. It won't." I finally say. She glances up at me through her eyelashes, but lowers her head just as quickly. I extend my hand down to her. "Up. We need to talk."

Clarissa makes no move to place her hand in mine. "If it's alright with you, I'd rather not look at you as you rip my heart out."

I hum deep in my throat, then lean back against the desk at the front of the classroom and cross my legs at the ankles and my arms over my chest. "You're choice," I answer, boredom coating my words. Her chest rises and falls as a slight tremor shivers through her frame. "I'm releasing you from your contract, effective immediately." Her eyes shoot up to mine—red and glistening with unshed tears. "You signed an NDA, and I expect you to uphold that. Everything that happened in this room stays in this room. Anything I've purchased for you is yours to keep."

She shakes her head as her chin quivers. "Why?" She swallows hard. "What does that *bitch* have that I don't?" The words slice through the air like knives. I go as still as a church mouse, and she notices.

"Watch what you say, Clarissa." My voice is calm, but my heart pounds in my chest like a tribal drum, and my hands twitch with the need to teach her a lesson in manners. I know how strong I am. I'm not as big as Julien and Wesley, but that doesn't mean I lack strength.

She scoffs and scrambles to her feet. "I've known you for three years. Three!" She holds her fingers up to emphasize her point. "Does that mean nothing to you?"

"Nothing personal, Clarissa." My voice is devoid of all emotion. "You and I had a contract, and now I'm ending it. It's business."

She scoffs. "Business? Business?" she repeats louder. "I love you, Zander!" Tears slide down her cheeks, splashing on her shirt. She steps into my space and drops in front of me like she's planning on sucking my dick. I shake my head when she reaches up for my belt, and her movements halt.

"You love how I *own* you, Clarissa. You love how I use you like my little fuck toy. I've never loved you, and you know it. You've always been a good stress reliever; letting me fuck you however I want because you're a pain slut. You seek humiliation because it confirms what you already believe—that you're nothing. You were never going to be my future, no matter how much you beg."

Her face twists into something truly terrifying. There is nothing worse than a woman scorned. "You've just met her! That's impossible!" she screams.

I've always enjoyed a pissed-off Clarissa. She puts up a fight before ultimately submitting to my every whim. I wonder if Riley will do the same. Is she going to let me beat her ass red before I shove my dick deep into it? I plan to do that tonight. Wesley hasn't had that hole yet, and I'm taking it before he gets any ideas. I want a part of her that no one else has ever had. I'm a possessive fucker like that.

"She's been around longer than you know." She's been part of Julien's plan for years. I may have only just met her, but I've known about her for the same time I've known Clarissa. All of us have done our research. She's an open book with an incredible online footprint. All that will change, though. I plan on wiping all traces of her from the internet. It will be as if she never existed.

Clarissa's hand comes up to slap me; but I grab her wrist, twist it behind her back and push her head down on the desk, smashing her cheek into the cool surface. She bucks like a bronco trying to stand, but I won't allow that kind of disrespect. I press my lower body against hers, trapping her against the side of the desk, and wrap my fingers through her hair at the base of her neck, holding her immobile.

"You know better than to hit me."

"Get off me," she growls in frustration. "I hate you," she spits out. "I hope she breaks you, and you fucking die."

Anger rises within me—warmth floods my belly and travels to my outer limbs. Clenching my hand tightly in her hair, she cries out in pain. I want to force the tears from her face. I need her to hate me more than she does because if she feels any amount of sorrow, she's going to come running back. She's going to beg for forgiveness, and I won't allow that. She needs to forget me.

I lean over her, putting my lips close to her ear. "This is your only warning, Clarissa. Do *not* make me hit you. Because if I do, I won't stop until you're lifeless on the floor. I've learned from the best. I know where to hit to inflict the most pain, showing the least amount of bruises." A sob passes her lips, and she squeezes her eyes shut. Her body trembles beneath mine. I feel the exact moment she decides what she wants and her body goes lax. "I don't want you. Our contract is over. Get the *fuck* out of here before I do something you'll regret. Don't contact me again. Do. You. Understand?" I punctuate every word, driving my point home. When she doesn't respond straight away, I shake her, her head hitting the table again.

She tries to nod, and I release her. She stays glued to the desk as her body racks with tears. Finally, just when I think I'm going to have to drag her out, she stands, refusing to look at me.

"Lose my number." She walks to the door, and as her fingers graze the handle, I stop her with my words. "One more thing. Riley's off-limits. If I catch even a whiff of you trying to do something to her, I'm coming after you, and you'll understand the full extent of what's taught in this classroom."

She stays frozen in place, but turns her head to the side,

looking at the torture instruments that adorn the wall to her right. Chains, brass knuckles, and pliers galore. The door opens, and she slips out without acknowledging me. I didn't expect her to, anyway.

FOURTEEN

RILEY

I'm pissed off at Zander for putting spyware on my phone, and also for having a side chick. Or maybe I'm the side chick? Either way, it turns out I'm not the only girl he's with. And in the back of my mind, I know I shouldn't be angry, because I'm also with Wesley. The difference is, he knew that before he screwed me. He knows I'm not going to drop Wesley, and he made it a point to tell me he wants the three of us to have something.

As far as the spyware goes, too bad for him. I had no problem performing a factory reset on my phone today when I finally had a few moments alone. Wesley hasn't wanted to let me out of his sight, and I can't deny the giddy thrill of knowing I matter to him. There's no way he should be able to track what I do or say on the phone now. Yet, there's still a small voice in the back of my mind that urges me to be careful. It's a warning that is so loud that my skin prickles. I bite my lip as I stare at my phone. It's only a matter of time before he figures out he can't track me anymore. I don't know what will happen when he does. I bite my lip and stare at the wall, at the possibilities.

Maybe I'll still ask James to get me a new one. I should've asked Dad today, but the words were stuck in my throat, my chest tight. I got the impression he already thinks I'm an idiot because of what happened. How would I explain that I was stupid enough to leave my phone lying around and someone put tracking software on it?

Taking a deep breath, I pull up Leah's contact. As long as we don't talk about the exposé, it shouldn't be a problem. I laugh, more to myself than anything. There's no way I'm going to pull this off. And the more time I spend with these people, the more I think there is a bigger story elsewhere. Something isn't sitting right; I just don't know how to explain it. I went from thinking Pointebreak was the story in itself to thinking it might be with the Kings. But now…now I wonder if it has nothing to do with Pointebreak at all. The students here aren't doing anything illegal, and the school, as far as I can tell, follows the guidelines put in place by the town and state. No harm, no foul, right? I rub my forehead, wishing I had the answers. I'll send her an email to fill her in on everything we can't talk about.

I pull up her contact and hit the call button. The phone rings, and just when I think it will switch to voicemail, she answers. Her warm, familiar voice makes tears rush to my eyes, and I swipe them away quickly.

"Hey, girl," she says, dragging out the greeting. There's a lot of noise in the background. It sounds like she's at a party or something. Suddenly I feel bad for bothering her.

"Hey, you busy? Got a few minutes to talk?" I ask.

"Never too busy for my bestie. Hang on." I hear movement on the other end of the line, and then the room falls quiet around her. "Sorry, there's a mixer going on here. And before you can apologize, I could have ignored your call. Don't stress it."

I love her. It feels like ages since we've talked. "How's school going?"

"Good! I'm meeting some nice people. How about you? What's going on with you?"

I heave a heavy sigh. "So, I've had a bit of a rough few days," I start.

She gasps. "Did you get knocked up by Mister Hottie?"

I choke on my spit mid-swallow and start coughing. "Excuse me? What? No!"

"What? You two could make cute babies." I haven't sent her pictures of Wesley, and I never told her his last name for her to look up. How did she find him? As if she can read my mind, she says, "You're friends with Ava. I found him through her. Not many people named Wesley out there."

I shake my head and laugh at myself. Of course. She's such an internet sleuth. "God, you're insane, Leah. I love you. No, I'm not pregnant," I look down at my flat stomach and rub my belly. *Would it be the worst thing? Ugh. Yes! Why am I even thinking about it? I'm only eighteen!* I shake my head and give myself a mental slap. "But I wanted to tell you what's been going on. My dad knows, but not many others. Please don't say anything."

"You know your secret's safe with me."

I know it is. I could trust Leah with my life. Closing my eyes, I take a steadying breath. It shouldn't be this hard to say out loud, yet shame burns through my entire being. "Someone tried to have me kidnapped the other night."

"What? What do you mean tried to?" she yells into the phone, and I have to pull it from my ear, wincing at her volume.

I wave my hand in a quiet down motion even though she can't see me. "Shhh. I'm safe. But yeah. We are trying to figure out who's responsible. It was…scary, to say the least.

I'm lucky I found a cabin that belonged to one of my professors."

"Jesus, Riles. I'm glad you're okay."

"I just wanted to hear your voice; I miss you. And I wanted to let you know I'm okay and we are trying to figure out who is behind it. I've got something I want to run by you, but not on the phone. I'll email you later," I say, trying to keep my message as cryptic as possible.

"Okay." She pauses, and when I add nothing, she says, "I miss you, too."

"I'll call you soon. Thanks for always picking up."

I hang up and open my laptop to email James. I can't have Zander watching my every move. Although I'd be lying to myself if I said it didn't turn me on that he's been listening to Wesley and me. I knew he was watching, but until recently I had no idea he could hear us.

I type a quick note, telling him my cell got damaged in the chase and ask if he could have a new one ordered and shipped. Then, I start an email to Leah when there's a knock on my door. I pause, spinning in my chair to face it. After saving a draft, I close out of the email browser, opting to finish it later. Slowly, I stand and shuffle over to the door, keeping as quiet as possible. My heart is beating so hard I'm sure everyone can hear it.

"Luna, open up," Zander calls from the other side. I close my eyes, taking a shuddering breath. My fingers wrap around the doorknob, and I pull it open. He stands there, still in his dark gray slacks, black button-down shirt, and red tie. He rolled his sleeves up to his elbows, displaying his full arm of tattoos. It's never been harder in my life to focus. The intricate designs swirl and swoop up and down his forearms, each part telling another story. He drops a duffel bag on the floor, and I stare at it, wondering what can be in it.

"Change," he says, running his eyes up and down my body.

I scrunch my face. "Change into what?" I ask, looking down at my leggings and sweatshirt.

"Your uniform. No panties." I go to protest, and he steps into my space, crowding me. "You want to know, right? Want to know what Clarissa and I did? I told you, you're mine, Riley." My heart skips a beat, and butterflies erupt in my belly as I nod. "You have your safe words you can use tonight." I nod again. "Words, Luna."

"Okay," I say breathlessly. I understand what he wants.

"Okay?" he asks, a hint of a smile lighting his face.

He closes my room door, walks to the bed, and tosses my uniform at me. Grabbing it, I turn and walk into the bathroom; closing the door and locking it behind me. I don't know why I'm so nervous. I've already had sex with him, and I've done stuff with Wesley here too. This should be easy.

I slide my pants and panties down my legs and pull my skirt up. Zipping it in the back. My cheeks flush red knowing I have nothing under it. Then, I pull my t-shirt up over my head and slide the black shirt over my arms, taking my time to button it. I take one look in the mirror and at the last second, undo my bra and take it off, sliding my shirt back on again. I leave the tie off and unbutton the top two buttons, hoping I look as sexy as I'm trying to. Of course, the stupid bruise on my face is making me feel a little less than beautiful, even though my makeup is doing the heavy lifting of covering it. I figured this would surprise him, even though he only said no panties. My nipples pebble as they rub against the soft cotton fabric, and I squeeze my legs together.

I push a quick breath through my nose and open the door. He's standing right where I left him, and he gives me no sign of how he's feeling. The only thing that gives him away is the bulge in his pants that wasn't there when he walked in. I smile inwardly and look at my feet.

"Unless I tell you to, you're to look at me. Do you understand?"

I calm my racing heart and lift my head, looking directly into his eyes. For some reason, I get the feeling that's not a command he gave to Clarissa. "Yes, Sir."

He pulls something from his pocket and holds it out for me to see. It's black and silicone with a wide, red-jeweled base and tapered end. The size is bigger than I expected, and I'm not sure it will fit.

"You're going to wear this tonight under your skirt. Do you know what it is?"

I nod slowly, not taking my eyes off it.

"I want you to get used to the feeling. Questions?"

Questions? I should have some, right? Like, how the hell is that going to fit in me, or how am I going to walk? My heart is pounding in my chest, and my legs feel like jelly, so it takes a moment for my brain to catch up with me.

"Ah. Lube?" I may not have a ton of experience with sex, but I'm not a complete imbecile. He's going to shove a butt plug into me, and I know I need lube for that to go there. I've had Wes' finger there, but this is definitely bigger than that. My breathing picks up as my anxiety rises.

"Luna, breathe." He takes my face in his hands and tilts my head up to look into his eyes. I blink up at him and place my hands over his, needing to ground myself. I breathe in for a count of four and then exhale for the same count. He breathes with me, and my heart slows, the pounding in my ears lessening.

"I have lube. It won't hurt. It may be a bit…uncomfortable, but you'll get used to it."

He hands me the butt plug, and I turn it over in my hands, examining it. He then pulls a small bottle of lube out of his pocket and holds it up for me to see. I can't help the smile that spreads across my face.

"You got cherry-scented lube?"

"You always smell like cherries and vanilla. How could I not?" he says, offering a rare Zander smile to me. Butterflies erupt, and I smile widely in return. This is the side of Zander he keeps hidden from the world. I love seeing this side. But the other side—his dark side—is what my body craves. I never knew it could be like this. We've barely scratched the surface, and already I want more.

He sits on the edge of the bed and taps his leg. "Bend over, hands on the floor. Let me help you get it in."

I do as he asks, my upper body facing down to the ground as my hands touch the floor, balancing my weight. I try to breathe normally, but I can't calm my nerves. He flips my skirt up and hums in appreciation as he sees my bare ass. His warm hand rubs over my butt cheek, and I take a few steadying breaths. He slaps my ass and I jerk in his hold, not expecting it. It wasn't hard, and it didn't hurt. It was just enough to make me squirm on his lap. I think back to the spanking I received the other day, and I moan. I hear him flip the lid of the tube as he spreads my cheeks, and the cool gel hits me. He massages it over my puckered hole with his finger, adding a little pressure at a time.

"Relax, push against me. This isn't meant to hurt," he reassures me.

I do as he asks, and slowly his finger slips past the ring of muscle. The feeling is uncomfortable, but not horrible, just as he assured me. I inhale a few deep breaths through my nose and exhale on a shaky breath.

"Good girl, Luna. I can't wait to fuck your ass." He works his finger in and out as I sigh in pleasure. "Are you going to let me?"

"Yes," I moan, pushing back into him. Every nerve in my

body hums in approval. His cock jumps under me, and I know he likes my answer. Knowing he's prepping me to fuck me there does all sorts of things to me. The urge to sit on his lap and ride his thigh is the first thought that pops into my head. I wonder whether he would ever let me do it. I've used my pillow before to get off, but I bet using his muscular thigh would be a million times better.

"Mmm, so needy." His words draw me out of my delicious daydream and back to reality.

He pulls his finger out, and I groan, missing the feeling of him there. I don't have to wait long, though. More cool lube is drizzled on my ass, and then I feel the blunt head of the plug pushing against me. I push back on it just like I did with his finger as I slowly open for it.

"You're doing so well. A little more." He pushes a little more, and I feel it slide into place. A little uncomfortable is an understatement. It feels like his dick is already between my cheeks and I'm being forced to cock-warm. As soon as that thought hits me, a wave of pleasure shoots through me. I'm panting by the time he helps me stand, and I cross my legs to stop from dripping down my legs. I'm soaked.

He rubs his fingers over his lips and jaw as he looks me up and down. "Do you trust me, Luna?"

"Yes," I say breathlessly, without hesitation. Because I do. I know he won't hurt me. He would have done it already.

He takes my face in his hands and turns my face up to him. His dark eyes shine with glee. "Remember your colors and use them if you need them."

I blink at him and finally say, "Yes, Sir."

His lip quirks up into a smirk. "It's Daddy to you, remember?"

I knew he liked the nickname.

FIFTEEN

RILEY

We're standing in the middle of a classroom, and I may have stepped out of my element with this one. Tables with restraints, handcuffs from the ceiling, and many assorted instruments line the walls. It looks like a mix between what I would assume a sex dungeon and a torture chamber would look like. We're the only ones here, and I don't know why, but that makes me disappointed.

"What is this?"

"Welcome to torture class." He spreads his arms wide and spins on his heel as he drops his bag beside him.

My mouth runs dry, and suddenly the type of school this is becomes real. I know I've had survival class and a shooting class, but this seems different. Dangerous. How many men and women have made it through this class without having a mental breakdown?

"Or, in this case, my playroom. I've been able to make it work for what I need."

Thoughts of him and Clarissa filter through my mind. I lick my lips and swallow hard. Best to pull the band-aid off, right? Honesty is the best policy? Not that he gave me the same courtesy, but I can't do anything else until I ask.

"Are you still with her?"

He shakes his head. "No. I met with her prior to seeing you and ended things with her."

Here. In this room. I look down at the ground, a sinking feeling hitting me like a freight train. I'm the other woman in this relationship. Shame burns through me and sours my stomach. The moments of passion and excitement from only minutes ago wash away instantly. "I'm sorry. I didn't mean for this to happen."

"Don't, Riley." He shakes his head, hooking his fingers under my chin, forcing me to look directly into his eyes. They hold so much emotion; so much sadness. I don't know how I haven't noticed it before. Zander has always been a mystery, but maybe I haven't been looking closely enough. "Clarissa was never a long-term investment. That was our agreement. Things have been different between us for a while."

"Since I arrived?" I dare to ask.

"Yes." He nods. I hate that his words make me feel important. Wanted. And I hate myself most of all for how quickly I light up.

"You're going to let me use you tonight like a good fuck toy, aren't you, Luna?"

Lust burns my face as I say the words I know he wants to hear. "Yes, Daddy, please." Admitting it out loud is…freeing. I'm panting. My pussy throbs, and the plug in my ass only adds to my burning need. I need to feel him, to let him use me. The walk over here was difficult, and I could barely concentrate on what I was doing. I want his dick inside me. I want to come around him.

"Um," I start, the realization hitting me all at once. I don't know a single thing about him sexually. Is he clean? Careful? Responsible? He's already had sex with me without a condom, and I sucked him off. God, I am out of my element. I should have found this out last week when he surprised Wesley and me. He watches me, waiting for me to continue. "Are you clean? Like I just realized I never asked, and now I know there was someone else."

"I'm clean. Only ever used condoms with her and haven't had sex with her since last year. I know Wes and you both are, and you're on birth control."

"Y-yeah. I am."

With a nod of approval, he crouches, rummaging through the bag until his fingers close on an item, then rises to his feet. "Arms out in front of you."

I do so without hesitation. He places the thick leather cuffs around my wrists, and I sigh when the soft material covers my skin. I'm ecstatic it isn't metal. When they are secure, he pulls me toward him, sealing his lips over mine in a heated kiss. I reach for him, but he keeps my arms pinned between us. He explores my mouth, taking his time to move my head in the direction he wants before finally stepping back. I sway on my feet, wishing he was still kissing me before opening my eyes and balancing myself again.

He pulls me with him to the center of the room and lifts my arms above my head, placing the chain over a hook in the center. I have to stand on tip-toes to avoid putting too much pressure on my arms. I pull at the restraints, but I'm stuck.

He digs through his bag and holds a ball gag out for me to see. It's all black with a leather strap. "Open your mouth."

I look at it long and hard, and he allows me time to decide whether I want it. Finally, I open my mouth, and he forces it in, buckling the straps behind my head. It's not completely uncomfortable, but my lips are stretched wide around it. Thoughts of that open mouth gag float through my mind, and for a second I wonder what that would be like.

"Snap once for yellow, and twice for red. Show me." I do as he asks, with a little difficulty, but still show him what he wants. A chilling smile curves his face. "You're in a lot of trouble, Luna."

My heart races and my stomach drops. What? Trouble? Did they find out about the information I've been feeding to Leah? Do they know what I'm up to? He's had the spyware on my phone for a while now. He could have overheard any number of conversations. I widen my eyes as fear spikes through me.

"You were naughty, weren't you?" With his large fingers, he undoes the buttons on my blouse, slowly working it open until my chest is on full display for him. He clicks his tongue in disapproval as I fight to keep my breathing under control. "I told you no panties; not no bra." I pant as he squeezes my breasts, and when he pulls my nipple, I let out a scream behind the gag, dropping my chin to my chest. The sting of tears fills my eyes, but my ass instinctively clenches around the plug. He reaches into the bag and pulls out a small set of clamps with small moons dangling from them. "Looks like we're using these sooner than later." I jerk back, but the hook keeps me in place.

What else is in that thing? If he keeps pulling things out, I'm going to assume he has an entire store's worth of items in there. He pulls and rubs my nipples until they are fully erect; bordering on pain. I cry out again as he keeps one squeezed between his fingers, staring down at me. By now, I can't swallow, and spit is dribbling down my chin. I turn my head to wipe it on my arm, but only clean half of it.

"Hm, you'd look so pretty with piercings." He flicks my nipple and I snap my fingers once as I shake my head violently, the direct no, sounding like nothing behind the ball. "No? We'll come back to that on a different day." He clamps my right nipple, and I cry out, my body flushing as it trembles. I wish I were sitting. It hurts, sharp and electric, yet sends a rush of heat straight between my thighs. I'm still shaking when he does the same to the left, stealing the breath from my lungs. He steps back, watching me. This adonis of a man—the one I know is going to ruin me. Zander is the epitome of perfection. My chest heaves as I pant, desire racing through me in relentless waves, leaving me trembling and exposed beneath his gaze. I whimper and drop my head.

"Welcome to my dark side, Riley." He puts his finger under my chin, forcing my gaze to his. "When you're here, I demand everything from you. Your pain, your pleasure, and your submission. Do you understand?" I nod, a line of drool dropping to my breasts with the motion. He kisses my cheek hard, then pulls away. His eyes are so dark they are almost black. The Zander I know isn't here in this room with us. This is the monster he hides from the world. The one only a few get to see.

"I'm going to make your ass red. I want you to remember who you belong to when you do anything for the next few days. You're going to be my needy little slut. And then I'm going to pass you off to my brother to do whatever he wants with you. I want you in a constant state of arousal, ready to sit on my cock at a moment's notice."

I nod. Yes, I want all of that. To want to feel wanted, and I want to be reminded of who I belong to. I'm not sure how I went from hating him to craving him in such a short time, but right now I can't concentrate on that. I rock my hips in the air, searching for any sort of friction, any touch to take some of this burning need away. My breasts are heavy and full, my ass keeps clenching around the plug, and if he doesn't touch my clit soon I think I might die. Patience is not something I've had much practice in.

He stretches my arms, releasing me from the hook, and I bend my knees, holding my weight. I expect him to pull me over his leg like before, only to lead me to a bench instead. He pushes me over it and I cry out when my sensitive nipples press against it. He tugs my arms in front of me and tightens them so I can't stand straight. Then ties something around my ankles, pulling them apart. I couldn't move even if I wanted to.

"My version of a spanking bench," he says. I drop my head to the side, my cheek resting against the smooth surface. My upper body is at a slight downward angle, and my ass is in the air. My entire body is shaking as I stand on tiptoe. Some of it is from the thrill, and some is from the pain from my nipples.

"Snap if it becomes too much for you. Show me."

I snap my fingers, and he hums his appreciation.

Something comes down on my ass, and I cry out behind the gag. It feels like a million tiny zings of electricity coursing through me. He hits me again and again. Each time in a slightly different place. The pain slowly morphs into pleasure, and I rock my hips against the bench, searching for more friction. I'm dripping after only a few strokes.

"You're never leaving our sights again." *Whack.* "You're not going anywhere without one of us with you." *Whack.* "It's my fault you were taken." *Whack.* I cry out in pain, the sound muffled by the gag in my mouth. This is more than I expected. This is too much for me, but in a sick way, I know this is what he needs. He needs control. Zander is grounding himself, knowing that I'm here and safe. This is his way of taking control of situations. It's like something clicks in the midst of him beating my ass red, and I get it. I grip the bench leg and hold on. Knowing I can't stop this because *he* needs it.

He drops the instrument, and I hear him undo his zipper.

"I need to fuck you, Riley. It's going to hurt. I'm so sorry, Luna."

Then he presses into me so hard I see stars. My pussy clamps around him as he pounds into me. This isn't about my pleasure right now. This is about him dominating me, owning me. And I take it like a champ.

"You take my cock so fucking well." He spreads my cheeks and pushes the plug back in and out of me, fucking me with it. It's all too much. I don't think I can hold out for much longer. I beg behind the gag for him to let me come as drool and tears run down my face. My body is slick with sweat, and it shifts over the bench. My nipples feel like they are being rubbed raw, and if I don't free them of their iron clasps soon, I think I might die. Then he slows down. I know he hasn't come yet. He pulls the plug from me and drops it on the floor.

"I'm going to fuck your ass. And you're gonna let my brother watch. Do you want him to watch, little Luna?"

I nod my head quickly, wanting desperately to see who is there, but unable to turn my head to look. Yes. I want him to watch. I want Wesley to see me with Zander again, knowing it turns him on as much as it does me. He pulls out of me, and I tense, knowing what's coming next.

"Relax, let me in," he says, pressing on my lower back.

I squeeze my eyes shut, focusing on breathing. It's a lot easier to relax when I'm not so nervous about what he's about to do to me. I will my muscles to go lax and focus on opening for him. His hard cock at my entrance, and I push back on him as he moves forward. The tip of his dick pops in past the tight ring of muscles as I push harsh breaths through my nose. He pulls out, squirting more lube over my ass, and then slides back in. This time it's with less pressure. It still feels strange, but not terrible. Each time he withdraws, a cascade of pleasure ignites nerve endings I never knew I had. I gasp, but push back against him. Wanting him deeper still.

He moans and holds himself inside me. "Fuck, you feel amazing. So tight. I love taking your virgin ass." I shudder at his words as he pulls out. "You're so fucking perfect, Luna. I'm going to fuck every hole of yours. You're mine. You're fucking mine to break and put back together." This time I can't help the moan of pleasure that comes out. "Good girl." His voice is deep and raspy—absolutely sinful sounding. It should be illegal how sexy it sounds.

I let out a trembling breath at his praise, my body already on edge, craving more. The pressure builds again, delicious and consuming, pulling me closer to the brink I'm aching for. I make a soft, needy sound behind the gag, frustrated that I can't tell him how badly I want this—how much I trust him to push us both over the edge. I don't want to stop—can't use my safe word.

"I'm going to come deep in your ass. Mark you as mine. Then I'm shoving the plug into you to hold it there," he growls. "Maybe call Wes over to fuck your ass, using my come as lube. Would you like that? Be our dirty slut?"

I sob around the gag and nod the best I can as my orgasm rises to the surface quickly. I want to come with his dick stuffed deep in me. He fucks me like he intends to break me, my body stretching to accommodate his size. I feel like I'm floating, and when he squeezes my nose, cutting off my only air supply, I fight. I rear up, intent on tossing him off me. He's fucking my ass so hard and fast now I know he must be close. Each slap of his balls against my cunt pushes me that much closer. I can't move, I can't breathe, and my heart pounds so hard in my chest I think it's going to break free. The edges of my vision are blurring, and if I don't get some air, I'm going to faint.

"Fuuuck," he groans. His release coating my insides,

warm and sticky. He releases my nose, and I suck in a deep breath, forcing the air into my lungs and coughing around the gag as my orgasm racks through my frame. I feel like I'm floating—weightless and boneless. This is the most intense orgasm I've ever experienced.

Zan pulls out and pushes the plug between my cheeks, just like he said he would. He stands behind me, rubbing my clit in small, gentle circles as he works me down from my high. My body bucks against the bench. I whimper when his touch becomes too much for my oversensitive body. Quickly, he undoes my restraints, then unbuckles my gag. I slowly push it out with my tongue, still unable to move my limbs. My jaw aches from being open, but I'm sure it will be fine soon enough. He helps me stand, steadying me when my legs quiver, and removes the clamp on my right side. I cry out in pain as a mini-orgasm racks through my body. I wrap my arms around his neck as he leans down and massages my nipple with his tongue. The blood rushing back is painful, and I groan in his embrace.

"Shhh, you did so fucking well," he praises. Then he applies the same careful attention to the other side. My nipples are flushed and so delicate that even slight contact is painful. Looking past him, I expect to see Wesley there, but we're alone. I frown, my brows pulling tight, and he notices.

"No one was ever here," he admits. "I knew it'd turn you on more." I blink at him, still a little slow to understand. Everything feels like it's moving at half speed. I've never felt this way before.

"I'm bringing you back to your room. We are going to shower, and then I'm going to tuck you in. Okay?"

I nod as words escape me.

"Words, Luna."

I move my tongue around my mouth before finally whispering, "Okay."

SIXTEEN

WESLEY

We still don't have leads on who tried to have Riley kidnapped. Derek still has yet to show his face on campus, but it's only a matter of time before he has to come out of hiding. He can't stay away forever, and as soon as he does, we will be ready for him. We may not be allowed to kill him, but we are all well-versed in torture tactics. Perhaps a few of the lessons here will prove beneficial. I have my own suspicions about who ordered the kidnapping, but I don't want to say anything until I know for sure. And if I'm right...well, let's just say I hope I'm not.

I overheard some of the conversation Zander had with Clarissa at the administration office today. And based on how he acted when he came home before grabbing a duffel bag and heading to Riley's, I'm guessing tonight didn't go smoothly. She was more attached to Zander than I think he even realized. At least he was smart enough to have her sign an NDA when they first started...whatever they did. I know he's into some Fifty Shades shit. That's not really my thing. Although the thought of tying Riley up has piqued my interest more than once now. Maybe I need to do a little more research.

I shake my head, ridding myself of my fantasies; and scour the internet for any clues I can find. Anything to connect the dots. Derek has led to a dead end, not that I'm surprised. He was just a lackey, never a major player in anything. He likes to play the big bad guy, but the truth is he's a beta piece of shit. It caught me by surprise when Julien told us he was giving him a chance to prove himself. Maybe his dad put him up to it; who knows. Clearly, it was a bad move, considering Julien had to break one of his fingers.

We had little background about him at the time, but Zander pulled a lot of information. Buried claims of sexual harassment, gambling debts discreetly settled, and a past DUI offense. He's a real winner, that's for sure. I bet the only reason he's here is that his family is trying to straighten him out. Good to know if he ever requests access to Contend to keep him as far away as possible. Only paying individuals gain entry. Not that I think he would be stupid enough to enter the belly of the beast. It's common knowledge that we are the ones who run the ring and all the bets. And after taking Riley, he would be stupid to think we aren't on the warpath. His uncle can only protect him for so long.

I rub my hands over my short hair and pull the ends, a tiny sting putting my mind back into focus. I feel like I've been at this for hours, and when I look at the clock, well, I guess I have. Pushing past my growing exhaustion, I keep searching. Up next is Michael Whittier himself. Color me surprised when he showed up on campus to scold Riley. I know none of us called him, and Dorian didn't either. So either Arthur called him, or someone else tipped him off. Something just isn't sitting right with me, and I want to know the connections he has in and outside of Pointebreak. Clearly, there are some powerful ones; otherwise, there's no way she could have gotten in here. There's a waitlist a mile long of families whose status isn't quite up to par, who want to send their kids here.

I sit back in my seat, placing both my hands on top of my head and stare at the colorful pictures on the screen. Instead of searching for more dirt on Michael, like I should be, I turn my attention to Riley. Her beautiful smile shining on the screen brings one to my face as well. She's been involved in his campaigns since she was young. I've seen pictures of her at ten, twelve, and now. She has stood by her father's side for almost as long as he has had a political career. There's a picture of her in a beautiful full ballgown, a delicate mask covering her upper face. She's smiling up at her father. The picture is from two years ago, and the headline reads *Governor's Annual Masquerade Ball Is A Success*.

I scan the article, looking for any clues. I can't help but wonder if Riley knows what these types of events are used for. I'm sure some of Michael's events are to rub shoulders with those who can help him in his career. But I can almost guarantee he used these events to make shady deals or shady connections. If he had the connections to get Riley placed here, he must have the right people in his corner. He's a shoo-in for the senator position. He's guaranteed that through his business dealings. There are enough powerful people to make sure they continue to get what they need; and Michael has assured them they can continue to do business as usual if that's the case. Even the candidate who is running for governor has been handpicked by crooked businessmen. The article is a fluff piece. Praising him for his good deeds and philanthropic endeavors. He donated half of the money raised to a local rehabilitation charity. I can't help but snort. He's probably the asshole who looked the other way when drugs were pouring into the streets until it was more convenient for a political move.

There are hundreds of articles about Michael. His political career, fluff pieces about his family and values, and then I find some about the death of his wife, Riley's mom, Grace. Riley looks so much like her. Same nose, shape of face, and pouty lips. I suddenly have an image of her in her late twenties. Older, but no less beautiful. Her hand covering her pregnant belly, a radiant smile spreading across her face. My arm wrapped possessively around her waist, protecting her and our unborn baby from the world.

I want that.

I've never pictured myself having kids; but suddenly the idea isn't so crazy. *That's if she doesn't walk away after all this shit.*

I push a heavy sigh out and look up at the ceiling. Things are working out a hell of a lot differently than I predicted. I'm usually great at reading people and determining odds. But Riley has done nothing but surprise me right from the start. So it shouldn't be a shock that she's making me rethink everything I've ever thought I wanted.

My phone buzzes on the table, and I place it to my ear without even looking at who is calling.

"It's Wesley," I answer.

"Hey," Zander whispers. "Can you come stay with her?"

My haunches go up, and I'm on full alert immediately. "Is she okay?"

"Yeah, she's fine. Things got a bit…rough. I don't want her to wake up alone, but I want to do some more digging into something. Just a hunch I have."

I want to ask him what rough is, but I know he wouldn't hurt her. Not on purpose, anyway. I wonder if his hunch is the same as mine, but I keep that thought to myself.

"Yeah, give me a few minutes to finish what I was doing, and I'll head over there."

I arrive in less than fifteen minutes and rap my knuckles on the door. I hear someone shift off the bed, and Zander's face peers out at me before he opens it completely. The light from the hall spills into her room and over her sleeping form. I grin at him, and he scowls back.

"One day, I'm going to see what you're actually into," I say, wiggling my eyebrows at him.

"I'm thinking of changing up some of the basement. The torture classroom isn't doing it for me like it used to."

"Get the stuff and I'll help you set it up," I offer. His lips quirk up in the corner, not exactly a smile, but close for Zander. He grabs the bag from the floor and tosses it over his shoulder; then glances back at her one last time, his features softening before his stoic expression forms again, and he brushes past me. She's wearing him down a lot faster than I thought possible. I toe my shoes off, peel my sweatshirt overhead, and climb in beside her. She smells so damn good and I need to get some of her body wash for my shower. The more she's around, the more Julien is letting his guard down. And while I know she belongs here at her dorm, I don't think it will be long until she is considering our house hers. Pulling her close, I snuggle against her and fall asleep within minutes, my mind calming for the first time today.

She shifts, and it jolts me awake. I'm immediately on high alert. I strain my ears, listening for anything out of the ordinary, then I kiss her shoulder when I realize nothing is amiss.

"When did you get here?" Her voice is raspy, still full of sleep.

"A few hours ago. Zan had some things to do, but didn't want you left alone." Her body sags against mine, and I know she's not happy about that. I want to know everything he did to her tonight. Clearly, she had a shower; even hours later her hair is still a little damp.

"Will you bring me to your house?" She fills her lungs with a deep breath and continues. "I think tonight was a little hard on him, too. He shouldn't be alone either."

I bury my face in her hair and smile. "You're gonna be good for us, Hellcat." I pinch her butt, and she shrieks, pulling away from me. "Come on, let's go."

She hesitates and nibbles on her lower lip. I stare at her, waiting. "I don't want you to think I'm pushing you aside for him. I'm not. But I think he needs me tonight."

Sitting up, I cup her face in my hands, drawing her eyes up to mine. "When you do right by my brothers, you do right by me, Riley. That thought never crossed my mind." My lips tick up in a sinful smirk. "I've actually been trying to figure out what fun I missed out on tonight, and I'm dying to be part of that show. Maybe next time you could invite me, even if it's just to watch." She sputters, and even in the darkened room I know her face is turning bright red. I laugh and pull her against me, pressing a kiss to her lips. She grabs my shoulders and climbs onto my lap.

Riley pulls on a pair of leggings as she is only wearing a t-shirt and panties, and we leave her room, locking it securely behind us. I open the passenger side door for her, and she slides in, smiling at me when I get behind the wheel and start the engine. The ride is quick, especially at three o'clock. When we pull in a few minutes later, I take her hand and hold it as we walk up the sidewalk and open the front door. The house is silent and dark, not that I suspected otherwise. Even when we can't sleep, we mainly stick to our rooms, or the basement gym. I pull her up the stairs behind me, and we both stop when Julien meets us half-way down the steps. They stare at one another, my hand firmly wrapped around hers, giving her my silent protection.

"All of us are dealing with our own shit," he says.

Riley nods. "I know."

"Don't make it worse for him."

"I won't," she promises.

Julien gives her a once-over before he nods and continues down the stairs without another word. Even though Julien doesn't want to admit it, she's wearing him down. He's falling for her, just like Zander and I have. Her magnetic pull draws us closer, and instead of pushing us away, she hugs us tighter. Her protectors.

I pull her hand, and she looks up at me, smiling. We stop outside Zander's room, and she knocks quietly on the door. I hear the lock unlatch moments later before he yanks the door open. His eyes panicked until they land on Riley, then he calms instantly.

"What are you doing here?" he asks, confused.

Riley drops my hand and wraps her arms around him, pressing her cheek to his chest. "I'm here for you."

SEVENTEEN

JULIEN

Friday afternoon, and I'm already in Scarboro's class, waiting for Riley to show up. I've been attempting to keep my distance from her since her mishap in the woods. I paid a visit to Stella, who denies any involvement. She all but shit her pants when I held her by the throat against the wall, cutting off her air, and demanded she tell me what happened. I made it clear that I don't need her. If she steps out of line again, I'll end her—permanently. I don't give a shit what connections her "daddy" has. She's worthless to me, and I'll make sure she knows it.

Students' families may hide a lot of secrets, but nothing stays hidden at Pointebreak for long. Secrets are just as useful as money, and depending on who has one, maybe more so. Riley doesn't know half the secrets her dad is hiding from her, which is why she is so useful. I've spent the past few days working with my dad and his men on a new plan of action, and I think we finally have something narrowed down.

And you're the asshole who suggested this current plan.

She's never going to listen to me, which is why I need Wesley and Zander to get her on board. And just in case that doesn't work, I need a Plan B. I'm working on it, but that is going to take time, and that's something I'm afraid we are running out of. Students filter through the door, and I keep my eyes trained on it, waiting for someone in particular. When Chloe walks in, I get her attention.

"Chloe," I say, barely raising my voice. She stiffens and turns to face me, blinking as she waits for me to say more. I raise my eyebrow and beckon her over with my finger. She visibly swallows but stops to stand right in front of me. "Derek Adkins"

She furrows her brow, and I lower my head, keeping my eyes trained on her. She gasps and covers her mouth with her fingers when it clicks. "Why?"

"No idea. Have you heard anything? Know anything?"

She shakes her head. "No. I barely know the guy. I know he's Mr. Adkins' nephew; but that's it."

I figured she didn't. She doesn't seem like the type to hang in his social circles. Not for nothing, she's kind of dorky. I'm surprised her family sent her here at all. I understand that for some parents, it's classes like these that's the reason for sending them. They want to make sure their kids have a fighting chance. For others, it's helping them into an arranged marriage. My gut is that is her deal. I haven't had Zander look into her, but if she's going to have anything to do with Riley, it might be wise to.

"Could you do me a favor?" She nods, her arms cradling herself. "Talk with Riley. She could use a few more friends around here."

Her lips curve into a small, gentle smile. "Okay. I'd like that. She seems nice."

"She is." I admit. She needs friends, and Chloe was the only one brave enough to come tell me what she knew about Riley's disappearance. Small gestures tell a lot about a person. I leave her to go stand in the corner where I have a clear view of the door. Riley walks in moments later, Wesley giving her a kiss on the cheek. She smiles up at him with stars in her eyes. I lock my jaw and push the anger simmering aside. Then I shake my head and berate myself for having a reaction. She's a pawn. Nothing more. Even as the words filter through my brain, I know it's not the whole truth.

She sees me and offers a small wave. I tilt my head to the side, examining her like some sort of insect instead, and she drops her hand, her shoulders slumping. Why does she want me to like her so damn badly? And why do I want to? She's the enemy's daughter. The key part of my masterful plan. This isn't Romeo and Juliet. Well, if things don't go to plan, we might both be dead, so there's that.

Riley stands in her usual corner, far away from me, and I watch as Chloe takes a step closer to her and starts talking. They are too far away to hear what they're saying, but Riley smiles, and that makes me feel marginally better. I know we haven't made it easy on her. And maybe if there are more eyes on her, nothing else will happen. Wes and Zan hardly let her out of their sight now, but that doesn't mean they can be there all the time.

The door opens and slams shut as Scarboro walks in, a scowl on his face. *What crawled up his ass and died?* He looks at me but says nothing. I guess we'll be chatting at the end of this class. He has to have an update on my dad. Either that, or something bad has happened. Neither option is good. He drops an empty box in front of him; the noise echoing off the walls in the large gymnasium.

"All right, listen up, everyone." The class steps in closer, surrounding him. "It's time for another round of hide and seek, but with a twist. Your attacker must keep you pinned until I get there. If they can't, congratulations, you survive. If they can, consider yourself dead. Once you're out, captors can go after other students."

Chaotic whispers fill the room as stress levels peak. He knows the can of worms he's opened. Whoever the lone survivor is, will have the entire class on him or her. I look at Riley, and she glances my way, her eyes wide with fear. I'm the lesser of two evils, and she knows it. Most of the first-year students take a step away from the older ones, and Chloe stays close to Riley's side. I swear most eyes land on Riley, and I don't like it one bit.

"I want to see how well you can fight your way out of this. Anything that can be considered a weapon stays here." He points to the empty box in front of him. "Empty pockets, leave your bags."

Everyone empties their pockets, dumping their belongings into their bags, which they deposit in the box. I'm not surprised to see a handful of pocket knives being put away. Despite the ban on guns at Pointebreak, it would be unwise to go without a weapon. Pointebreak does a good job of making sure feuding families stay away from one another, but accidents happen.

"First years, you get a thirty-second head start. Make the most of it." He puts his whistle to his lips and blows.

FWEET

Whispered curses, gasps of unease, and the sound of sneakers on the tile floor fill the room. First-years take off in a flash, traveling in different directions. Everyone around me is champing at the bit to capture someone. I won't lie; I love the rush, hunting her down, stalking her like prey. It's the sweetest part of breaking Riley. The way her body coils with fear, her breath ragged, her eyes wide and wild—it drives me mad. I crave her fear almost as much as I crave her body. She races further into the gym, avoiding the same direction as others, breaking from the pact. It might have been smarter to stay with everyone; but it's too late now. Glancing to my right, Silas, another third-year, winks at me as a devilish smile takes over his face.

When Scarboro blows his whistle again, the rest of us take off in search of our victim. Shrieks and laughter quickly fill the air as the female students are captured. Only an idiot would assume they tried their best. I hear Scarboro telling them they're out, and even scolding Chasity for her lack of effort. One by one Scarboro checks off his list of those who couldn't get away. Riley is still out here, though. My Princess likes to run and hide; I know she'll be one of the last ones.

"Two students left," Scarboro announces as I continue my search, each container coming up empty. I haven't heard her scream out yet. I've heard multiple versions from her, including fear, pleasure, and pain. Zander gave us access to the camera feed and audio from her phone. I've seen and heard it all. And I'd be a liar if I wasn't jealous of my brothers for bringing her so much pleasure. For using her body to take away a fraction of their pain and frustrations.

Her scream has me pulling up short, and I jerk my head to the right, listening for her again. She cries out, and this time I run as fast as I can in the direction it came from. I slow to a walk, shoving my hands in my pockets to avoid smashing his face in. To anyone observing, it appears I don't give a shit. Silas stands directly in front of her, his hand wrapped around her neck, while Bruno and Adam hold her arms out, pinning them against the metal wall. Silas lowers his lips to her ear, says something, and her face blanches, all color draining from it. Her eyes water and her chin quivers as her chest rises and falls so fast I think she's hyperventilating.

"Let her go," I say, taking a step closer.

"Uh-uh. She's my captive, Azarian. You can't keep her safe forever," he sneers before focusing his attention back on her.

"Isn't that right?" She frantically shakes her head as the first tears fall down her face. Bruno and Adam hold her arms in place as Silas pulls her body; it bows toward him at an almost unnatural angle. Her chest rises and falls with a ragged, almost panicked rhythm.

"Let her go," I growl, the sound low and menacing.

I lower my head and grit my teeth, ready to charge when Scarboro comes into view and blows the whistle. The three of them let her go, and she drops to the ground like a sack of potatoes, hugging her knees to her chest, rocking back and forth as she hides her face.

Silas kicks her upper leg, and her body jerks. I stand over her as the three walk away laughing. I glare at Scarboro, but he says nothing. He walks away, giving us some time alone.

I drop next to her and pull her small body into my lap. She rests her cheek on my chest but keeps her face hidden from me. "Shhh, Riley. You're fine. It's okay. It's a drill, not real." She shakes uncontrollably in my lap as I rub the back of her head. "I've got you. You're safe." I'm not sure how much my mantric reassurance is helping, but I know she needs something right now, and I'm all she has.

She'll never be safe with me though. I will break her over and over, while my brothers build her back up. It's fucked up, but it's what needs to happen. She's not meant to be mine now. Maybe once long ago, but not now. I know there were plans for us at one point. An arranged marriage of sorts. But then my mom was murdered, and that was the end of that. Alec and Michael were on the outs, and Riley was none the wiser.

After several minutes her body stills in my arms and I think she may have fallen asleep on me but she lifts her cheek from my chest and looks up at me.

"Why can't you always be this nice to me?" she asks,

running her index finger along the curve of my jaw. "Why do you hate me?"

Her body feels good in my arms. I want her to explore me more, but now it's neither the time nor the place. I ignore her questions and ask one of my own instead. "How long have you suffered from panic attacks?" Because that's what that was. Did they just start, or has she had them for years? It's possible it's a trauma response to being kidnapped, but the way she knew how to handle it and bring herself down from the brink tells me it's probably been going on for a while. I'm surprised she hid it for this long. Wesley or Zander would have told me if they knew.

She stiffens in my arms and crawls off me, putting some much-needed distance between us. I've been hard as a rock since she crawled into my lap, and I know she could feel it. I'll blame it on the chase; but I can only fool myself for so long. I want her as much as Wes and Zan have her. Sooner or later, Riley is going to find out the truth, and I just hope she's strong enough to handle it.

EIGHTEEN

RILEY

I notice he didn't answer either of my questions, instead asking his own. It shouldn't surprise me; that's who he is. He's always in control. Hates having his authority questioned. Even when I've tried to talk shit about him to Wesley or Zander—question his motives—they always shut me down. I'm sick of it. For once, I want answers to *my* questions. And if he's not going to, then neither am I.

"Never mind. I should have known you wouldn't answer me." Standing, I wince at the slight pain in my thigh, thanks to Silas; and brush dirt off my legs and skirt. I'm going to have yet another bruise there. Soon enough I'm going to look like the poster child for abuse. I mentally shake that image from my mind. Julien gets to his feet and towers over me, making me feel small in comparison.

His green eyes bore into mine, daring me to refuse answering him. "Do Wesley and Zander know?"

I close my eyes and count to four, calming my frayed nerves. I know today was an exercise, and that nothing bad would have happened to me, but I couldn't help slipping into an episode. Silas is an asshole. He proved it today when he and his lackeys held me captive. I understand that was the assignment, but the crude things he told me weren't. And unfortunately, because of recent events, my mind dropped into a bottomless black hole. Especially when he told me that if he ever caught me alone, he'd send a message to the Kings. Yay for me for being used, yet again, for someone else's agenda. The free groping didn't help either.

"Riley," he repeats. This time there's a hard edge to his voice. He hates being ignored, and I almost want to do it longer just to twist the knife. But I won't be doing myself any favors if I do that.

"I'm fine. Thanks for the save, but it looks like I'm a dead girl today." Then, I give him my back and wander through the maze of crates to the front of the room again. Scarboro is still talking, but as soon as Silas sees me, he grins and winks. I grimace as bile bubbles up in my throat. I know he was being an ass because he wanted to get a rise out of Julien, but his words hit a little too close to home, considering my recent night run through the woods. Chastity pops her gum and rolls her eyes at me like I'm an annoying fly she wants to swat away. Whatever. I hate to say she's jealous, but I know she is. She's been vying for Julien's attention since the beginning of the year, and he barely glances her way.

So when Julien comes up behind me, I can't help it when I stand on tiptoes, pressing a feather-light kiss to his cheek. He turns his head, my lips colliding with his, and he holds me in place. His hand wrapped around the back of my head, fingers curling into my hair. His tongue darts out, exploring mine, and I sink into his touch. Not exactly the best location for a bit of PDA, but I suppose we could do worse. Scarboro clears his throat, and Julien releases me. I flush red as he wipes his mouth and peers over my shoulder at the rest of the class, who are waiting for us.

"Come to my fight this weekend," he whispers.

I suck in a deep breath, surprised by the request. No, not a request, but a command. I'm sure Wes or Zan would have brought me, but it hits differently coming from him. Something in the back of my mind gives me pause. What if this is a trick, or he's planning something? Maybe I need to give in a little if I want him to come around. Things have been different between us lately, and maybe if I extend the olive branch, it will make him less combative.

"Okay."

"You two done?" Mr. Scarboro calls out to us, and I jump in surprise. Julien's hand goes protectively around my waist, as if he expects to have to shield me at any moment.

"Yup," Julien answers, pushing me toward Chloe, and he takes up his usual spot as far from me as possible. Chasity locks her jaw around the gum, and I swear steam billows from her ears. In my haze of lust, I had momentarily forgotten about her and her venomous looks. She crosses her arms tightly over her chest and glares back at Mr. Scarboro, ignoring us once again. I'm not sure if he did that on purpose, but regardless, it puts a little pep in my step. I stand next to Chloe, who beams at me.

"I wish I were you," she says in a dream-like voice.

"Trust me, Chloe, you don't."

She keeps her voice low. "Are you kidding me? It's like a fantasy. Julien was frantic when he couldn't find you last week."

Now, that bit of information causes me to pause. I knew he ran to my dorm; he told me as much, but he never told me he spoke with anyone. "What are you talking about?"

"The night you were…," she trails off, turning her finger in a circular motion, wanting me to finish her thought. Straightening, goosebumps covering my flesh, as I blink at her. I'm at a complete loss for words, and she must decide I look lost, so she continues, "He was pounding on doors, asking if anyone saw anything. I was in the bathroom when he came by, but I met him outside and told him I saw you pushed into a van with four guys."

Looking at Julien, I let her words sink in. He was frantically searching for me. He was scared. I knew he came to find me, but I assumed it was out of obligation, not fear. Something has been going on with him. His eyes lock with mine, and we stand there, frozen, in some sort of battle of wills. Mr. Scarboro continues to talk around us, but I hear nothing. All my attention is on Julien. Why wouldn't he have told me that? He never mentioned pounding on doors for more information. I offer a small smile, and I swear I see his lips twitch in response before he drops my gaze.

At least I did something right today.

Saturday morning, I rush to the on-campus post office to retrieve my package from James. He ordered me a new phone and had it sent directly to me. It looks the same as the other, so hopefully I'll be able to fool Zander for a while. Even though I did a factory reset, I don't know if that's enough, and I don't want to take any chances.

I lock myself in my room and rip open the box, turn on the new phone, complete the setup, and download my contacts from the cloud along with my apps.

I bury the old phone under blankets and put some music on my computer to drown out any additional noise. I don't want to leave anything up to chance when I speak with her.

"Hey, girl," Leah says as she answers my call.

"Hey. I have some stuff I want to tell you. Do you have a few minutes?"

"Hang on, let me get my computer open." I hear her shuffling some things around. "Okay, whatcha got?"

"Well, remember I told you I was kidnapped last week?"

"Duh, like I could forget that. I've been dying for more details. What did Wesley do?" She gasps, "Did he murder someone for you? Was he all like, she's mine, hands off?" she asks, her voice dropping in octave to match his timbre.

I snort and lay back on the bed, covering my heated face with my hand. He didn't murder anyone, but I will say I've never felt more protected in my life. Between him and Zander, I've hardly had any time to myself. But Ava needs me too, and I miss her. I made the guys go home last night and spent it watching a movie and eating popcorn with her.

"No. But things are interesting in that department."

"Oh?"

I bite my lip, then inhale a sharp breath. "I'm also seeing Zander."

"Sexy diner man? Jesus, you go away and get two guys and I still can't even get one. I definitely went to the wrong school!" she complains. "Can I show up next semester?"

"I mean, there are a lot of really nice-looking guys here."

It's crazy to think two guys want me, when prior to coming here I could barely hold down a boyfriend. Something in the back of my mind questions that piece of information, too. Julien seems to know me, or at least know of me. It wouldn't be hard to believe. I've been in the public eye almost as long and as much as my dad. Michael paraded me around at all his functions, parties, and campaigns. Even more so when mom died. I was good for his image.

"So, has anything changed with our plans then? Like do you think there's something better out there?" she asks, breaking into my thoughts.

"I feel like there's a bigger story here, but I haven't been able to figure it out yet."

"You'll figure it out. In the meantime, I want details about boning two guys, you slut!" she teases me, and I smile wide.

"Um, really crazy. Like it's weird, but in a good way?" Sighing, I add, "I don't know what I'm doing. I'm so far out of my element."

"Well, I'm not the one to ask. I only have one guy I'm fawning after."

"Oh?" I perk up at this new information. "Tell me."

"It's nothing much. We've gotten coffee a few times, but I really like him. He's in my history class. His name's Corbin. Cute, a little goofy, but we mesh well together."

"I'm really happy for you, Leah. That's awesome, and I can't wait to meet him. If he does anything to you, I'll send my mafia boyfriends to kick his ass."

She laughs at that. It's only a half-lie though. Because I will really find a way to make him miserable.

"Hey Riley?" she asks.

"Yeah?"

"I'm glad you're safe. I don't know what I would have done if something had happened to you."

"Me too. Miss you," I say, biting my lip to stop from crying.

"Miss you too. Talk soon."

I sit straight up on my bed, a sharp knock on my door. My heart pounds in my chest and my stomach drops. I need to get this under control.

"Riley, it's me," Zander says from the other side.

Closing my eyes, I sigh in relief. Since Derek came to pay me a visit, I don't like that I can't see who is on the other side of the door. I twist the handle and drink in his tall form. He's in a pair of jeans, a black shirt, and a black leather jacket. He has a bit of scruff on his face that I decide straight away I like. It adds to his dark and mysterious personality. I reach my fingers up, trailing them along his jaw, and he hums his appreciation.

He drops a bag at my feet and closes the door behind me. It's the same bag from the other night when he made me wear the plug and clamps and my pussy aches at the thought. I wonder what other fun things he's brought for me today.

"I'm here to help get you ready for Julien's fight," he says.

"Oh," my face falls. "I was planning on getting ready with Ava. And you're wicked early. The fight isn't for another three hours, right?"

His lips twitch in amusement. He hardly ever smiles, so when he does, it makes my heart stop and I melt a little more. I'm well aware I barely know anything about him; but Ava and I have talked, and what I have gathered, her home life wasn't the greatest. Which means it was probably worse for Zander. I can only imagine the type of things he had to endure to become such a hardened man.

"You can still get ready with Ava. I just have a few," he pauses and rubs his jaw as his eyes trail up and down my body, "requests."

I suck in a deep breath and push it out on a shaky sigh. "Like what?" My belly flips, and I keep glancing down at his muscular forearms, covered in tattoos. His muscles jump and dance as he clenches his jaw, and suddenly I'm thinking about how he choked me. How he controlled me to his liking. I suck my lower lip between my teeth and bite down, quashing the impending need.

"Hmmm, is my little Luna hungry for me?" His voice is low, with a hint of danger.

It feels like I could melt into a big pile of goo and never get up. I don't even know what's coming over me with the three of them—well, the two of them at least. Julien is still a work in progress. It's as if fate bound us in the same darkness, and the only way to survive is together. Together involves Julien. He's the last piece of the puzzle. My future is in his hands, and I know there's nothing I can do to stop it.

"Yes," I respond with a sigh. "Please," I whisper.

The muscles in his jaw twitch, and he raises a brow in my direction. "Mmm," he growls deep and lustfully, "I love when you beg. Makes me so fucking hard."

I glance down; a defined bulge filling his jeans. "We have some time," I say, hoping to entice him enough to take me.

"I'm not looking for a quick fuck." Frowning at his reply, he continues. "I want time to play with you. Don't worry, we'll make you feel better soon enough." He removes items from his bag and places them on my bed. Dildos, plugs, handcuffs, scarves, and the last item—a gag. My jaw already aches just looking at it. It's not like any I've seen before. It's a big metal ring with leather straps. And if I had to guess, this is the open-mouthed one Julien talked about.

I worry my bottom lip between my teeth, looking at everything, and frown as a thought hits me. "Um," I start, looking at my feet, feeling so embarrassed. "Are these new, or are they…hand-me-downs?" God, I feel like such an idiot even asking the question. My face flames and I rub my cheeks to hide the stain of color.

His smile is so bright this time that it covers his face. He finds humor in my discomfort, and it makes me want to bury my face and hide. I groan and hate myself a little for even asking the question.

"All new, and all for you."

I sigh in relief and nod. Then I point to the gag. "I'm not sure how I feel about that."

"All these are for you to keep here. We don't have to use anything you're not comfortable with. We'll work up to it. Now, about that request. I want you to wear these." He holds out a pair of small, round balls that are connected. "Ben Wa balls," he explains. "They're small and shouldn't be uncomfortable." He licks his lips and bites his bottom one. It's the cutest thing I've seen because it's so flirty, and so unlike him. "I want you dripping for me tonight. I want to smell your arousal at the fight, and when we bring you home you're going to come all over our dicks."

My stomach tightens at that, and I nod. "Um, y-you said requests?" My voice comes out breathy as I wonder what else he wants me to do.

"Hmm, I did, didn't I?" I nod; keeping my eyes trained on him. He unzips the front pocket on the bag and pulls out a butt plug and lube. My heart thunders in my ears, and thoughts of the other night filter through my mind. I wonder if Wesley would be involved this time. I guess he said dicks so I assume Wes is part of the plan. In a twisted way, I want Julien to know what Zander and Wesley do to me—how they make me feel. I want him to be part of it.

"Be a good girl, Luna. Lay back on the bed, let me help you put them in."

NINETEEN

RILEY

Getting ready for tonight is proving to be a little harder than I thought it would be. Between the balls in my pussy and the plug in my ass, I feel like I'm being stretched open. I don't know how I'm going to survive until after the fight. Every slight move and my nerve endings fire at once; bolts of warmth and electricity course through me. I also had to tell Ava…everything. Well, not everything as far as exactly what depraved things I've done with her brother, but that we are seeing one another. I thought she was going to be mad, but yet again, she surprised me and gave me a big hug instead.

"Listen, I love you like a sister already. You're amazing. But I'm also going to say this as his actual sister. I will still cut you if you break my brother's heart."

I smile wide and shake my head when she draws her thumb across her neck. "That's the last thing I want to do to him, to any of them."

She has a sly smile on her face. "Yeah, how is that working, anyway? It's like you're living in a smutty book or something."

"Um," I duck my head, hoping to ward off the blood rushing to my cheeks. She's not wrong, though. This isn't a normal relationship…or whatever it is we are doing. I don't know how to describe it. All I know is that it feels right. "I don't know, it just does."

She makes a face, then smiles warmly. "Gross, but I'm happy for you."

I pull the black, lacy tights up my legs, smoothing them out. Then pull my leather skirt up and top it off with an oversized cream sweater. I have a pair of low-heeled booties I tugged on to complete the outfit. I look in Ava's mirror and smile at myself. I look good; and it's going to drive the guys crazy tonight. Almost as crazy as I feel right now.

One thing Zander forgot to tell me is that the plug in my butt has a small vibrator in it. Imagine my surprise when it popped on. He got a nasty text from me and all I got back was a wink eyed emoji. Wes must have sent that because that's not Zander's style at all. Okay, so I don't think I'm going to survive the night. For a hot minute I thought about removing everything; just to see what would happen, but thought better of it. I don't know if I could handle more bruising on my butt along with the other parts of my body.

Right on time, someone knocks on the door, and Ava jumps up to answer it. Nick stands there with Zander, the two of them in a heated stare-down. Wesley must be with Julien, helping him prep for the flight. I told them I could show up with Ava and Nick, but that idea was shot down before I could even finish it.

I roll my eyes and push Zan away. He allows it, but walks backward, keeping his eyes planted on them. Nick hesitates before kissing Ava's cheek, and she closes the door behind her, following us down the hall. Zan is driving all of us to Contend, and thank goodness it's a quick ride.

We slide into our seats, Nick and Ava in the back, and

Zan adjusts the mirror to watch them as he drives. He says something to her in Russian, and she snaps back at him. I don't even have to know what he said to know it pissed her off. Nick kisses the back of her hand, and they lace their fingers together.

"Ava," he warns.

She rolls her eyes and crosses her arms over her chest, brewing in her own annoyance. I don't want to get in the middle of the two of them; but he needs to release the reins a little. He throws the car into park after a few more tense moments. Then he places his large, rough hand on my leg, holding me in place while the others get out. When the doors close behind them, he locks them, trapping me in here with him.

"I'm not the asshole you think I am, Riley. I'm protecting her. Nick…I don't know. His family is close with ours, which means nothing good can come of it." He gives a heavy sigh; like the weight of the world is resting on his shoulders. And maybe it is. Maybe he is carrying too much of a burden, and he needs to let some of it go. "She's my sister. I'm need to protect her from the monsters in the world. Even those you wouldn't suspect, are good at hiding until it's too late."

This is big. I know him opening up to me, even if it's only a little, is an enormous step. Wrapping my fingers around his, I offer a slight squeeze, and he looks at them. "I know you're trying to protect her; but you need to give her a little space."

He shakes his head. "How much has she told you about our father? Growing up?"

"Not much. She's mentioned it was rough sometimes, but hasn't gone into details."

He huffs out a dry laugh, shaking his head, "Rough. Nice way of putting it."

"We don't have to do this right now. Julien has a fight and I know he needs you in there. We can talk about this later." I place my hand on his cheek, drawing his attention up to my face.

"Do you know why I enjoy spanking so much?" I shake my head. I assumed it was just a kink he had. I never thought of a deeper meaning to it. "My dad used to beat me. Kick me, use me as an ashtray. You name it, it's probably happened."

I can't help the horrified look that crosses my face. Who would do that? Why would anyone think that's okay; especially to their own child? "I'm—"

He holds up a hand, cutting me off. "He told me once, probably when he thought I was unconscious, that he did it to toughen me up. That the only way I'm going to rule anything is to be ruthless. A monster. Men needed to fear me, and that could only happen if I had nothing to fear; and would stop at nothing to get what I want. I was fifteen when he stopped beating me up and started training me to be ruthless like he is."

"Jesus," I whisper under my breath. "Is that why you watch everyone?"

"There are no surprises when you know what to expect. When you understand everyone's motives, you can't be surprised."

"So what is it about Nick that you don't like?"

"He likes my sister."

"So, no reason."

"There's something. I just haven't found it yet."

Contend is packed tonight. We missed the first fight because we were in the car, but there's another one before Julien's; who is the main event. There are more students here than I remember seeing last time. Or maybe it's the same amount, but I recognize more people now; I'm not sure. The energy is just as intoxicating as the last fight, and I smile wide as we walk into the warm space. Boisterous voices surround us as Zan leads me through the throng of bodies to the side of the ring where Wesley and Julien are getting ready for his fight. Julien has a light robe draped over his shoulders as he wraps his hands, securing the black material securely around his wrist.

"There she is," Wes says, pulling me into a hug and kissing the top of my head. He dips his head so his lips brush the shell of my ear, "You smell amazing. I can't wait to eat you later."

I pull my lips between my teeth and smile. I don't even know how to respond to that, so I press a kiss to his cheek and pull away, focusing on Julien. "Who are you fighting tonight?" He stands at the side of the ring, the current fight in the last few seconds. Both men look worn down and bloody; but they keep grappling for a hold on one another.

"Nico."

"Have you fought him before?"

He gives me a bored look and pops his mouth guard in as they ring the bell, signaling the end of the fight.

"Winner, Sean!" The referee holds up the short man's arm high in the air as he sways off balance. The crowd cheers, with a few boos mixed in. I don't think he was a favorite to win tonight, which means those who bet on him won a lot. They clear the ring and mop up the blood on the white padding as the crowds place last bets and order more drinks.

"Are there more students here today than last time?" There's got to be. Everywhere I turn, there are students watching us.

"Julien's trying to draw Derek out of hiding and opened

tonight up to all students. They got a text with the code last minute," Zander says, helping Julien into his gloves and securing the velcro.

"You think he'd show up?"

Julien shrugs. "He's not the brightest bulb in the box. We've got eyes out for him."

"What are you going to do if you catch him?"

He gives me a long, incredulous stare before pounding his gloves together and climbing through the ropes into the ring to a round of cheers and chants of his name. Julien Azarian is in his element and is a superstar. He feeds off the energy of the crowd, and when Nico, his opponent, enters the ring, I see the switch. Something predatory sharpens behind his eyes; and I'm glad I'm not his target.

"Welcome to the main event," the referee starts, and the crowd yells a little louder. "In this corner," he motions toward Nico and his group, "we have Nico!" Several boos trickle through the crowd along with more cheers. "And in this corner," the crowd gets louder, and I can't help the smile that tugs at my lips, "Julien!" I scream along with them and jump, only to have the Ben Wa balls shift and I open my mouth in a silent "O". Julien is too busy scanning the crowd to notice, but Zan sure as hell does.

He says something to Wes, who looks at me with interest and licks his lips. It feels like I'm on display at a market, and I'm top prize.

"Shouldn't you be paying attention to Julien?" I chastise.

Wes offers me his casual, playful smile. "Why? It seems the better show is right in front of me."

The bell dings and the men circle each other. Nico throws the first punch, which Julien dodges effortlessly. Jab. Block. Cross. Block. It's a warmup round, each fighter learning the other's moves. Julien sweeps his leg out and knocks the other man off kilter before swinging his fist, landing it in his gut. The crowd groans, and Julien instinctively steps back, steering clear of Nico. He scowls and grinds his teeth, his nostrils flaring in anger. He reminds me of a bull in a china shop, and I know Julien sees it too.

His eyes dart in our direction, and he says something to Julien, then gives him a cruel smile.

"Has he ever fought Nico before?" I ask Wesley.

He shakes his head. "No. He's a first-year, but he specifically asked for Julien, so we humored him and set the match up. He has a small following online for his fights, so he's not a complete nobody."

The bell rings, and the first round is over, with Julien landing the only hit. He comes into the corner, snags his water bottle from Zander's outstretched hand and rolls his neck.

"He's fast," Zan calls out. "Quick punches, solid form. Keep your guard up. If he lands one on you, you're not walking away unscathed."

"He won't."

The bell rings for round two, and Julien strikes hard and fast this time, barely giving the referee time to move out of the way. He gets Nico in the jaw with an uppercut, and his head snaps back with a sickening noise. The crowd groans, and I grimace, burying my head in Wesley's chest. He laughs, but rubs my upper arm all the same.

Three more jabs and a roundhouse kick to his neck, and he crumples to the ground. Julien is breathing hard, and the tendons in his arms and neck protrude as he stands there watching, waiting for the call we all know is coming. The referee counts to three, and they ring the bell once again in Julien's favor.

He leaves the ring without a backward glance, Nico still down, blood trailing from his face.

TWENTY

RILEY

I'm not entirely sure what I witnessed tonight, but that wasn't like the last fight. That was...personal. He said something to Julien to make him snap, but no one is talking about it. Wes and Zan have had a few quiet words passed between them; but other than that they are busy tallying out the night. It seems student night was a bigger hit than they expected, based on the glimpses of smiles and numbers I saw when I was trying not to be nosy. Okay, I was totally being nosy.

The crowd has thinned out now, with a few stragglers milling around finishing drinks and having a few good laughs. I'm ready to leave, but we are waiting for Julien so we can all head back to the house together.

"He didn't show up," Zan says more to himself than to anyone in particular.

I don't know Derek well, but I didn't think he would be stupid enough to show his face in the lion's den, regardless of them allowing all students in. I still don't understand what's in it for him. He wouldn't put his life on the line for no good reason. You don't cross the Kings.

Julien comes out from the back room, showered and changed, his dark hair still damp. He has a duffel bag slung over his shoulder. As he approaches us, he gets a few shoulder claps and words of congratulations thrown at him, but he doesn't stop to exchange pleasantries. I stand, my gaze glued to Julien as a cage bunny throws herself at him as if she has a claim. He shifts her out of his way without a word. Satisfaction burns through me when his eyes never leave us.

I didn't realize they had a locker room of sorts. I suppose that makes sense. Most fighters don't want to go home bloody or sweaty after a fight. I know I wouldn't want to.

The plug in my ass vibrates on a low hum, and I glare at Zander, who only offers me a slight curve of his lips. Wesley notices, and his eyes sparkle with glee. Not that I had forgotten about the toys stuffed inside me, but my mind has been elsewhere. Derek. Julien. The green monster of jealousy rears its ugly head when it comes to Julien. Everything that's led up to now is…confusing. The push and pull amongst us. I know Zander, Wesley, and Julien are a package deal. It feels like a game of tug-of-war, and I'm the rope—yanked in opposite directions, fibers tearing one by one. Who will ultimately break me?

Wesley pulls me onto his lap and buries his face in my neck, taking a big inhale. "I can't wait to bury my dick in you. Maybe I should pull you into a locked room, rip your tights, and fuck you against the wall. Actually…" He stands, forcing me to my feet and takes my hand in his, pulling me with him, hellbent on doing exactly what he's described.

"Don't you dare," Zander warns on a low growl.

Wesley stops and gives him a boyish grin, and he tucks me under his chin, wrapping his arms possessively around me. "Fine, but I want your ass," he whispers to me.

I stiffen in his arms. Wes is bigger than Zander, and I'm not exactly sure how he's going to fit. Wes kisses the back of my hand and drapes it over the back of his head as he plants tender kisses on my elongated neck. I lick my lips and sigh in contentment.

"Get a fucking room," Julien grumbles.

"That's the plan, stud," Wes winks playfully and smiles widely. "Gonna stick around and watch?"

Julien shakes his head and storms off, taking his things with him.

"Come on, let's go," Zan says, taking my hand in his and leading us to the door. Wesley follows behind, his fingers on my waist. We pile into the car with Wesley in the back with me. Ava and Nick left right after the fight, and I know Zander wasn't happy with that arrangement, but the alternative was that he would have to take her back to the dorm; and he said he didn't want to leave me. I would have been fine with Wesley until he got back, but I know better than to argue with him when he's made up his mind.

Zander's confession tonight has me mixed up. I have so many questions, including whether Ava experienced the same treatment. They are only a few years apart in age, so it makes sense that she could have been the subject of her father's abuse too.

Wesley rubs his fingers down my nose, and I blink at him in surprise. "Whatcha thinkin' about, Hellcat?"

I scrunch my nose and turn my head to look at him. "Oh, nothing, really. Just…" *How my heart breaks for Zander, and for you. How no kid deserves to be treated like garbage.* It wouldn't surprise me if Julien had a rough childhood too, and that's why he is the way he is. I mean, his dad is in prison, and from what I've read, he was a black market dealer and possibly killed his own wife. I'm sure that would screw anyone up.

Wesley lowers his head, catching my attention, and places

a gentle finger under my chin. I squirm in my seat. "Just what?"

"Nothing." I lean in close, my lips grazing the shell of his ear. "I—I'm dying to get these toys out of me," I whisper. Which isn't a lie; it's just not the whole truth.

Wesley smirks, and I already know he's up to no good.

Zander opens the door to his bedroom, and I stop in my tracks. I've only been in here once, and it was dark when I arrived. We cuddled and slept, and then I left the next morning with Wesley to train. I didn't have time to really *look* at his space. And the only way I can describe it is one hundred percent Zander. Dark.

His multi-screen computer sits on his desk, darkened, but the low hum of the machine tells me it's on and he could wake it at a moment's notice. His bed is against the opposite wall, adorned with a hunter green spread and four padded cuffs lying in the middle. He has a deep blue oversized chair in the opposite corner, and when Wesley sits, I know the exact purpose of it—to watch. His dresser and nightstand are the same shade, dark, nearly black in the dim light of the room.

Zander pulls a knife and lube out of the bedside table, and I tense; unsure what the knife is for. He notices my change and flips it open, the blade glistening in the low lamplight. He walks up to me, and I crane my head back to look into his eyes. Wrapping his hand around my hair, he holds my head immobile. He runs the blunt side down my cheek as I hold my breath, my body trembling.

"Take off your top." He releases me, and I do so without hesitation, dropping it on the floor by my feet.

"Skirt." I reach to the side, unzipping the skirt and letting it pool at my feet. Wesley sucks in a quick breath, and I look at him. He rubs his hand up and down over his covered dick as my mouth salivates. I clench around the Ben Wa balls and moan. Everything moves agonizingly slow. I've been dripping for hours, imagining how this night would go.

"Wes, get the restraints."

He grins as he stalks toward me, the soft cuffs dangling from his hands. I offer him my wrists, and he places tender kisses to the inside before securing the strap. Then he offers my other wrist the same attention before kneeling in front of me to secure the cuffs to each ankle. The sight of him on his knees for me makes my stomach flip, and I run my fingers through his blonde hair. He looks up at me, a warm smile spreading across his face. My stomach clenches and I swallow hard, knowing this is going to be intense.

"Bed."

I back up, my knees hitting the edge, and I lower myself to the mattress, resting my hands on either side of me. I shift when the plug pushes against the balls.

"Do you want them out?"

My face heats and I nod. "Yes."

"Move up the bed and lie back."

I do as I'm told, and my breathing picks up when I feel a dip on the bed. I look down my body and Wesley has a hold of one of my ankles. He secures it to the restraint on one end, while Zander takes care to secure the other one. I test the movement, and they hold strong, my legs splayed open.

Zander drags his finger up the side of my body, and my skin breaks out in goosebumps. Wesley wraps his hand around my wrist and pulls it out, giving it the same attention as he did my ankle. My breathing picks up when I try the restraints, and I can hardly move. I'm splayed out for them like I'm a dessert platter ready to be devoured.

"Safe word?"

"Red," I reply without hesitation.

"Good girl. Wes, have a seat. I want you to see what this does to her."

I lock eyes with Wesley as he pulls his shirt over his head, tossing it on top of my sweater. He unzips his pants and pulls the waist open before splaying out on the chair to enjoy his front-row seat. I can see his bulge and I lick my lips, wishing he was standing here instead.

Zander removes his shirt, and I get a glimpse of his tattooed chest and abs, along with the scars and bruises. Even in the dim light, I can pick out the fresh ones. I'm not looking forward to those torture classes. I reach for him, seeking any sort of touch, but I can't move more than a few millimeters, and I huff in frustration. His husky laugh has me clenching, and I wish I could rub my legs together to ease some of this tension.

"Soon, Luna. You're going to ride my cock as Wesley fucks you from behind."

He runs the tip of the blade down from the middle of my lower lip to the delicate spot on my throat where my pulse is fluttering out of control. I close my eyes as the cold metal travels further until it reaches my waist. The first tear through the lace has me gasping in surprise. I don't know why this is so erotic, but it is. Zander tugs at the fabric with the blade again, adding another hole to them. He bends down, his scruff tickling my leg as he kisses the exposed flesh. He bites my clothed core and my back bows up off the bed, wanting more.

"Please, Zan," I whisper. I'm not sure what I need, but I know it's more than what he's giving me.

He pushes me back down and kisses mc again, this time attempting to push his tongue through the material. I'm drenched.

"How's she taste?" Wes asks from his spot on the chair. I had forgotten he was there, watching. He catches my gaze and holds it as his hand caresses up and down his length, his boxers covering him.

"Like fucking heaven," he answers before digging the knife under the tights and ripping a gaping hole over my left thigh. He does the same to the right, no longer teasing me, teasing us. Then he places the blade under the seam of my panties and pulls up, ripping them away from one leg, then the next. It's the last thing I expect, but I bite back a groan as the cool air hits my heated flesh. I watch as he shoves them in his pocket before leaning down and inhaling my scent. My body flushes and I close my eyes, embarrassment washing over me.

"Open them," Wes commands from the chair. I do, watching him as Zander lifts my hips and pulls the soaked Ben Wa balls from me. My pussy spasms around nothing as the plug in my ass vibrates.

"Oh God," I moan as I rock my hips up, seeking Zander's mouth, anything to put an end to this constant edge he's had me on. He slides two fingers inside me, searching for that sweet spot that he knows will make me come. He plays with me and I'm there. I'm so close it borders on pain, only for him to pull out and the vibrator to turn off.

"No," I sob out. It's too much now. I can't do this anymore. "Please, Daddy, please let me come." Tears fall down my cheeks, and he leans over, licking each one, devouring my pain and pleasure.

"Shhh, Luna. We're gonna make you feel so damn good." He kisses me hungrily, his tongue exploring my mouth as I lay splayed open for him. I open my eyes to watch Wesley, who is still lazily stroking himself.

"Take the plug out. If I don't get in her soon, I'm gonna blow my load," Wesley says.

"Didn't know that was a problem for you, Wes. Maybe

you should get that checked out." Wesley huffs out a laugh. "Come on, help me."

I laugh at that, and I'm graced with a full Zander smile.

After releasing me, Zander pulls off his pants and boxers, throwing the articles of clothing somewhere, and I'm speechless. This is the first time I've seen him completely naked. Every other time he's kept most of his clothing on. It's a vulnerability I don't think he allows himself often, and it warms me knowing he is sharing this with me.

He sits at the edge of the bed and pats his thigh for me to sit on him. He leans back, supporting his weight on his hands, and looks up at me when I crawl into his lap. I line him up with my slit before sinking down on him completely. Just like when he had me tied to the bench, I feel so full with him and the plug filling me.

"Fuck," Wes says, placing his hand on my back. I turn my head enough to capture his mouth before Zan lays back, taking me with him.

Zander lazily pumps his hips up into me, and I'm on the verge of coming.

"Please, Daddy, let me come."

"Not until Wes is buried deep in your ass, Luna." He stops moving, knowing if he doesn't, I'm not going to hold it.

Wes opens the bottle of lube and rubs it up and down his length, then tugs the plug. I clench around it, holding it in place. It's been in there for so long that he needs to reopen me. Little by little he pulls it until it pops free.

"Ready?" he asks, the blunt tip of his cock at my asshole.

I lift myself off Zander and arch my hips the best I can, allowing him some space. When he presses into me, I clench my jaw and focus on breathing through my nose. He holds my hips in place as Zander sits at my entrance. Zander peppers my cheeks and neck with kisses and licks. Moaning, I push back on Wesley, the tight ring of muscles relaxing with each micro-thrust into me. It doesn't burn, I just feel so full.

"How ya feeling, Hellcat?"

"So good. I want you deep; don't stop." It's torture not to move my hips; to feel Zander right there, but not in me.

"You're so fucking tight, I don't think I'm gonna last." Wesley pushes all the way in and holds himself steady. I'm panting as I wait for him to move. He leans over and kisses my shoulder, sliding out, just as Zander thrusts up. When Zander pulls out, Wesley presses back in, over and over. Our breaths and moans penetrate the surrounding room. The blend of ecstasy and pure need is a heady burn, setting my nerves on fire. Zander crashes his lips to mine and holds me immobile, exactly where he wants me, while Wesley grips my hips with a punishing force, slamming into me each time Zander withdraws.

I feel both their dicks rubbing inside me and it doesn't take long for my orgasm to rear its head again. I whimper against his lips as my body locks up, pleasure spiking through me.

"That's it, baby. Come on our dicks like a good girl," Zander says in a husky voice. The sound extends my own delicious release.

Wesley goes first, holding himself deep inside me as he releases everything in me on a guttural groan. Zander follows, pulling my ear down to him, whispering something in Russian to me. Then, pulling my lips to his in a final, sweet kiss. He moves lazily in and out of me, but when Wesley pulls out, I wince. Yeah, I'm definitely going to feel that for a few days.

I lay on Zander, my cheek pressed to his chest, listening to his racing heart. Wesley comes back into the room with a few towels, tossing one to Zander, who catches it with ease. Wesley grabs my hips, pulling me up and helping clean me.

Then he grabs a t-shirt from Zander's drawer and pulls it down over my head. He's already back in his jeans, the waist still open, but his boxers are gone. I run my fingers down the trickle of hair that disappears into his pants. His abdomen tightens instinctively, sucking inward as a laugh escapes.

"That tickles, Hellcat."

I blink at both men, lost for words in my sex-drunken haze. What just happened, and how am I ever going to let them go?

TWENTY-ONE

ZANDER

Riley lays sprawled out on my bed, the early morning light filtering through the partially open window, bathing her face in golden light. She's perfect. Riley Whittier is the final jagged piece of my heart. Her breathing is still deep and even; her eyelashes rest delicately on her cheeks. She's going to leave us when she understands what this is, and I don't think my heart can take it. I know she wants to know what's going on, and maybe it's time to let her in.

She stirs and blinks her eyes open, only to smile widely when they lock on mine.

"Morning, beautiful," I say. Then in Russian tell her, "You've ruined me for everyone else."

"I'm going to take it you said, I trust you slept well," she teases, and stretches her arms above her head.

"Something like that," I admit. She gets up to use the bathroom, then climbs back into bed, snuggling close to me.

"What time is it?"

I pick up my phone to look. "Just after seven-thirty."

The silence stretches between us, not at all uncomfortable, but serene. A lazy Sunday morning. She fell asleep last night between Wesley and me. Once her breathing evened out, he went back to his own room for the night, giving us some privacy.

She traces the tattoos on my chest until she finds the Russian phrase and stops. "What does it mean?"

I hold her hand. Stroking my thumb lazily over the back. I say the words in Russian first, then repeat them in English for her. "Lord Jesus Christ, son of God, have mercy on me, a sinner." A harsh breath escapes me, halfway between a scoff and a laugh. "Hell is already promised to me. Reaching for heaven feels like rebellion."

She crawls on top of me, resting her legs on either side of me. Her blonde hair falls over her shoulders, and she tucks it behind her ears, so I get an unobstructed view of her gorgeous face.

"Will you tell me?" she asks, her small hands resting on my chest. She has so much hope in her gray eyes.

I sigh, knowing she's going to get everything she wants from me. "What do you want to know?"

"Everything." Her eyes bore into mine, a quiet prayer for answers. "Tell me how many scars you have."

"Too many to count. Each one at the hand of someone else. Mostly my father. New ones are from the classes here, but they're superficial. Hardly anything at all. They'll heal without leaving a scar." I sit up, dragging her with me so I can settle against the headboard on my bed. Might as well get comfortable. She settles back down in my lap, and I have the urge to flip her and sink deep into her again, listening to her moan my name as I bring her so much pleasure. But I know now isn't the time or place for that. She waits patiently as I collect my thoughts.

"It started when I was about eight. Maybe sooner, but I can't remember. He never showed affection for me anyway, always cold. My mother, on the other hand, was my world.

To her, I was perfect. She would snuggle with me on scary nights, sing Russian lullabies to sleep, and play with me. I respected my dad, but I don't think I loved him. Mom always told me he had a stressful job, and to keep out of his way, that she would give me all the love he couldn't. And I believed her.

"Imagine my surprise when I broke a dish in the kitchen one night after dinner by accident and he backhanded me, then demanded I clean it up. I remember sobbing and running into my mother's arms. It was the first time he had ever truly hit me. Nights of being yelled at and hit turned into days too. Slowly he became colder, more merciless with me. Bruises, cuts, and burns were always in inconspicuous spots so my school uniform would hide them. Any emotion I showed earned me some sort of punishment. I learned to watch him and those around us. He had spies who reported back to him. I worked out and grew stronger because I knew if I didn't, no one else would protect my mom or Ava.

"I took the torture, buried it down, let it morph me into a monster. Dad's role in the Bratva is as an enforcer, or he used to be."

"Wait, Ava told me he was a numbers guy," she interrupts me.

I snicker at that and shake my head. "No, Luna. The only numbers he deals with are in dead bodies. He's too fat and out of shape now since he outsourced his work. He thought he could maintain his wealth without doing the shit work anymore. Unfortunately, it worked for him." I take a deep breath, knowing this part is going to be difficult for her to hear. "It started with simple tasks—cutting off body parts, pulling teeth, or slicing flesh down to the bone. Then it became more complex once I could stomach that. Little by little he stole the light in my soul until it was as black as his. I still remember the night I killed my first man. When I think about it, I remember the stench—his breath, his piss-covered pants. He was strung up from the ceiling like a rag doll. His feet barely touched the floor, his wrists bleeding, droplets running down his arms, soaking his light-colored shirt."

He begged me, like they all do when they know they are about to die. Begged me to have mercy on him; but I couldn't, especially that night. Not when the threat to Ava coiled in the air like smoke, choking every rational thought. "Mikhail, my dad, promised to hurt Ava and my mom if I didn't complete his dirty work. That night was his first true test of loyalty."

Her fingers fly to her mouth, and I know she wants to say something, but gratefully she stays quiet, allowing me another minute to gather my thoughts.

"I shut down, letting the darkness consume me as I sliced his flesh bit by bit until his entrails were hanging from his stomach and the floor was stained crimson." I drop my head back, looking up at her with tired eyes, her own innocent ones searching mine.

"How old were you?"

"Fourteen."

"Four—Jesus. Fourteen?"

"Yeah." I run the pads of my fingers up and down her thighs, needing her to ground me. "He brought me home and told me to shower before going to bed, like we had just watched a baseball game together. I managed to make it upstairs, locking myself in the bathroom and puked. I locked that scared little boy up after that. If I wanted to make it out alive, I couldn't be weak. I haven't killed in four years, and that's not from his lack of trying. He would pull me out of bed in the middle of the night and force my hand. The few times I fought back, he battered me. The last time was when he beat me within an inch of my life."

"How did you get him to stop?"

"Dragged his ass into the basement one night when I regained my strength and strung him up, offering him a taste of the monster he turned me into. My mom was the only one who pulled me out of my stupor," I add quietly, remembering the night like it was yesterday. The terror in her eyes still hits me when I least expect it, dragging me right back to that moment. That night she wasn't seeing me, her son; she glimpsed the devil—empty of emotion, stripped of feeling, fueled by pure, unadulterated hate.

If she hadn't found us, I would have killed him. Instead, I made it a lesson to him not to touch Ava, my mom, or me ever again. But that doesn't mean my mom and sister are safe. There are many ways to do harm that aren't physical. And while I protested Ava coming to Pointebreak, I know it's the best option for her. She'll learn to protect herself when I can't be there to do it. When all this is over, when I'm done at Pointebreak, I'm going to kill him; and anyone else who thinks they can harm my family.

Riley digs her fingers through my hair as I run my hands up and under my t-shirt she's wearing.

Her tongue pops out, and she sucks her lower lip, securing it between her teeth. "I'm so sorry, Zander. I don't even know what to say."

I shake my head. "There's nothing to say. It's in the past. It's taught me a lot about people. Everyone has a secret; it's a matter of prying it out of them."

She lowers her voice. "What's your secret?"

"Hmm," I hum. If she knew the power she held over me, it would be disastrous. Riley has always been the key to Julien's future, but never in my wildest dreams did I think she would have the same pull on me.

She rolls her eyes and huffs when I refuse to answer. She knows me better than that, though. "Fine. How did you, Wesley, and Julien become so close?"

My lips quirk at the corner. "I think it was always going to happen. Our dads came to Pointebreak and were in the same graduating year. Never exactly friends, I would say, but mutuals who formed a bond with one another. More of an "I scratch your back, you scratch mine" type of thing." She nods. "They worked together while at Pointebreak and then went their own ways. My father went back to New York, Wesley's to Connecticut, and Julien's stayed in New Hampshire."

"Okay, so now that brings us to you three. How did you meet?"

"Orientation. Mikhail and Christos saw one another and introduced us. I don't think they expected us all to become close."

"And Julien?"

"His uncle dropped him off. There were whispers from the moment he stepped foot on campus about who he was, and we all clicked. Our fathers may not have been close, but maybe it's our shared tragic pasts that have brought us together. We all want a version of the same thing, and will work together to get it."

She offers a sad smile and bites her lower lip. "And, um, what about spanking?" Her face flames, "The kinky stuff?"

I smirk. "Mmm, you're full of questions this morning. Maybe I should stuff your mouth instead. I'm not used to all this talking. Looking for another round, Luna?" I shift her over my lap, so her clothed pussy rests right on top of my dick.

She shakes her head before dropping her gaze, focusing on my chest. "No. But you said you enjoy spanking because your dad used to beat you."

I nod. I told her that yesterday in the car. "Yes. I like rough sex because it gives me control over the part of myself that could do actual damage otherwise. The monster I keep tucked away has time to breathe, if only for a little while. Every detail is mine—the pain, the pleasure, the intensity. I can push hard, take out my frustration, and still end it exactly where my partner needs to be. When everything is controlled, nothing can go wrong."

"You're not a monster." She touches the side of my face, and I lean my head into it. "That's a lot of pressure you put on yourself, Zander." She wraps her arms around me in a tight hug, her warm body pressing against mine. "So where do I fit into all of this?"

I knew the conversation would ultimately return to this. She's the missing piece, the one person who can make this all work. I know this is Julien's story, and he can tell her when he's ready, but she needs something to hold on to. She needs to know when everything is over, and the pieces fall, that she won't be forgotten in the rubble.

"You're the key to victory, Luna." A knock on the door pulls us up short. "What?"

"Breakfast."

"Okay, we'll be right down."

I don't want to move her from my lap. I wish we could stay cocooned in my room. Away from the pressures of the world. But even I know that dream can never be a reality.

"Come on, let's go eat."

"Please, Zan," she places her hand on my cheek, directing me to look at her. "You need to give me something more than that. Why am I here? Why am I the key?"

I force a breath past my lips. "How much do you know about your father's political career?"

"Dad's been in politics since I was a baby. He's been governor of New Hampshire for the past eight years, and he was mayor before that. He's running for senator now."

"Michael's already won, Luna. He may still be on the

campaign trail, but he knows he's the next senator. He's worked a lot of shady deals to make sure it would happen."

She shakes her head. "No, voting isn't until November. And poll numbers show him coming in a few points behind his opponent."

She doesn't get it, or she chooses not to. I'm not sure which. I watch her, trying to figure it out and say the next words carefully. "Why does he back Pointebreak so strongly? He has no personal ties to the school." Maybe she will put two and two together if I give her enough hints.

"He's always said it's a prestigious school that turns out some of the brightest students. He always touts it as being a positive thing to have in the state."

I nod. "Okay, and who goes to this school? And what do their parents do?"

"Mafia kids. Selling drugs, weapons, money laundering; that sort of thing."

I stay silent, letting her work through it on her own. I see the moment she figures it out, too. Her hands fly up to her mouth and she covers it. "No."

"People think votes win elections; they're wrong. Favors win elections. As long as he keeps letting drugs and weapons pass through the ports while looking the other way, he's safe to do whatever the hell he wants. He could run for President, and if he owes enough favors, could win. The underground syndicate runs everything. It hasn't been the power of the people in a long time.

"You weren't supposed to be here. You were supposed to go to Dartmouth and not know about us until the time was right. I don't know why that changed, or what Michael's reasoning is for sending you here; but you're part of the plan now. You can't escape, no matter how much you try. We will always drag you back. Even if it's kicking and screaming."

TWENTY-TWO

JULIEN

My alarm goes off at four-thirty, just like it does every other day. I rarely vary from my day to day routine, especially my morning one. I get up, get dressed in shorts and a t-shirt before heading into the kitchen to make a protein drink, which I bring down to the basement with me so I can get a one-hour workout in. Usually, it's a combination of the heavy bag, the treadmill, and some weights.

So color me surprised when I open the basement door to the sound of grunts and bodies colliding.

"Good. Try again," Wesley says. "This time the goal is to get me off balance."

I walk down a few steps to watch their interaction. She bounces on her feet with her arms raised, protecting her face. She's in a pair of black leggings and a bright pink sports bra. Neither is breathing heavily, so they couldn't have been at this for that long. The private room Zander's constructing is nearly complete, and I wonder if Riley has asked about it.

They circle one another, and when he reaches for her, she sidesteps and leans forward, pushing his shoulders. He stumbles backward but catches himself quickly.

He chuckles. "Good. That's perfect. The goal is to get your attacker off balance and get away quickly."

She balls her hands into fists and places them on her hips before blowing a loose strand of hair from her face. "Yeah, but I might not outrun the person. So what then?"

"You need to get a head start, anything to delay," he instructs. "Yank his clothing, push him off balance, or even shove him into an obstacle. Anything to help give you an advantage. Work smarter, not harder. The more you fight, the less likely you are to come out on top."

She nods, and they move around the mat again. This is torture watching her, especially when Wesley grabs her around the waist and the two of them crash down to the ground and his lips crash down over hers. I clench my teeth so hard I'm afraid they might crack. She's fucking with my head.

I descend the rest of the stairs and stop at the edge of the mat. I cross my arms over my chest and wait for them to realize they have an audience as they practically dry-hump one another.

"If you're going to fuck one another in a public space, at least let me set up a camera to make some money off it." They freeze, and she cranes her neck back to look up at me. I wiggle my fingers at her in greeting. "Don't stop on my account."

Riley pushes on Wesley's shoulders until he finally climbs off her. "You already have some material to use if that's the case," she says. Wesley stands and extends his hand down to her, helping her to her feet.

"One video is just a tease, Princess. I'm sure the world would love to see what a whore the senator's daughter really is. Come on, I'll film it and then let you suck me off as a reward for being such a good girl. I'm sure Wesley wouldn't mind, would you?"

"Julien," he warns, the tendons in his neck straining with the effort not to hit me.

I hold my hands up in defeat and take a step back. I know how Wesley is when he's being the protector. Honestly, it's how we all are. The only difference is that they have the luxury of opening up and letting her in. If I do that…well… let's just say I won't receive the same response of open arms and falling into bed with me.

Soon.

She will know soon enough. It's getting harder and harder for me to remain detached from her; from them. The three of us falling for the same girl is unexpected, but we work as one unit; it's not entirely surprising. I run my gaze down her body, tilting my head to the side as I examine her. The large bruise on her face is better. More yellow now than purple; and with makeup, I'm sure you can't see it. And the superficial scratches she had on her chest and stomach are all but faded.

"Come on, Princess. Fight me instead. Wesley is an easy target. He won't hurt you. I can't promise I won't."

"Not sure that's a good idea," Wesley interjects.

"Why? If she ever finds herself in a similar situation, she needs to know how to fight off an unknown attacker. You're training her, right? Don't half-ass it, Wes."

She steps between us and lifts her head to meet my gaze. "No, it's fine. I've got this. If I take you down, you back off. Leave me alone."

I rub the stubble on my chin in contemplation, then lift my brow. "Oh yeah? And what do I get if I pin you?"

She shrugs. "What do you want?"

Now there's a loaded question. There are a lot of things I want, including my dad out of prison, her dad in prison, to be balls deep inside her.

"You're going to help me. No questions asked. Be a good girl and do exactly as you're told."

She shakes her head. "Not *no questions asked*. I have a right to know what I'm getting into."

"You lost any rights when you made this bet. Those are the terms; do you accept them?" I hold my hand out for her to shake. She stares at it, then shifts to look up at Wesley. He hasn't taken his eyes off me. His tight jaw, strained arm muscles, and rigid posture scream everything he thinks about this bet.

"For how long?" she asks skeptically.

I shrug. "How long is leave you alone?"

"Forever," she answers honestly.

She couldn't have walked into a more perfect trap if I had tried. My face lights up, and I can't help the grin that tugs at my lips. "Forever it is."

"Riley," Wesley starts.

"No, no. Let her make her own decisions." I turn my attention to him. "You've been training her for some time. She got away from four captors; this should be easy. We can even put a time limit on it. If she can avoid being pinned under me for one minute, she wins the bet."

He shakes his head. He knows she's going to lose. The surge of adrenaline coursing through my body makes my fingers twitch in anticipation.

"You're not allowed to film me."

I lick my lips and stare down at her. "Shame. I could split the profits with you, seventy-thirty," I motion to me and then to her. Her mouth pops open in shock as she scrunches her face. "I'm kidding, I'd be nice and split it fifty-fifty. My half is the finder's fee."

She crosses her arms over her chest. "No filming."

I roll my eyes and make a spectacle that she's really putting me out here. "Fine."

"Wes, start a timer."

I had hoped she stuck her hand out to shake mine, but that would have been too easy. She would have been pinned in under twenty seconds flat. I reach for her and jump back when she tries to knock into me, to throw me off balance like she's been practicing with Wesley. One minute isn't a long time, and I need to make my move now or risk losing this opportunity.

I grab her wrist, tugging her to me, and drop to the ground, wrapping my arms around her. She struggles in my grip, but I wrap myself around her like a boa constrictor, not letting her get in a hit. Then I roll us, pinning her tightly under me just as the timer goes off.

She closes her eyes, a pained expression crossing her features.

"Looks like you're mine, Princess," I whisper. "You should know I always get what I want. My room after classes today. We're gonna have a little chat."

I stand and offer her my hand. She ignores it and stands on her own. "I hate you," she grumbles.

"Shouldn't have made the bet."

Rumors are really flying regarding Derek's disappearance. He's not well known around campus, but the longer he stays away, the crazier the gossip gets. My favorite one is that I chopped him up and brought him to a farm in the next town for the pigs to eat his remains. I mean, it's not a bad idea. I might have to find a farmer who will strike up that kind of deal for the future. Others are saying his uncle has something to do with it. He'll show his face sooner than later, and when he does, we'll catch him.

I expect Riley to be waiting for me, like I told her when I get back home, but she's not here. Her tracker shows she's at the library. It didn't take long for her to fall into old habits again. A part of me wants to go to the library and carry her back here. Another part of me wants to see just how long she's willing to hold out. Broken promises mean death in my world.

The sun fades into darkness, and the blue dot moves along the screen. Before long she's at our front door with Zander by her side. I pull it open before she even touches it.

"You're late," I say.

"You said after class. You never specified how long after."

Zander smirks, but slides into his nonchalant demeanor quickly. "I told you not to test him."

She rolls her eyes and walks into the house, her bag draped over one shoulder. Dropping it by the front door, she then toes off her shoes, leaving them next to ours.

"My room. Now. Bring your phone."

She huffs but follows me up the stairs and to the end of the hallway. I push open my door and stand to the side, letting her walk in before me. Then I close the door, locking her in with me. Riley tenses when the latch clicks into place, but does her best to remain unaffected.

"Best two out of three?" she asks. I shake my head. She shrugs indifferently. "Worth a shot," she mumbles to herself.

"Sit."

"I'm not a dog."

"No, but I bet I can make you beg."

She looks disgusted. "What do you want, Julien?"

"You're going to help me."

"Help you with what?" She sits on the edge of the bed and crosses her legs.

"Getting my dad out of prison."

A derisive noise escapes her throat. She thinks I'm joking.

This is the plan we came up with. And it's either this, or we force her father's hand. At least this way he can save face with the public for longer. He's been blocking an appeal for years that would allow my father to be out on bail. I raise my brow in question.

She stops laughing and takes in my stern expression. "Oh, you're serious. And how the hell do you expect me to do that?"

"You're going to ask Michael to do it."

She stands. "Listen, I'm sorry your dad's a criminal and got caught," she starts. I have half a mind to cut her off and tell her all about her hero daddy, but let her go. "My dad isn't going to pull any favors to get him out because I asked him to."

"Yes, he will. Tell him Julien Azarian is forcing you to."

"And why would he care about you?"

"Trust me. He's going to think he's seen a ghost." She searches my face, questions written all over her features. "Get on a FaceTime call with him."

She huffs. "This is crazy." She picks her phone up from the bed and opens FaceTime. Only instead of calling her dad, she starts a call to someone named James.

"I said your dad, Princess. Ears not working today?" I tap my ear for emphasis.

She huffs and rolls her eyes before glaring up at me. "Dad won't answer my call, but James can get him on the phone."

"Riley, are you okay?" the man's voice comes through the phone. I stay out of view.

"I need to talk to my dad. It's urgent."

"He's in a meeting. Can I have him call you back?"

She looks at me, and I shake my head, mouthing no to her. "No, I really need to speak with him. Can you please go get him?"

"Okay. Hold on." The phone goes silent as she continues to stare at it. Not even a minute later, Michael is on the line.

"Riley, I'm busy. This can't wait?"

Annoyance crosses her face before she shakes her head. "No. I need you to do something for me."

He huffs. "What?"

"Alec Azarian. Get him out of prison."

"And why the hell would I do that?"

I move quickly, knowing I have a small window of opportunity. Pulling a gun from the back of my pants, I aim it at her head. I cover her mouth with my hand and hold her immobile against me, making sure he can clearly see the glint of silver pressed against her temple.

"What the fuck is this?" Michael bellows at the same time Riley screams behind my hand. Tears slide down her cheeks and her breathing shallows as she struggles in my hold.

"Shhh, you don't want me to blow your head off, Riley. Hold the phone higher now; let him see me."

I watch his face contort from anger to fear, and I know the moment he recognizes me—the boy who was supposed to be dead. The one he was *told* was dead. "You have three days, or I'll start mailing you body parts in a pretty box."

I kiss her cheek and end the call just as Wesley pounds on the door and Riley screams again.

I drop my hold on her and toss the gun onto my bed as she races toward the door, pulling it open and falling into Wesley's arms.

Wesley looks at the bed and back to me. I roll my eyes and shake my head in exasperation. "Oh, relax. I borrowed it. It's not even loaded." I pick the weapon up and show him the empty magazine. "Which she would have known if she had disarmed me like she should have. Seriously, are you two just fucking, or are you actually teaching her anything?"

"Now? You couldn't have given us more warning that you were doing this?"

I shrug. "We're in a time crunch, and I might as well make use of my winning bet."

She looks up at Wesley, and the look of betrayal on her face hits hard. "You knew about this?"

"I told you betting against him was a bad idea."

TWENTY-THREE

RILEY

I feel like a downright idiot. Julien is only ever about his endgame, and I played right into his hand this morning. My inner voice screamed at me not to take the bet, to just let him keep harassing me; but somewhere deep down, I thought maybe I could win. That maybe, just maybe, I could get him to open up and tell me what's happening, and I could decide if I would help from there. Not that he would have given me a choice. I see that now.

Zander stands in the doorway, leaning against the frame, watching the three of us. I pull away from Wesley to wrap my arms around myself. Just when I think I'm figuring things out, they pull this shit and I'm back at square one again.

"You both knew?" I look between Wesley and Zander, the deep feeling of betrayal weighing heavy on me. Of course, they did. They have been warning me since the beginning.

"I told you, you're the key to victory, Luna."

I nod my head and pull my bottom lip between my teeth, biting hard. "Right. The key to victory," I repeat somberly.

My phone rings on the bed, and I jump, reaching for it.

My dad is calling back. When I try to answer it, Julien pries it from my fingers and taps the green answer button.

"Did I not make myself clear the first time? Or are you having trouble understanding orders?"

He places the phone on speaker so that I can hear everything.

"Listen here, you punk-ass piece of shit, if you harm one hair on the top of her head, I'll make sure you never see the light of day again. I want to talk to my daughter."

"You're not in any position to be making demands," Julien counters.

"Damn it, boy. Give her the phone, or so help me, I'll make sure your father dies in that cell and it will look like an accident."

"Best not to say anything incriminating, Senator. You never know when calls are being recorded." Julien nods at me. I take a step closer to him and reach for the phone to take the speaker off. He shakes his head and holds it firm.

"Daddy," I whisper.

"Baby, I'm going to get you out of this, do you hear me? Don't give them anything. I'm going to fix this."

I look around the room at the three of them, and the pit in my stomach tightens. They have been using me from the beginning to get what they need, but I don't fear them nearly as much as I fear my dad. The Kings may have omitted information, but they haven't straight-up lied to my face. And it's becoming more and more apparent that he has.

"What's going on, dad? How do you know him?"

"Julien, you let my daughter go!" he bellows. "She isn't part of this. I'll get him out, but it's going to take longer than three days. There's a process I have to follow not to raise suspicions."

"Hmm. That sounds like a *you* problem, Michael. Get it done."

He hangs up the phone and drops it on the ground before smashing it to pieces under his heavy boot.

"What the fuck are you doing?" I scream, attempting to push him away. He allows me to shove him when the last flicker of light leaves the screen. Looking at the broken screen and bent frame of my phone, I feel something snap within me. "I need that!" That's the new phone, the one without the tracking on it. The one that I've been keeping hidden. I've only had it a few days. I figured I would at least be able to get through a few weeks before they were none the wiser. Julien holds out his hand to Zander, who places my original phone in his hand.

My shoulders slump. When I think I'm two steps ahead of them, I'm really three behind. I can't even begin to describe how frustrating it is! I wipe at the tears filling my eyes as I fight past the burn in my throat.

He holds it up for me to see. "Here's your phone, Princess. Next time, don't try to pull a fast one on us. We'll always know. Zan will get the service set back up on it." He hands it back to Zander, who puts it in his pocket. "I'm blocking your father and James. I don't want them talking with you until my father is out."

"I hate you," I spit.

He doesn't respond. He only stares at me like I'm nothing more than an annoying fly on the wall. Wesley takes my hand and leads me out of his room. Willingly, I go with my head down, looking at my feet. I want to be alone. I don't want to be here with them.

"When can I leave?" I ask. I don't think Julien is planning on keeping me locked up here at the house. It's not like I have a place I can run to, and they can find me easily enough. Wesley runs his hands over the top of his head. He has this worry line between his eyes, and I reach out to run my finger along it. "Why won't you just tell me?" I whisper.

"Why do you keep letting him get the upper hand?" For once, I'd like to feel like I can beat Julien at his own game.

"Zan will be done with your phone soon, and then I'll bring you back to your room."

A breath slips out through my nose, thin and hollow, the last echo of hope leaving with it. I nod absentmindedly. "Right."

"Ril—" I hold my hand up to stop him.

"Just don't, Wes. I don't want to hear it right now, okay?" The resignation in my voice runs deep.

One step forward, two steps back. We can't keep playing this game. At some point, one of us, most likely me, is going to fall; and I don't know if I have it in me to get back up. I walk down the stairs to gather my bag and tie my shoes. Zander comes down a few minutes later and hands me my phone.

"How did you know?"

He shakes his head. "I didn't. I would have figured it out soon enough, but Julien is the one who discovered it this weekend."

I nod. Finally, I say, "I trust both of you, but I can't keep doing this. I need answers. I need to know what I'm falling into if I choose you." My chin quivers, and I bite my lower lip hard to stop it. "Just tell me one thing?" They look at each other, then back at me. "When all is said and done, am I still going to be alive, or is this plan Julien's concocting going to kill me?"

"We won't let anything happen to you, Riley."

Right. Well, that's not exactly the answer I was looking for.

Wesley doesn't put up a fight when I ask him to leave after he brought me back to my room. I change into pajamas and knock on Ava's door, and she opens it and ushers me in, but she's on the phone. I take a seat on her bed. She's speaking a mile a minute in Russian, and I hear her mutter the word Papa, so I know who she's on the phone with. After a few more minutes, she hangs up the phone.

"Everything okay?"

She sighs and plops down next to me. "Yes. No. It's fine. I'll figure it out. How was your day?"

"Sucked, you?"

"Same. Wanna watch a movie?"

I shrug and pull my knees to my chest. "Sure. Something funny? I could use a few laughs tonight."

She scrolls through Netflix until she finds a stupid rom-com and hits play. We sit in silence for a bit before I finally speak. "Julien's trying to get his dad out of jail." She glances in my direction, then looks back at the movie. "He's using me to blackmail my dad." I add.

That catches her attention, and she turns to face me. "What did he do?"

"Julien or my dad?"

"Julien, obviously. And your dad. What happened?"

I tell her how Julien made me call my dad and pulled a gun on me and demanded his father get released from jail. How he needs to make it happen in three days. I'm not entirely sure what he will do if it's not done in the time Julien gave him because I have a hard time believing Wes or Zan would let Julien actually kill me and chop me up. Hell, I'm having a hard time believing Julien would do it cither.

"Damn. Sorry, Riley." She pauses, the movie filling the silence between us. "My dad found out about Nick and called to scream at me tonight. Called me a whore. Told me

I'm no use to him." I take her hand in mine. She scoffs, "the funny thing is, we haven't had sex."

I'm not sure why that surprises me, but it does. "You haven't?"

She shakes her head. "No. My whole life I've been told I need to wait for marriage because he's going to want a virgin. And as much as I like Nick, I can't bring myself to go there…yet." She pauses, looks at the screen, and continues. "He's great though, Riles. He's been so patient. I mean, we've done other things, but he's just happy being with me." Then she lowers her voice to a bare whisper. "I'm terrified he's just using me."

"Hey," she looks at me. "For what it's worth, I think he seems like a great guy—genuine. I don't think he's using you."

She nods, hearing me, but I'm not sure she believes me. "Zan doesn't trust him."

I chortle. "Zander doesn't trust anyone. So I wouldn't base your relationship on him."

One side of her lips twist up into a smirk. "Yeah, I guess you're right."

"I'd tell him, though. What your dad said. He told me a bit about growing up." I lower my eyes. "I'm sorry."

She shrugs, feigning indifference, but I know she's anything but. "Zander's always had it worse. He's protecting me, and I love him so much for it. I know he's the reason I'm here. I told him I wanted to come here. Regular college was off the table, but I knew this would be my chance to live a little. To have some freedom before ultimately being roped back in to push out babies for some Pakhan wannabe." Her words are clipped, full of disgust.

"Nick's family isn't Russian, right?"

She shakes her head. "No. Irish. Weird, right?"

I furrow my brow, wondering how the hell that works

out. "I thought everyone from different crime families hated one another. Or at least couldn't be friends."

She laughs. "This isn't the Hatfields and McCoys. It happened kind of organically. Same gala events, same social circles. When you're put in the same room as one another long enough, relationships happen. They just sort of became friends, I guess."

"So is there any chance your dad would let you be with Nick?"

Her smile fades. "I don't know. He was really upset tonight when he found out, so it's hard to believe he would be okay with it."

"Don't give up yet." She nods, but doesn't say anything else. "Hey, could I crash here tonight?"

TWENTY-FOUR

WESLEY

"Julien, you've got to tell her. I'm telling you, she'll help. You can't keep playing these mind games with her, otherwise you're going to lose her." We're going to lose her. She looked so defeated when I dropped her off at her dorm last night. She wouldn't look at me, wouldn't talk to me. It was damn hard to walk away and leave her alone for the night. Even though that's what she needed. I watched her on the cameras go into Ava's room, but she left her phone in her room.

"She's fine, and I needed her surprised; otherwise, it never would have worked."

I run my fingers down the front of my face. "Yeah, *she* needed the surprise, not us, asshole."

"Listen, she's safe, right? Michael is doing what I need him to do, you and Zander are getting to fuck her, and I'm getting my payback. Everything is working to plan."

I shake my head. "She's pissed, Julien. What aren't you telling us about her? There's more to this than you hating Michael. You hate her too, why?"

Zander stands in the doorway, watching us, listening intently.

"I don't hate her. She's useful. Riley Whittier is the key to ruling the upper New England area. Her dad, Michael, has had a hold over imports and exports for the past eight years. He wrongly sent my dad to prison; and now someone else is moving into the area, attempting a takeover. I won't fucking allow it to happen on my watch. Michael is working with someone else, and my dad needs to be free to put a stop to it."

"How long has this been going on for?"

He plops down on the couch and drops his head back against the headrest. "The past six months. My father's men have been tracking it. Until recently it hasn't been a problem. Well, it's becoming a problem now."

"What would you have done if Riley wasn't here at Pointebreak?"

He sighs. "Dartmouth would have had a missing person on its hands." He looks up at us, his focus bouncing between our faces. "I need you to trust me. I promise she'll be fine."

"Did you have anything to do with her kidnapping?" Zander asks.

Julien focuses on him. "No. I think her dad had something to do with that."

That's what I think too, but I haven't found anything to tie it to him. Why would he do that to his own daughter? What gain does he get from it? All it would do is make Pointebreak look bad and open an investigation; and the students' families will not let that happen. It would turn into a national disaster overnight. We're missing some pieces to this puzzle. And where the hell is Derek? We've had our guys searching high and low around campus with nothing to show for it.

There needs to be a way to draw him out. The more

time passes, the less likely we are to get answers. Plus, there's only so much pull his uncle has with keeping him enrolled. If he keeps blowing off his classes, someone will send a motion to remove him.

"Where the fuck is Derek?"

I knock on Riley's door at four thirty in the morning, ready to head to the gym for our training session. She spent the night in Ava's room because I checked the cameras myself before coming over. She's pissed about yesterday, and if I'm being honest, I am too. Julien shouldn't have pulled that shit, especially without giving us warning. I know he has his reasons, but we're a team. Going into all this, I knew he needed her, and that there would come a time when he would make a move we wouldn't like. That's the way this was always going to end. The problem is, I never expected myself to fall in love with her. Yeah, the big L-word. I've never had this feeling before—the urge to rip someone apart for simply looking at her. Isn't that what love is?

A craving.

An obsession.

An addiction.

Riley is the only woman I've been with who elicits these raw emotions. Everyone else has been a distraction. The necklace I designed for her came in. I wasn't planning on giving it to her now, but I'm hoping it can help smooth things over between us. It's a beautiful white gold chain with a crown pendant at the end. A queen can't stand beside the Kings without her own crown.

I unlock the door and let myself into her space. She has to come back at some point. While I'm at it, and I have access to her computer, I might as well get Zander to hack into that so we have access to everything.

The screen flashes a few times before static covers her background. I sit on her bed and lie back, giving him the time he needs to complete the spyware transfer. The screen returns to normal, and my phone buzzes with a text.

I slip the USB back into my pocket and wait. Then I doze. I haven't been getting enough sleep, and it's catching up with me. But I'll sleep when I'm dead. Riley walks into the room a little after five-thirty, and I sit upright when I hear her key in the lock.

She stops when she sees me, but quickly closes the door behind her, trapping us together. Riley leans her weight against the door, maintaining as much distance between us as possible.

"I came to get you for training. You weren't here."

She shakes her head. "No. I don't want to train with you anymore."

I clench my jaw and pull a deep breath through my nose. "Those lessons are non-negotiable, Riley."

"Then I'll find someone else. I need some space, some time to wrap my head around everything. And the three of you up my ass constantly isn't helping."

I stare her down, letting her words sink deep into my soul. I know she's struggling. She has been since she started at Pointebreak, and we've only made it more difficult for her. She needs to do this on her own terms, and I think it's time to take a step back. Give her a taste of the freedom she's craving.

"I'll find someone for you to train with."

"No—"

"That's the offer. Take it, or the deal's off, Riley."

She winces, and I don't know if it's from my tone, or that I've now used her name twice instead of the nickname I usually use with her.

She huffs, but nods. "All right, fine."

"Good. Now, the other reason I'm here." I pull the chain out of my pocket and dangle it in front of her. She steps closer for a better view in the dim light. "I designed this for you, and I want you to wear it."

She eyes it suspiciously, but slides her hand under it to hold it. I release it, letting the full weight settle into her palm.

"Every queen needs a crown," I admit softly.

"It's beautiful. Thank you, Wesley." She holds it out for me to take, but I step away, my hands raised in surrender.

"I want you to have it. No strings. I'm here for you when you're ready. You're the only one I've ever felt the need to open up to. You allow me to feel, Riley. Please don't take that away from me. I'll keep you safe, and we'll navigate these murky waters together."

Her rigid stance softens and her shoulders slump. When I reach out to pull her into an embrace, she allows it. Her vanilla and cherry scent fills my nose as I breathe her in. After Alec is out of jail, Julien is going to tell her everything. I refuse to let her go, not like this. I will not lose the only woman who I've ever needed because Julien is a stubborn, pig-headed asshole.

"Will you help me put it on?"

I take the necklace from her, and she turns, giving me her back. I unclasp the chain and pull it around her neck, securing it in place. She turns to face me, placing her fingers over the necklace. The gold crown rests in the hollow of her throat.

"Thank you." I nod, not trusting myself to say something that will cause a visceral reaction. "Just give me a little space. That's all I'm asking for, Wesley. Please," she adds meekly.

"Okay. A few days. If you need anything, you know where to find me."

Her lips turn up into a sad smile, and I wish she'd let me wipe the sorrow away. I don't like her feeling alone in this. She's not. I lean down, kiss her on the cheek, and leave her room. When I'm out of the building, I pull the video of her room up on my phone and place an earbud in to listen to her. She's lying on her bed, curled into the fetal position, crying. I could have stayed, let her cry in my arms, reassure her she's not alone, even if it feels like she is.

Today's the day Julien told Michael to have Alec out of jail. So far, it's been crickets. I've barely seen Riley too. We've been respectful of her wishes, which has been a trial in itself. Zander and I follow her to class to make sure she makes it without incident. We also have some of our guys keeping a watch on her in places like the cafeteria and the library.

I've caught her a few times smiling at me when she sees me behind her, and she touches her necklace. It's torture not being able to scoop her up in my arms and hug and kiss her whenever I feel like it. Plus, people around campus are talking, which is never a good thing. The longer we stay away, the worse it's going to be for her. Even if the other students aren't vying for our attention, that doesn't mean she's off scot-free.

I sit in the quad, basking in the sun. It's a warm fall day, and students are enjoying the burst of heat before the bone-chilling cold sets in. My ears perk up when I hear Derek's name, but I don't move, straining to listen. He's been missing for a little over two weeks now. I've got to hand it to the guy; I didn't think he could hold out this long. I'm impressed. Unless he's actually dead, that might be a problem. We still do not know who he's working with, and Arthur is too smart to admit to anything.

"I heard from him last night. He texted me. Said his uncle is demanding he come back to campus," the guy says.

"Really?"

"Yeah, he said he's holed up in a safe house somewhere close."

We haven't searched off campus. That could get messy fast, especially if we ended up with bad intel. It makes sense that Arthur wants him back at Pointebreak. It's a terrible look for him if his own nephew isn't participating. I text the guys what I've overheard and put my phone down, closing my eyes again. After a moment, a shadow covers the light on my face. I pry open an eye to see Lucas looming over me.

"She's hurt," he says.

My heart gallops in my chest, and I bolt upright, getting to my feet in record time. "Where is she?"

TWENTY-FIVE

RILEY

I'm lying on the uncomfortable cot in the infirmary, the faint stench of antiseptic making my nose twitch. The nurse shuffles around me, and my saving grace is that I'm the only one here. There are three other empty cots in the room, along with an assortment of medical supplies—bandages, ointments, wraps, and medications. The only thing that sets this place apart from a typical school nurse's office is the X-ray machine and the neatly labeled cabinets stocked with casting supplies. It makes sense to treat patients here instead of sending them to the hospital for care. Police file reports outside these protective walls. The number of lies to keep the truth hidden runs deep.

I'm so embarrassed I'm even here. It was stupid. I was standing by the pool, ready to jump in for laps when someone knocked their shoulder into me as they walked by. Definitely a guy, based on the height, but I didn't see who. I lost my balance and down I went, headfirst into the damn water. I hit my shoulder on the floor and maybe my head? My head aches, and I don't remember falling in, so I assume I did. The professor dove in and pulled me out, and got me over here to be checked out. I'm thankful for the blanket that is wrapped around my body, keeping the chill at bay.

Ava popped over with my bag and personal items and stayed for a few minutes to make sure I was okay, but then left. I'm not sure who called her to tell her what happened, but I'm thankful. I close my eyes, fighting the urge to take a nap. Would it be so bad? Just a tiny one? It's been a rough few days, and I haven't been sleeping well, thanks to the boys keeping their word and giving me space. And you'd think I would sleep like a baby, but no. Any little sound jolts me awake. So I'm sure me slipping into the water has something to do with that too.

"Stay awake, Riley. You have a concussion. Sleeping is the last thing you should do," nurse Bethany says. She's an elderly woman with graying hair and wrinkles. Kind eyes, though. It's a sharp contrast to a lot of the professors here. I could see her going home on the weekends and spending time with a bunch of grandbabies, spoiling them rotten and getting all the love.

What I wouldn't give to have a hug right now. *No.* Stop it, Riley. You don't need anyone else. Since when did I become so damn dependent on those three...well, two. Julien can fuck off to hell for all I care. I'm actually surprised no one has tried to email me to make sure I'm actually okay after the last phone call with my dad. I would have expected at least James to reach out, but...nothing. So either they aren't buying his threat, or they've given me up for dead.

"How long have you worked here?" I ask, needing the distraction instead of stewing in my own thoughts.

"Twenty years. I've seen my fair share of injuries over that time. You got lucky if all you did was trip."

Yeah, trip. I don't even know who was responsible for my fall. It all happened so fast. One minute was listening to the professor, the next, I'm being dragged out, gasping for air.

I'm a decent swimmer too; I think that's why I'm so angry at myself. I should have been able to pull myself out of the water and give him a piece of my mind.

Someone knocks on the door. "Come in," Bethany replies. Wesley fills the frame and my heart stutters. "Mr. Bastian, you shouldn't be here."

Does she know everyone's names, or has he been here before? Maybe he's come in to get something bandaged up?

"Is she okay?" he asks, ignoring her.

Bethany purses her lips and stands in front of me, blocking me from his view.

"I'm fine," I answer as Bethany looks back at me, unsure. "Is it okay if we talk for a few minutes?" I ask her. She looks at him, and then back at me, her eyes softening a smidge.

"You've got five minutes and then you need to leave, Mr. Bastian."

He nods in understanding, and she leaves us alone, returning to her office and closes the door. While she might not be listening in on our conversation, that doesn't mean she's not watching us intently.

"Who did this to you?"

"Oh." I'm not sure why that catches me off guard so much. "I don't know. One minute I was talking with someone waiting to jump into the pool, the next I was being dragged out by the professor."

"Why didn't you text us?"

"Ava came with my bag of stuff. I figured one of you asked her to bring it to me." He shakes his head, and I frown. "So how did she know to bring me my bag? Let me text her."

I pull my phone out, and he puts his hand on it, pressing it down. "No screens. The light isn't good for a concussion. I'll find out."

"Mr. Bastian, your time is up. Ms. Whittier needs a little more time to rest, and then I'll release her."

He kisses the top of my head with such gentleness that it makes my heart ache. I've missed them these past few days. I shouldn't. They have put me through hell and back, but something about them draws me in like a moth to a flame. I'm not sure I can ever escape them, even if I wanted to. Which…I don't. Call me crazy, but I think I'm actually falling for these guys.

"Zan or I will be back later to get you." He turns to look at Bethany, "Please call me, and I'll make sure she makes it back to her dorm, along with following any discharge directions." She nods, appeased by his answer, and quickly jots down his phone number.

Just as he said he would, Wesley is there to take me back to my room. I changed back into my uniform, but Bethany is sending me with a thin, but warm blanket draped around my shoulders. The chill is settling into the air now, and there's even talk of an early winter.

"No phones or computers for a few days. If your symptoms get worse, come back here and we will do a full workup. You should be okay in a day or two. Any questions?"

I shake my head. "I don't think so."

She nods and sends us on our way. I glance at my phone to see the sun slipping behind the treeline. My stomach gurgles, and Wesley smiles.

"Shut up," I mumble. "Where's Zander?"

"Working on a project."

"Does he know who pushed me into the pool?"

He licks his lips and nods. Which I'm understanding as

yes, but not here. He clicks the unlock button on the fob and helps me into the car. It's still warm, and I settle into the comfortable seat. He gets into his own and pulls out of the lot.

"Who pushed me?"

"Bruno."

"Huh?" I ask, my brow furrowed. "He's not even in that class. You'd think I would have noticed that." He nods, but remains silent. Slumping in my seat, I say, "I'm terrible at this, this mafia crap, of watching over my shoulder at each turn. I hate this. I hate my father for sending me here. And I hate the fact that when you guys aren't around," I pause. There's no going back if I admit this out loud. He glances at me from the corner of his eye, waiting. I lick my lips and swallow. "I miss you."

I might as well be honest with myself. It's been bubbling for a while, and these last few days without them cemented it. I don't want them to leave me alone. Well, I wouldn't mind if Julien backed off because he's a dick, but it was lonely without Wesley and Zander.

"I've been on edge these past few days, and I haven't been sleeping well." I shrug. "I-I guess I just, I miss you," I say again.

"We're still here, Hellcat," he says as he reaches over and takes my hand in his, giving it a gentle squeeze. "You honestly think you've been alone this whole time?"

"Well, I mean, I know I've seen you around campus, and I've had class with Zander and Julien, but you haven't been with me, or walking me to classes. I didn't realize how much I actually enjoyed having that. You make me feel like I'm part of something; something bigger than just myself. It's…nice."

"Riley, you haven't been alone at all. We've had our guys watching you. That's how I knew about the pool incident.

Lucas found me and told me where you were. He saw the whole thing."

My stomach drops. I know these three well enough to know that means nothing good for Bruno.

"You're not gonna kill him…are you?"

He smiles wide, but it's not the carefree smile I'm accustomed to seeing on Wesley's handsome face. This one is sinister; the hairs on the back of my neck stand at attention. "Of course not." I let out a breath I didn't know I was holding. "We're going to make him wish he were dead."

He pulls into a parking spot and kills the engine. Peering up at the familiar building, I swallow the lump in my throat. I don't want to go in there. I don't want to see what they're doing to him. But I recognize the building. This is where torture class is. Where Zander showed me his dark side, the side that demands an audience. I don't want to taint the pleasurable memories with whatever I'm about to witness.

My heart pounds in my chest as my breathing shallows. My vision blurs around the edges as my panic attack pushes to the forefront. *Fight it, Riley.* Breathe through it. In for four, out for four. "Please don't make me go in there."

"He needs to pay. He'll learn that you're not to be fucked with, in any capacity."

I shake my head, my breathing becoming more labored. I'm falling into the darkness; I won't be able to fight this one. It came on so hard and fast that I'm not strong enough to push it down.

"Please, no," I repeat over and over like a whispered prayer. I rock in my seat with my eyes closed. I'm lifted out of my seat and dragged across the middle like a rag doll. It feels like I'm drowning.

"Riley, look at me," Wes says.

I open my eyes to look at him, but I can't focus on him. I

keep shaking my head as tears stream down my eyes. "Please don't make me go."

"Shhh. You don't have to go." He places his large hands on either side of my face, then pulls me in for a hug.

We sit like that, with me on his lap and his hand running soothing circles along my back for a few minutes until the darkness fades and my vision returns to normal. I curl into him and breathe deeply, filling my lungs with Wesley's scent.

When my body stops shaking and my breathing returns to normal, he says, "what just happened?"

"Julien hasn't told you?"

"Told me what?"

I inhale on a shaky breath. "About my panic attacks."

I'm so embarrassed, I can't even lift my head to look at him. They aren't any worse than normal, per se, but I feel smaller things are setting it off. There are too many fight-or-flight situations here, and if I can't control it, I fear it will happen in the wrong place, and I won't come out of it.

"No. When did he find out?"

That's surprising, considering Julien doesn't keep secrets from the others. I figured they knew. "Before the fight. I had one in survival class when Silas, Bruno, and Adam caught me."

He kisses the top of my head and presses my ear back to his chest, the steady rhythm of his heart helping to calm me further. He digs his phone out of his pocket and lifts it to his ear.

"Meet us at home when you're done. We need to talk."

TWENTY-SIX

ZANDER

The plastic crinkles under my weight as I circle around Bruno. I wish I could kill the fucker right here and now. He's tied down to a heavy wooden chair bolted to the floor. The coppery tang of blood swirls in the surrounding air. Julien sits in a chair off to the side, with a bored expression on his face and his arms crossed over his chest.

Julien has already punched Bruno a handful of times, and now his face is swollen, one eye completely closed. He's lucky he didn't lose some teeth. If I had it my way, I'd pull them all out with the pliers currently hanging by my side. I know how I must look to him, his tormentor. From the moment I walked in here to find him tied down, I've felt the darkness ripping at its cage. He hurt Riley. She's never going to be safe with us, but I can't bear the thought of losing her.

"Who put you up to it?"

He spits blood and it lands next to my black shoe. I glare at it before raising my eyebrows at him. He's already missing one fingernail, and he was a little bitch about it; a blubbering mess. His hand jerked against the restraints, a strangled sound tearing from his throat as the nail gave way. The blood still oozes from the open wound. Pressing the pliers into the soft flesh, an inhuman sound falls from his lips as his eyes water, but he still hasn't talked. I haven't seen him in torture class, but I guess this school has taught him something.

"Fuck you, Fedorov. When I get out of here, I'm going after your whore *and* your sister."

"Big talk for a man who's tied down," Julien says, tilting his head to the side.

"When I tell them you two were behind this, you'll hang."

"Hmm, I don't think that will happen. Bruno Moretti, son of Anthony and Veronica Moretti. You have an older sister, Bianca Castellano, who's the Don's daughter-in-law. Before coming to Pointebreak, you," he pauses dramatically, "oh shit, really? You fucked your sister-in-law and got her pregnant?" Julien laughs as he reads from his phone. "Haven't you ever heard wrap it before you tap it?"

"That's bullshit," Bruno responds through clenched teeth.

"Not according to the information my buddy, Zander, dug up about you. Oh," Julien continues to scroll on his phone, and I roll my eyes at the theatrics of it all. "Oh, you are a bad boy, Bruno. Looks like you also racked up an enormous debt with him," he offers a dry, humorless laugh. "Shit, how are you not dead already?"

Bruno stares daggers at Julien, but keeps his mouth shut. The thing is, we've dug up a lot more than that, and this is just the icing on top of the cake.

"Oh, it looks like you're Massimo Castellano's bitch for all the harm caused, and the only reason you aren't dead is because of some deal your family worked out, no doubt. I'm sure that tidbit of information would be horrible for you if the other families got wind of it. Shall I continue?"

"No," Bruno grits out.

"Then who the fuck made you push her into the pool?" I ask again, ready to pry off another nail.

"It was an accident."

I shake my head, my patience wearing thin. Attaching the pliers to his middle fingernail, he struggles against his bindings. I'll stay here all night doing this if I have to. Bruno isn't going anywhere until we get answers.

"You know, Zander may have the patience of a god, but I don't. And you're starting to piss me off," Julien says as he rises to his feet and comes closer. "Who the fuck put you up to this?" he screams in Bruno's face.

"I don't know. Called me from a blocked number and wired a large sum into my account. Told me I'd get the rest when it was done," he finally responds and drops his head.

"Good boy," Julien taunts and smacks his cheek. Bruno winces from the pain and struggles to free himself.

"I told you. Now let me go."

"You know nothing about him? Name, location, reason?" I growl. I hate not getting full answers, only vague details.

He shakes his head. "No."

"Not good enough, Bruno." I pry his fingernail off so quickly that it takes a moment for his brain to react to the pain before he finally screams.

Julien places his hand on my shoulder, and I step back, bringing the pliers to the sink to clean and sanitize them. "You're going back to your dorm and will fix yourself up there. If you end up in the infirmary, and you utter a single word of who did this to you; I'll make sure your secret ruins your entire family. Stay the fuck away from her."

Julien cuts through the ropes, nicking Bruno's arm, just for good measure. He scurries out of there; the door slamming shut behind him. We take a few minutes to clean up the room before heading back to the house. I need to fuck Riley. I need her to help bring me down from the high I just experienced, but I know I shouldn't. Julien takes the keys from me, knowing I can't drive when I'm in this state.

Who the hell is involved in this? Is it the same person who put Derek up to it? Is it even related? Fuck, I need answers. I push the door open to the house and stride into the kitchen, where Wesley said they were. Riley sits there in sweatpants and a sweatshirt with a mug clutched tightly in her small hands. I kiss the top of her head, and she startles, spilling a bit of her tea. I look at Wesley for an explanation, and he looks at the chair, asking me to sit.

I do so and pull the chair in, being careful not to touch Riley again.

"Julien," Wesley says. Julien looks at him over his glass of water as he takes a large gulp and places it on the kitchen counter.

"Wesley?" He leans over the counter, watching him.

"Mind telling me why you knew Riley suffers panic attacks but didn't think to tell us?"

Riley keeps her eyes trained on her mug, refusing to look at any of us. I lock eyes with Wesley. "I'm sorry. Say that again?"

"Riley suffers panic attacks. She said she's had them since her mother died. Julien found out in class last week and didn't think it was something we should know."

"I never thought it was something you shouldn't know. I was giving the Princess here a chance to tell you herself." Riley grinds her teeth at the mention of that nickname and glares at him. "Looks like I'm not the only one who has kept secrets."

"I figured you told them. No secrets among you, remember?"

"Hey, why are you getting mad at me?" he accuses. "I kept your secret. I figured that's what you wanted."

She sighs. And puts her head down on her forearm.

"I brought her by the classroom—"

"You brought her there?" I snarl, the tendons in my neck straining as I rein my anger back. I'm still on edge from the events of the night.

"I wanted her to get answers. Or be able to hear them with her own ears. But when I told her, she begged me not to bring her inside."

Of course she didn't want to go in there. Who would want to be a witness to what we were doing to him? She doesn't need to see that. I know there's a lot of shit in our world, and eventually she'll take the class, but she doesn't need the exposure yet.

"Riley?" I ask, rubbing her back. "What happened?"

"I didn't want to ruin the memories I have of that place. And it all came rushing in so quickly." Her arms muffle her voice. She sits up again and looks between us. "Did you kill him?" I shake my head no, and she visibly relaxes. "Can I go to bed? I was told I could as long as someone monitored me."

I nod and hold my hand out to her. She takes it and stands, so I lead her up the stairs and into my bedroom as the guys talk downstairs. I don't want to touch her until I've had a shower, so I help her out of her sweatshirt, and she pulls her sweatpants off, dropping them in a heap on the floor, then crawls into my bed, pulling the covers up to her chin.

"I'm going to shower, and then join you soon." She nods, keeping her eyes closed.

I take the fastest shower, not wanting to touch her until every single trace of Bruno is off my skin. I towel-dry off and step into my room. Her quiet snores pull at my lips, and I smile down at her. I leave, closing my door behind me, and jog down the steps. Wes and Julien are still in the kitchen talking.

"No, the fucker didn't get him out today. I sent him a

little present that I'm sure will kick his ass into gear," Julien says.

There're some containers of takeout food sitting on the table. I grab a plate and load it up as the two of them continue their discussion. Today was day three of Julien's threat, and Alec wasn't released from prison. Julien arranged for a package to be delivered to Michael's office with a severed finger inside. He had the fingerprint burned off, so it's going to be difficult not to think it's Riley's.

Both James and her father have been sending her emails since they can't get through on her phone, but I've deleted them. The last thing we need is for her to spoil the surprise for Michael. This whole situation isn't making sense though. First, Derek is involved in the kidnapping. Now an unknown source sets Bruno up to attack Riley. As far as I know, there has never been this blatant type of attack on any student at Pointebreak. So what exactly is going on? This doesn't have to do with Riley. This all comes back to Michael somehow.

I clean up my plate and the three of us head to our rooms. Riley is still sleeping when I tear off my shirt and sweats and climb into bed behind her. At some point, she ditched the t-shirt and undies and is lying completely naked in my bed. I pull her warm back against me. She curls up, placing her ass right over my straining dick. I groan deep in her ear. She shivers and presses back against me harder, her deep breathing still steady.

I lift her leg up and angle myself so the head of my cock sits at her entrance, and I achingly slowly push into her. She's so tight like she always is, but feels amazing. I rock into her in a gentle rhythm, letting her ground me, burying my demons once again. When she whimpers and presses back into me, I flip her onto her stomach and pull her hips up, slamming back into her. I let go of the careful control I had. My hips snap into her over and over again. Each bounce of her lithe body pushing the darkness further and further from my mind.

She cries into the pillow and I reach my fingers around her, rubbing her clit the way she likes. Before long she clamps down on me and comes with a cry. I can't hold back any longer.

"Fuuuck, Riley." I still behind her, holding myself deep as I coat her insides. Thoughts of being able to do this every night filter through my brain, and I cling to that fantasy. I want that. Riley is the light to my darkness, and I can't let her go. I pull out of her, and she slumps down with her arms tucked under her. I clean up quickly and get a facecloth to clean her.

"You wanted to get fucked tonight, Luna?" I whisper as I kiss her shoulder.

She says nothing at first, but then says, "will you help me?"

"Help you with what?"

"My panic attacks? I don't like that they're happening around people. I've been able to control them for so long, but lately, I can't. I-I don't want to be weak."

I lie on my back and pull her on top of me, her head resting on my chest. She drapes her arm over me and settles down. "You're not weak. Will you tell me about them?"

"They started after my mom died when I was eight. It was strange, and I didn't know what was happening. They weren't frequent, and probably only happened when I thought too much about the accident. My dad brought me to the doctor, and she gave me a diagnosis of panic attacks because of stress. I remember not really understanding it then. But we were told to keep the stress levels down and eventually they would go away.

"My dad got mad the first time he saw me have one. It

was when he was campaigning. I was with him at the event and all but passed out on stage."

"How old were you then?" I run my fingers up and down her back.

"Ten. That was the last time I had one around people until recently. I got good at hiding before one could pull me under. But they got better for a while. Things at home stabilized. I knew what was expected of me, and I maintained that perfect persona. I had my best friend, Leah; and I spent a lot of time with her. Things were good. Then, James, my dad's bodyguard, brought his nephew over to hang out during summer. I was thirteen, and he was a few years older. God, I had such a crush on him."

I tighten my hold on her, and she laughs before patting me.

"He lived in a different town and went to summer camp the following year. I was crushed. I tried writing him letters, but they went unanswered. I felt like we had this connection. It sounds so stupid now. But when I was sixteen, he showed back up. He snuck into one of my dad's masquerade parties —he's known for them."

"I'm aware, Luna. Research, remember?"

She hums. "Right. Well, I slept with him that night. He was my first, and until recently, only. We fell asleep, and when I woke up, he was gone. I begged James to get letters to him, but he refused and told me to forget about him. I tried to find him on my own, with no luck. After a while, I forgot about him, except the attacks became more frequent after that."

"Riley, I don't want to hear about you sleeping with someone else. Do I need to remind you who you belong to now?" I'll gladly take her over my knee and teach her a few lessons so she doesn't forget. Hell, the basement is nearly done, the last walls are being painted and soon I'll have the perfect space to play with her and make her understand she will never belong to anyone else but us again.

"The point I'm trying to make is that there's something wrong with me. I-I think I'm afraid of being alone. Of being forgotten about."

"No one could ever forget you." She gives me a sad smile. "You want help to control them?"

"Is it even possible?" Her eyes are so full of hope, it's cute.

"We can try."

TWENTY-SEVEN

RILEY

Zander's already out of bed by the time my eyes flutter open. He's watching me as he buttons up his black shirt.

"Morning," I say, sleep still heavy in my voice.

"Morning, beautiful. How did you sleep?"

"Like a rock." And it's true. After sex and the conversation with Zander, I slept really well. I don't know if it was because I was next to him, or the prospect of kicking my panic attacks, but I feel refreshed this morning. I get up and pull his t-shirt over my head before using the bathroom. Checking the time on my phone, I panic when I see how late it is. I won't have enough time to get to my dorm, get my uniform, and make it to class on time.

As if Zander can see my mental freakout, he points to the chair by the desk. "Your uniform is there, along with some clean underwear and toiletrics."

"Wow, you're not gonna steal these ones?"

He shrugs and his lips quirk up. "Thought about it, but no one needs to see that magical pussy of yours." I groan as I feel my face light up. He pulls me into his arms and kisses the top of my head. "Get changed and come downstairs."

He leaves and closes the door behind him. I get dressed and brush my teeth in record time, and meander down the steps. The guys are all in the kitchen, and Wesley hands me a coffee mug when I walk in. I take a sip and smile up at him. Then take a seat, and Zander puts a plate of food in front of me. Buttered toast, cut-up fruit, and scrambled eggs.

The three of them eat with few words spoken between them, so I do the same and focus on the food in front of me. For once, Julien doesn't scowl at me. Then I remember what day it was yesterday.

"Did my dad get yours out of prison?"

Julien looks up at me and swallows his bite of food. "No."

"Oh." I slump into my seat. "So, what does that mean for me?"

"Nothing good."

Always with the cryptic messages. I'm getting really tired of this shit. "Julien—"

"Let it go, Princess. You're still alive, but let's just say he thinks you're missing a limb."

What the hell does that mean? You know what, nevermind. I have a pretty good guess, and I don't like it. So why hasn't he tried to contact me through other means? Or storm the campus like he did last time. I wish I had answers instead of being stuck in limbo.

"Have you found anyone to train you?" Wes asks. And I'm sure he knows the answer because he smirks.

I stab a strawberry with my fork and point it in his direction. "No, but you already know that." I pop the fruit into my mouth and chew as he continues to grin at me.

We finish breakfast and pile into the car. Julien drives and pulls into a parking spot in the center of campus since we have classes in different areas. I grab my bag and heft it over my shoulder as Wesley interlocks our fingers together. I smile up at him, and we walk in comfortable silence to my class. He stops me outside the building and pulls me around the corner, shielding us from prying eyes.

"Hey, so I overheard some people talking yesterday, and supposedly Arthur is making Derek come back today."

I tense up at his name, but push a harsh breath out and straighten my shoulders. "Okay. I don't have any classes with him, so I should be fine."

"Even so, I wanted you to know."

"Thanks, Wes."

"Hey, why don't you use my nickname anymore?"

"Sugar plum?" I snort. "Want me to?"

He shrugs and smiles widely. "You call Zander Daddy, and when Julien pisses you off, you call him Cupcake. Why not?"

"Okay, Sugar Plum. I've gotta get to class. I love you."

The world freezes as my heart thumps wildly in my chest. Sweat beads at the corner of my hairline, and suddenly it's too hot out despite the cool temperatures hanging in the crisp autumn air. I've been hiding those feelings, even from myself. Anytime the thought filters in, I crush it down and shove it back into a tiny mental box to contain it. It can't be a genuine feeling. It has to be some sort of Stockholm Syndrome response. I've just ruined everything, and I don't know if I can take it back.

Do I backtrack? Maybe pretend I didn't say those words? I could play it cool, make a joke about it; but the moment I risk looking up into his handsome face, I know he feels it too. His eyes are bright, as he holds me prisoner with his gaze.

"I love you too, Riley." He bends down and kisses me as he wraps his arms tightly around my waist, pressing my body to his. "You've become an obsession to me. I don't know how or when it happened, but you're all I think about."

And I believe every word out of his mouth. Wesley may be a lot of things, but a liar isn't one of them. He's always been truthful with me, even when I didn't want to hear it. This scares me. Knowing he reciprocates my feelings makes this thing between us real. This isn't some crazy fantasy I'm dreaming up; but with this admission, it means I will do anything to protect him. And protecting him means protecting his brothers and Pointebreak.

"I really wish we were somewhere alone right now," he presses his lips against mine again, and I melt into him.

I do too, and I never thought I would say this, but I want to help. I want to know what they are hiding from me; and I want to help them rule. Not only this school, but outside as well. They haven't told me their plans for after college. I don't know if they are planning on building their own empire together, or splitting ways after this. Wesley hates his family, and he's not taking over for his dad. He's probably planning on staying by Julien's side. And as long as Ava is safe, I think Zander would be comfortable anywhere.

We break apart, both panting, and I help straighten his shirt from my death grip on it. "I'm grabbing you after class, Hellcat. We aren't done yet."

"I have target practice after this before my shooting class." I haven't been doing it long, but I'm getting decent. I'm finally able to rebuild a gun, which means they are finally showing me how to aim and shoot it correctly. That's a win in my book. I hope I never have to use it, but I suppose it's a useful skill to have.

"I'll meet you there." He pushes me toward the door and swats my butt. I rub the sting and smile widely at him as I push my way through. I take my seat, and Ava spins to look at me. "Girl, you have so much to tell me."

I have a dull headache behind my eyes, and I'm sure a lot of it has to do with the concussion. It was mild, at best, though; but Bethany said bright lights or screens can cause an onset. It's too hard to take notes in a notebook, though, so I power through. I'm constantly checking over my shoulder as I walk to the gun range. I wonder if the Kings guys are still keeping watch on me. Looking over both shoulders, I don't see anyone with me, and a sudden chill runs down my spine. I pull my phone out of my bag and immediately call Zander.

"What's wrong?" he answers immediately.

"Nothing. I don't think. Maybe something?"

"Riley," he warns.

"I'm walking to the range. Do you still have your guys watching over me? Wesley told me about Derek today."

"I know, and yes. Lucas is in your area now."

I stop and turn a full circle, looking for anyone around me. I see a few students, though most are moving away from the range. It's on the edge of the property, so there aren't many students who venture out this way. If he is watching, he's damn good at hiding.

"Riley," a voice calls out, and I see a large man jogging toward me.

"That's Lucas. He'll walk with you," Zander says to me as if he could see the confused look on my face.

"Thanks," I sigh. "Okay, I'm gonna hang up. See you later." The urge to tell him I love him is there, but I know it's too soon for that. Zander is…intense. And while I don't think I'd be far off base if I said it; I don't want him to feel he has to say it back.

"Hi Lucas," I say, putting my phone away. "It's nice to meet you." I hold out my hand to him, and he looks at it for a beat before finally shaking it. I wonder if that "no touch" rule is still in place. Then I mentally slap myself, because of course it is. They've said it over and over; I belong to them. A thrill runs through me at that thought.

"Zander told me to stay during your lesson, maybe give you a few pointers."

I smile warmly up at him. He's big, like he could be a bouncer type of big. With shaggy, light blonde hair and light green eyes. If he weren't a mafia kid, I could see him on the cover of a magazine. He has the right look for it. "I'd appreciate that, thanks."

We walk into the range, and Mr. Barone is there waiting for me. He nods at Lucas and hands me safety goggles and headphones. Lucas collects his own safety gear and comes to stand next to me again.

"You've gotten the hang of a .22, now I want to move you up to a 9mm and see how you do." I nod. "I'm going to show you how to take this one apart, and you're putting it together again before firing it. First rule?"

"Point away and make sure it's not loaded." I say.

He nods. I watch as he checks the chamber with practiced ease before starting. He methodically separates the main components, laying each piece out in a neat line—slide, barrel, recoil spring, frame. When he looks at me, I nod in understanding. Then he reassembles the Glock with ease, proving he's done this a million times over.

Great, my turn. I take a deep breath and hold it, mentally running through taking it apart. It's not much different from the .22 I've been handling, so I know I can do this. I check the chamber, just like Mr. Barone did. Then, with a slight tremble in my hands, I take the rest of it apart, laying the pieces in a neat row. I smile up at him.

"Good. Now put it back together," he instructs.

I do so with more confidence this time until I put the slide back into place. He hands me a magazine to load, and I smile wide to myself. I look over at Lucas, who smirks at me and nods. I'll take that as approval. Placing my headphones over my ears, I load the magazine and take my stance. Staring straight ahead, I pull the trigger and, oh wow. That's different. The shot goes high as the gun kicks back into my palms a bit. Placing the gun down, I take my headphones off to talk.

"Different gun, different approach. Each one is unique, and you have to understand the difference. You've gotten used to a .22, so this is a bigger gun with a bit more kick behind it," Mr. Barone says.

"The heavier the gun, the more recoil?" I ask, hoping I'm right.

"Not exactly. There are more parts to it, but for this lesson, we won't go into that. The key is to find a gun you're comfortable holding and get used to shooting it. In an unfamiliar gun situation, try your hardest. Line up again, you now know what the recoil is like."

I shoot again, and this time the shot doesn't go as wide, and I hit the target, even if it is the outer ring. I shoot another few rounds off before putting the gun down and stepping away. It's almost time for class. Lucas left at some point, but there are a few students milling around the large space. I pull my phone out of my bag, fully intending to text to guys and tell them how great I did, when there's a text from Wesley.

WESLEY:

Great job, Hellcat! You should be proud of yourself.

Attached to the text is a picture of me with the biggest

grin on my face right after I put the gun back together on my own. Lucas must have snapped it without me knowing. I'm glad someone was here to share in my accomplishment, even if it wasn't one of the Kings.

TWENTY-EIGHT

RILEY

I'm exhausted and my head is pounding by the time I make it back to my dorm, and I pop a few Advil hoping it touches the throbbing pain. Maybe I pushed myself a little too hard today, despite being told to take it easy. I already feel behind in basically every subject; I don't want to fall behind any more. This is my new normal—Pointebreak, the Kings, and the underground battlefield. Okay, so battlefield may be a bit dramatic, but sometimes that's how it feels. I don't know who to trust, and I don't know who has it out for me.

Thanks Dad.

I hoped Wesley would have found me by now, especially after our talk this morning, but I only got that text from him and a promise to see me tonight. So I strip out of my uniform and get into my favorite pair of sweats and a hoodie. The nights are getting cold now as the cooler weather sets in. Soon, we'll get snow, and it's going to be harder to get to the guys' place. I won't be able to get there through the woods unless I'm willing to trudge through the snow, which I'm not.

I open an email to Leah, but squint at the bright light on

my screen. Even with the brightness almost off, my head begins to ache. Maybe I'll give it a few more days before I tell her I'm backing out of the exposé. I'm going to make it through Pointebreak, and I'm going to make my guys proud. I might have been forced into coming here, but it doesn't mean I can't excel and prove people wrong. Just like how Julien calls me "princess", I know that's how a lot of others perceive me, even outside these walls. I've been my dad's perfect daughter, and you know what? I'm sick of it.

For once in my life, I don't want anything handed to me because of the people I know. Half of the reason I got into Dartmouth was because of my father, even though I had the grades and extracurriculars to qualify. I'm not an idiot, despite what some people would believe. I haven't spent my time trying to figure out who tried to take me and for what reason, but I've decided now's a good time to piece things together.

I pull out a notebook and pen and sit on my bed cross-legged. I write down all the facts I know and the bits I can remember from that night. It's hard to believe it's only been a few weeks since then. The one that still gets me is my dad showing up. Zander already told me I can't have contact with them. My phone buzzes, and I look down at the screen.

ZANDER:

Luna, we have something we have to do.
Stay put. We'll swing by later to check
on you.

I deflate. Oh. Well, I guess I can rule out any time with the guys tonight. I huff out a breath and respond.

ME:

Okay. Be safe. 🖤

WESLEY: 

We will be. Love you. 🩶

My stomach flips as I read the words. Has he told the others how he feels, or is this the first time he's admitted it to them? I shake my head and chide myself. This is stupid. I shouldn't be this excited to read a few simple words. But right now, those words mean everything to me. I want to say it back to him, but I don't know how Zander would feel about that. I haven't admitted it to him yet, even though I feel the same way. I'm way over-thinking this, but I heart his reply instead of sending one.

I stare at the list I've made, including a few names I've circled. My dad, Bruno, and Derek, of course. Silas chased me, but that was in class. Outside of that, I haven't had interactions with him, so I don't think he's involved. I've hit a dead end with Derek, and Arthur has no online presence that I've been able to find. None of the professors have an online presence. And maybe that's by design. I'll have to look more into Bruno when I feel up to it. The letters W-H-Y are scrawled across the top of the paper, and I've underlined it a few times. I really wish I had the answers.

I sit straight up in bed, my ears throbbing and my heart pounding in my chest as the fire alarm blares overhead. I cover my ears, hoping to dampen the piercing sound. There's no way anyone is sleeping through this racket, and I toss my covers off. I flip on my light and search around the floor until I find my sports bra and a pair of sneakers. I pull it over my head and slip my feet into them, the laces still loose. Then grab my phone off the charger and leave my room. Ava opens her door at the same time and stumbles out into the hallway.

"If this place burns down, I'm gonna be pissed," she says, shutting her door tightly behind her.

I don't think it's an actual fire; I think it's a false alarm. We will all stand outside in the cold until the fire department gets here, and then they will give us the all-clear. It happened once when I was on vacation with my family. I remember being so scared, but my dad told me everything would be fine, and it was.

But this doesn't feel like that time. Something doesn't seem right about this. Maybe I'm just paranoid because of my experiences. I try to shake the uneasy feeling that consumes me as Ava and I walk side by side down the stairs. Other students join us in the hall and grumble about the late hour. I didn't even look at the time, and when I pull my phone out of my pocket, I see it's just after eleven.

Did anyone come by to check on me? Zander said they were going to, but I don't remember hearing anyone. Maybe I was just really out of it. Or maybe they are still busy with whatever they were doing. We step outside, and the cold air sends a chill down my spine. I wrap my arms around myself, hoping to ward off the bitterness of the night. We follow the other students down the path to the muster point.

That's when I notice it. This isn't a fire drill for Graton Hall. All of Belknap Hall is here, too. I slowly step into the space, surrounded by first-year students, most of whom are still sluggish from sleep. Hushed conversations circulate around me, and slowly tensions rise. The air changes around us, becoming electrified as we start to figure something isn't adding up. I circle where I am, keeping a tight grip on Ava and looking at the familiar faces around me.

First-years.

It could be a fluke. In the orientation paperwork, this was

a muster drill location, so it makes sense all of us would be here, right? Whispered words die down, and an eerie quiet takes over the group. On the horizon, among the treeline, there are figures, barely visible in the darkened sky. There's no moon tonight, and while the stars above provide a semblance of light, it's not enough to see clearly.

A gunshot cracks through the night, disturbing some sleeping birds who flutter into the black sky as the dark figures run closer to us. The distance between them and us closes quickly, and I have enough time to see they have on different masks, covering their faces; making it impossible to determine who they are. Are they students, or is this some sort of coup? My brain is too foggy to give me a logical answer; all I know is we need to run.

"Ava, run," I say as I push her in the direction I want her to go. Chaos and confusion ripple through the crowd as everyone moves. Bodies slam together as everyone scatters like roaches, wanting to get away from whatever threat this is. Some students have their phones out, using the flashlight to see. And I know without any doubt, that's the wrong thing to do. Screams and cries of panic ricochet around the open space and disappear into the night.

Ava turns her head to make sure I'm still with her. "Don't look at me," I warn. If she doesn't pay attention to where she's going, she's going to either get hurt or get caught. We make it away from the crowd and into the woods. My body fights the urge to double over and puke. Between my head and the exertion, I don't know if I'm going to make it out of this situation.

I slow as my steps falter, and Ava turns, grabbing my hand to keep me upright. "Nope, you're not going down," she huffs between labored breaths. Rustling leaves encircle us, and I don't know if it's the people trying to capture us, or if it's other first-year students attempting to avoid capture.

Just when I think I understand how Pointebreak operates, they throw this shit into the mix.

I look down at my clothing, and then at what Ava's wearing, and mentally kick myself. She's in dark gray and dark green clothing. She'll blend in well. My sweatpants are light pink with reflective stripes down the sides, and my sweatshirt is black. The black is great; it's the pants that are going to screw me over. So now I have to decide if it's worth keeping them on. I push Ava toward a large fallen tree trunk and crouch down, catching my breath. My pulse races, and with each beat of my heart and the sound of blood rushing past my ears makes it almost impossible to hear anything else. I'm sweating and shaking from the cold all at once.

"Ava, I need to take off my pants."

"What?" she huffs. "What the hell for?" She keeps her voice low as she forces her breathing into a regular pattern.

Another scream, and this time it's a guy begging for mercy. I cringe when he goes quiet moments later. That settles it. I pull the sweatpants over my hips and kick them off over my feet. Mentally, I say a prayer of thanks that I'm in boyshorts and my butt isn't completely exposed. I shiver in the cold as the dry leaves and sticks press into my flesh.

"We need to stick together," I say, attempting to convince myself it's for the best and not just because I'm scared shitless right now. I use Ava's presence to ground me, to keep me in the moment, and to keep me focused on what we have to do. I tie my shoes and get back into a crouching position. Glancing up and over the trees, I notice a few men walking around. One of them laughs and mimics a scream, which causes some girl to run from her hiding place and dart away. They are after her instantly, and I hear her fall to the ground with a thud.

How many are there? We've got to be outnumbered three-to-one.

"Ava, why didn't Nick stay with you tonight?" I whisper quickly, working through a thought.

"He said he had a study group, but I'm starting to think that was a lie."

I nod. Yeah, me too. I guess the only thing we can do now is play the game, because that's what this is; some stupid, twisted game. My phone buzzes in my pocket on the ground, but I don't pull it out. The light will give our position away.

"Okay. On the count of three, we're going to run. I say we head toward the King's place. If you lose me, just keep running. It's straight out that way." I point down the path that students have forged over the years.

She nods, but I know she doesn't like the idea of being alone any more than I do. We're going to get through this, because I haven't gone through so much crap to be taken down now. I close my eyes and take one more deep breath. The muscles in my legs ache as I stand and run as fast as I can. Ava keeps pace beside me, and the crunching of steps behind us gets louder and louder. Ava takes a sharp right. It catches me off guard, and I almost trip as I watch her break away. That was *not* the plan, and I hope she knows what she's doing.

I stumble over some roots but catch myself before I smash face-first into the ground. "Shit," I hiss. Scrambling back to my feet, I notice movement to the right. I pull my hood over my head, covering my light hair, and focus on making myself as dark as possible. My head pounds in time with my heart, and spots dance in my vision. This is definitely not what Bethany had in mind when she said rest for a few days. I want to scream in frustration, but those are precious moments I don't have.

I left my phone in my pants and now I wish I had it on me. At least I could call them and scream or something. And at least they'd know where the hell I was because they can track it. Do the Kings know this is even going on? Do they know the students are being hunted like prey?

Finding a rock, I hide behind it for a second, making myself as small and invisible as possible. Shaking my head, I work on getting my eyes to focus, but everything feels like it's moving at half speed. I know I can't keep this up for long, and I'm not sure if the best way to go about it is to stay and fight when I am found, or keep trying to run to the house. I'm not stupid. It was pure luck I found Mr. Scarboro's house last time; no way karma is on my side twice.

I can't keep running like this though. I won't make it much longer and I'll be even more exhausted than I already am. Staying to fight seems like my best option. Plus, if I'm running and get knocked down, it's a lot harder to get out from under someone. I stay low and listen. I can't tell if my mind is playing tricks on me or not, because I don't hear any movement around me. No crunching of leaves, labored breathing...nothing. But I know I'm not alone; there's no way.

The spots in front of my eyes have cleared a little as my heart rate slows. At least I know I'm not doing more damage to myself. I hype myself up with a pep talk and decide on the direction I'm going. Then I stand, and as soon as I run, a familiar voice startles me.

"You're a tough one to catch."

I stumble and stare at him—Derek.

TWENTY-NINE

JULIEN

This doesn't feel real. I sit in the SUV with the guys as we watch the front of the prison. This has been my dad's home for the past five years. Because I was supposed to be dead with my mother, I haven't seen him in person for just as long. We have conversations, and I've had pictures sent to me, but a picture isn't the same. I'm not some sentimental asshole, but it was hard to lose both of them at the same time. I was a fucking kid; I wasn't prepared to be an orphan.

"Where the fuck is he? We're going to be late," Wesley says impatiently from the back seat. Zander sits in the driver's seat, and I'm in the front passenger seat. I couldn't drive tonight, and he knew it. There's another SUV parked next to us, and that's the one Alec will get into, if they ever release his sorry ass. I got word today that it was happening. Apparently Michael got his present in the mail and it seems to have lit a fire under his ass.

Tensions are high in the car, and for once I bite my tongue instead of tossing a sarcastic comment at him. Wesley's in too deep with Riley. He loves her—fucking loves her—which means being here tonight, of all nights, is torture. I tried to convince Dorian to change fright night, but he said it was out of his hands. I could have let Wesley stay with her, but I knew if any of us stopped her from going outside, there would have been hell to pay.

Fright night is what it sounds like. The first years get the shit scared out of them as they run around campus attempting to flee from unknown attackers. It's fun for the older students, though. The school calls it a training lesson, and the teachers watch the students through drones and night-vision goggles. It's stupid, if you ask me. How can you grade someone on their ability to evade capture?

The door in the gate opens, and two officers step out behind my dad. They hand him a bag, and he walks to the other vehicle before climbing in. I needed to see it with my own eyes to believe it was happening. He looks a bit beat up, but no worse for wear. I'm sure the guards gave him a little parting gift to remember them by. Zander puts the car in drive, and we follow the other one to the house.

My childhood house. I haven't been home in a long time. After my mom was murdered, my uncle took me in while they hauled my dad in for it. The accusation didn't stick—he wasn't even home when it happened. So they called it racketeering and slammed the door in his face. The courts have denied every appeal for the past five years. He's still been running his empire from behind bars, but things are changing a lot sooner than we thought.

I'm glad my brothers are here with me tonight, but their minds are elsewhere. I sometimes wonder if it was a mistake dragging Riley into all of this. I could have ignored her, not said a word about her to the guys. They might have found her on their own. But the chance was too good to pass up. So I told Alec, and he agreed to move on it. Speed things up for the greater good.

We pull into the driveway, and I look up at the darkened home. There's a light coming from the downstairs window, glowing behind the blinds. The house has stayed in my dad's name, and he has a cleaner who goes in once a month to dust and air out the place. I haven't stepped foot in here since that night. I was supposed to be dead after all. Shaking my head, I refuse to travel down that path of destruction. I open the car door and come face to face with Alec Azarian. He opens his arms for a hug, and I give him a quick one. No need to get too sentimental. He feels thinner than I remember, but I've also bulked up.

"Good to see you, son."

We pull apart. "You too."

The group of us walk inside the house, and I realize this is the first time Wesley and Zander have met my dad and have seen my house. My dad's men take over searching through each of the rooms, and when everything is clear, we settle. I pull the sheet off the couch, and we all sit down.

"Dad, this is Wesley Bastian and Zander Fedorov. Wes, Zan, this is Alec Azarian," I introduce.

Alec's lips twitch up in the corner. He shakes both their hands, and the three of them exchange pleasantries. I wonder if he remembers his own time at Pointebreak and their fathers. Glancing down at his ankle, I see the monitor attached to it. I expected it, and I'm sure he did too. No one knows he's out except those who have to know, and we plan on keeping it that way.

"Lucien Moreau is expanding his operations and is encroaching in New Hampshire. Montreal is cracking down on his shipments and he's working on some shady deals with our guys to steal the cargo and redistribute it to his area. His operations are growing in size, and unless we fight back, we're going to lose our guys and the district," he says.

I take a slow breath, processing what he's saying. This has

been our area for over thirty years. Even behind bars, he's kept control of it. Part because of favors, others because of having the right crew. "How long has this been going on?" I ask. This is the first time I've gotten straight answers from him. They recorded every call we've had, and he has always chosen his words carefully. Plus, he has me involved, but has wanted me to focus on Pointebreak and finishing school.

"About a year." I nod again, letting that information sink in. He told me six months, not a year. How could I not have known this? Why didn't anyone tell me? "Julien," I look at him, "this isn't your fight now. Soon, but not yet. You'll be ready when it's time."

He looks at the three of us and offers me a grim smile. "Keep Riley close. She's proving to be more useful than I thought."

I gather a few items that I'd stored in my old bedroom, and we leave shortly after. I give him a last wave as I close the door and lock it behind me.

"We're never gonna find her," Wesley growls in frustration as Zander races back to campus. Despite Zander's silence, I know he's just as worried about her. It's not ideal, this whole situation. Including the fact that she's still recovering from a concussion. The added stress of the night is going to mess with her even more.

My phone pings with a new camera notification for the house, and I open it. Ava's made her way onto the property and gets in with her code through the garage door.

"Ava made it to the house." Zander's shoulders relax a hair.

"Fuck. Either the tracker's not working, or she dropped her phone," Wes says.

"We'll find her, Wes. Calm down."

"Fuck you, man," he growls. "I should have been there tonight."

I turn in my seat to look at him. "We'll find her. Zander, call Ava. Find out if she knows anything."

Zander dials her through the car, and Ava answers on the third ring. "Zan?" she asks, relief coating her words.

"Good job tonight. Have you seen Riley?" he asks.

"Yeah. We were in the woods and separated at one point. She told me to run here. I thought she would have made it by now, but she's not here."

Zander looks at me and presses the gas pedal. "Stay put. We'll find her."

"You knew, right?"

"Yeah, we all knew."

We reach campus and get out, jogging to the last signal we have for her phone. Son of a bitch, she's not wearing pants. I pick them up and pocket her phone. She was running toward the house, so we all take off down the path. The woods are relatively quiet. This has been going on for a little over forty-five minutes. Anyone who evades capture gets a text that will ping their exact location, provided they have their phones on them.

"Get off me," Riley's shrill voice cuts through the air like glass. We all stop and listen for her again. A gun shoots off in the distance—the ten-minute warning. This is when things get frantic. Those hunting know they only have a few minutes to get their captures to the meeting point; but those hunted do not know this cat-and-mouse game is almost over.

Even with barely any light, I see her light hair and the pale skin of her legs. Whoever is on her hears us and snaps his head in our direction, before taking off at a sprint. Riley lays motionless on her side, her knees pulled tightly to her chest.

Wesley's going to kill me.

THIRTY

RILEY

The footsteps fade as I lay on my side, my brain at war with my limbs. I know I need to move, but I…can't. I'm frozen in place. The night presses in around me, too loud and too quiet at the same time, the rush of blood in my ears drowning out everything else.

He's gone.

The sound of approaching footsteps reaches me, yet I'm paralyzed, unable to act. Maybe if I stay still long enough, they will go away. I scream at the top of my lungs, but no sound comes out. I'm trapped inside myself.

Leave me alone, I scream, but again, I'm met with silence. I will my body to move, to do anything but lay here. Somewhere in the back of my mind, I know I'll freeze if I can't snap out of this soon.

"Riley!"

Wesley's voice cuts through the haze—panicked and close. I blink, slowly at first, and then it becomes more rapid. My fingers tingle as the feeling begins to return. A numbing feeling continues to crawl up my arms and legs, bringing awareness to where I am again. Bit by bit I become aware of my surroundings, and a sudden chill wracks my body. The ground beneath me is cold and unforgiving.

"Jesus, Riley. You're frozen. Give me her damn pants," Wesley yells. I flinch at the harsh tone in his voice, and I'm vaguely aware of the soft fabric being pulled up my legs. He cradles my head in his lap. Closing my eyes, I let the first tear slip. Feeling has returned to my arms and legs again, but I can't move; I might as well be a rag doll for the good they do me.

Safe.

He's safe.

I repeat the words like a mantra. My brain scrambles to make sense of everything that's happened tonight. I'm aware of them talking. Zander, Julien, and Wesley found me. The three of them are here. My dark knights. The boys you don't want to be on the wrong side of; but the ones who will protect each other until death if needed. And they're here— for me.

My chest tightens, and a sob breaks free. I shake in Wesley's arms and cling to him like he's my lifeline.

"I'm so fucking sorry, Hellcat," he murmurs into my hair. He scoops me up bridal-style and stands as if I weigh nothing. "We were supposed to be here."

"We couldn't protect her even if we were," Julien says.

"No," Wesley seethes, "I could have. We could have made it work without interfering."

I can't stop shaking in Wesley's grasp. He hushes me like one would a scared child, and I hate that I'm not strong enough for them. I hate myself for this involuntary reaction. I should have been able to kick Derek in the nuts and kept running for safety. Instead, he got the upper hand. I was seconds away from being dragged off, and there wasn't a thing I could do about it. I feel the tension rolling off Wesley as he carries me to the edge of the woods.

"It's over," Julien says from behind us. "Good job, Princess. Looks like you're one of fifteen who survived."

I don't even know what that means. What the hell happened tonight?

"Can you stand?" Wesley asks me when we reach the car. I nod, and he places me on my feet. I wobble as I stand, and he helps me stay upright.

"What happened?" I ask when all of us are in the car. Wesley hands me my phone, and I stare down at it. Wesley sits next to me in the back, Zander drives, and Julien is in the front passenger. It seems like these are more or less their normal seats.

"Fright night. They were testing your survival skills." I shake my head, not sure I fully comprehend. "Every year, the student body tests the first-years by chasing them. Capture the flag, student style."

That's absolutely insane. What kind of sick place would teach that?

"And the point?" My mouth is dry, and I'd kill for some water right now. As if reading my thoughts, Zander hands a water bottle back to me, and I drink it greedily. The cool liquid slides down my throat, taking the edge off the fire that still coats my insides.

"Hey, slow down, you don't want to get a cramp," Wesley says, tipping the bottle down and taking it from me. He's probably right. The last thing I need now is a cramp.

"The point is to test you. School's been in session for a little over a month now. How much have you learned?"

You know, Julien's voice is really irritating me. My phone rings in my hand, and I look at my dad's familiar number. One of them must have unblocked it at some point tonight. A little late for a phone call, isn't it?

I hold it up for them to see, and Julien nods for me to answer it. I put it on speaker because I'm not dumb enough to think I'll have a private conversation.

"Hello?" My voice is small and unsure, and I'm sure he hears it.

"Riley, I've been calling you for three days. Where are you?"

I turn my head to look at Wesley, then meet Zander's eyes in the rearview mirror. Neither of them coaches me on what to say, so I figure I'm free to answer how I want. "Pointebreak."

"I know that," he answers with an exasperated sigh. "Is he there? I want to talk to him."

After all this, he doesn't even want to talk to me. I don't know why that is so surprising to me. Nothing should surprise me about this man now, but it does. I lock eyes with Julien and stretch my arm out for him to take the phone, too tired to argue with my dad.

"Got my present, I see," Julien answers with a bit too much venom in his voice.

"He's free. Let her go, you son of a bitch."

"Dad—" I stop speaking when Julien glares at me. I'm too tired for this anyway. I close my eyes and rest my head back against the seat. Wesley pulls me over to him, so I reposition myself so I can snuggle under his arm.

"Not how this is going, Michael. He will have his appeal, and you won't interfere. If I catch wind of you trying to pull a fast one, I'll make sure videos of her in precarious situations go public. She's become a bit of a slut since starting here. Already has two different guys fucking her. Wouldn't want that stain on your image, would you?"

Wesley's body goes rigid under mine. I hate Julien. I hate how he makes me feel less than myself, or how he's using

Wesley and Zander in his own twisted game. I want to scream at him, punch him, kick him…anything!

"Riley, I'm going to get you out of there. You don't need to stay there anymore. We can get you enrolled at Dartmouth. I've pulled some strings," he rambles.

Julien barks out a laugh. "Are you fucking stupid, old man? I *own* her. You do what I say, and nothing else bad will happen. Understood?"

"Riley—"

He hangs up the phone without letting me answer. Just as well; I had nothing to say to him. Why did I need to come here in the first place? He never gave me a reason, but more and more I believe he had a motive behind it. It wasn't only for his campaign. Whether it's for my well-being or not is to be determined. Zander has already given me some clues who my father is. So my guess is this is more for his benefit than my own.

"You could have let me say goodbye," I mumble. Wesley's body is still tense under mine, and I place a gentle kiss on his chest. He kisses the top of my head and rubs my shoulder in a soothing motion, which I think he needs more than I do. I see the house up ahead. I want out of this car, and a nice warm bed and pillow so I can go back to sleep.

"He doesn't give a shit about you, Riley." Julien's voice remains calm and quiet.

"You don't either. At least I know he won't kill me if I step out of line. Can't say the same about you, Julien."

"Ah. That's where you're wrong, Princess."

"Julien, stop," Wesley growls. "Enough for the night."

Zander parks the car, and we all get out. Wesley wraps his arm around my waist, steadying me. Ava stands in the doorway and pulls me into a hug when I reach her.

"Thanks for helping me tonight," she says, holding me tight.

"What are friends for?" We break apart, and she looks at me from head to toe. I'm sure I've got dirt all over me from lying on the ground. "What happened?"

"Derek." Those two syllables have the men freezing in their spots.

"What did you say?" Zander answers first.

She stares blankly at him. "Looks like he's back."

THIRTY-ONE

WESLEY

Derek was there, and he slipped right through our fingers. How the hell could we have let that happen? One of us should have gone after him, preferably Julien. I'm sick of this shit. It's all about the fucking plan with him; but that's not good enough anymore. Since day one, Riley has been the target; a means to an end. But not anymore. She is going to fight beside us; I've been saying it since the first week of school. Still, Julien pushes her away. How much more can she take before she breaks for good?

I help her to the couch, and she sits, resting her head in her hands. "What happened tonight?" I ask, taking a seat next to her. I need her within arm's length of me now. Zander stands in front of her, his arms crossed over his chest, and Julien leans against the wall on the opposite side of the room. Ava sits beside her with her hand on her back.

"The fire alarm went off. We went to the meeting spot. That's when I saw them at the tree line and a gun went off. When everyone started advancing, I pushed Ava toward the house. I knew if we got here we'd be safe. We had people following us; I have no idea how many. I refused to look back, but Ava thought it would be better if we split." She turns her head to look at Ava, "Congrats on making it here."

Ava gives Riley a sad smile. "This was your idea, so I have you to thank."

I glance at Zander in time to see his eyes light up, if only for a moment. Riley tried to protect Ava. That's all Zander has ever wanted for his sister. Someone to look out for her as much as he has.

"Anyway, I was being chased and fatigue was setting in, and I thought maybe if I could take him down, it could give me a few minutes to get a lead again." She sits back, dropping her head on the cushion behind her, staring up at the ceiling. "Derek said you're a tough one to catch and started grabbing at me. He managed to get on top of me, pressing his weight into me. He said something about he won't stop until he gets me, maybe?" She sighs heavily. "I'm not sure that's exactly what he said, but something like that. I was too busy fighting him to really listen."

That makes all of us perk up more. He won't stop until he gets her. Now, who would that be regarding? Julien has had enough conversations to confidently state that Alec has nothing to do with this. I still have my doubts, but so far there is nothing that's happened that would suggest otherwise. Most students are from out of town, and the local politics in New Hampshire are of no concern to them.

Christos and Mikhail have no clue who Riley is or would even care about her. She offers no benefit. Arthur might try to pull a fast one on Michael to ensure some type of funding or spot in his inner circle, but blackmail wouldn't be the way to handle that. So that leaves Michael.

"What did you mean by a present?" she asks Julien.

He licks his lips and stares at her, deciding whether or not he tells her. *You'd better tell her, you son of a bitch.*

He takes a deep inhale and says, "I sent him a finger and

made him think it was yours." She flexes her fingers, examining them, and he adds. "The fingerprint was burned off. No way to trace who it belongs to."

She nods sadly. "Got it." After another beat of silence, she adds, "can I lie down? My head is killing me and I just want to forget tonight." Her words snap me out of my thoughts, and I focus on her again. No visible bruises, cuts, or broken limbs; so it's a combination of everything over the past few days coming to a head. She needs to be put in a damn bubble for a few days.

"Come on, Hellcat. Let's get you upstairs. Ava, you can take over the guest room," I point to the bedroom on the first floor. She nods, and Zander walks with her to the room. I glare at Julien, and he knows we aren't done for the night.

"Can I take a quick shower? I'm dirty from the woods and it will help me warm up."

"Yeah, give me your clothes; I'll get them washed for you." I walk into the bathroom and start the water for her. She comes up behind me, stark naked, and I give her a once-over again, searching for any injuries.

"I'm fine, Wes. Stop fussing. I just want to get clean and go to sleep."

"Let me help you." I pull my shirt over my head, knowing damn well after I'm done kicking Julien's ass tonight I'll need another shower, but not wanting her to be alone. Riley nods and steps under the warm spray as I get in behind her. She spins and drops her head to my chest, listening to my steady heartbeat. She hardly moves, and I fear she's fallen asleep. I tilt my head to see her better, and she's staring blankly at the wall.

"Tell me," I urge.

"Tell you what?"

"What you're thinking."

We stand in silence, the running water drowning out any other noise. "I hate him."

"Who?"

"My dad. I hate him. I-I hate that he sent me here, that he doesn't care. I hate that it took Julien sending a random body part to him to finally listen. Not that I was potentially being held captive, but that he's afraid I'm missing a finger." She blows out a broken scoff. "I don't think I've mattered to him in years."

"For what it's worth, you matter to me. I'm so sorry about tonight. We were supposed to be there; but those plans got fucked up."

I tilt her face up to mine and lower my lips to hers. She opens and I slip my tongue into her mouth, deepening the kiss. I pull her body flush with mine as she wraps her arms around my neck and clings to me like I'm her rock. I pepper kisses along her jaw, cheek, and neck.

"I love you, Riley. I'm so fucking sorry I wasn't there tonight."

She drops her head back as I kiss lower, finally pulling her erect nipple into my mouth. "Make me forget." She inhales on a shaky breath, "Please make me forget."

I lift her up, pressing her back against the wall as she wraps her legs around me. Then line myself up as she slides down on me and hisses at the tight fit. I pull out and spit on my hand to rub against her and try again. This time there's less friction and she moans when I fit all the way inside her.

"Make me forget," she whispers like a prayer.

I don't like that she's using sex to forget. She doesn't need vices; she needs to fight; but I also understand sometimes it's too much. I thrust up into her, fucking her like my life depends on it. Taking away a fraction of the pain and confusion she's feeling. Her nails dig into my shoulders as she holds me tight, kissing me with everything she has. The muscles in my legs strain from the hard thrusting up into her, and when she knocks her head back against the wall on a gasp, I know I've found that sweet spot inside her. Over and over I drill into her, the muscles in my body tightening as my climax is on the precipice.

"Oh God, Wes!" She drops her head to my shoulder and bites hard as she grips me like a vice. I go off, coming deep inside her.

I hold her tight, keeping us wrapped as close as possible. "I love you."

"I love you too, Wesley."

I tuck her into bed, making sure she's asleep before I walk downstairs. Zander sits on the couch alone. He must have sent Ava to bed already. Then he looks at the door to the basement. I'm going to pummel Julien. This has gone far enough. She's no good to him if she's dead, and it seems someone wants that to happen.

Julien sits by the punching bag, wrapping his hands. He's lost his shirt and changed into a pair of sweatpants. He looks up when he hears us coming down the stairs and stands to his full height. All I see is red. Anger flares hot inside me, and I know I shouldn't, but I can't help it when I walk straight up to him and send my fist across his face. Pain jolts from my fingers and radiates up my arm. I don't even care. I go to hit him again, and this time he blocks it before I can do more damage.

"You're not mad at me," Julien says.

"The hell I'm not," I seethe. "If it wasn't for you, she wouldn't be in this fucking situation." I lash out again and catch the side of his head. He steps back, dodging a kick to his nuts. He tries the same, but I shove his knee away with my hands, circling him once more. "Riley isn't just some fuck toy. She's my future. Our future." I lash out again, hoping to catch his nose, but he blocks the punch. "You want her as badly as we fucking do; but you're such a pussy you won't admit it."

I've built my entire reputation on luring people in with a smile or a joke. At being the guy who shrugs it off and moves on, without a care. But there's nothing charming about the thing crawling up my spine right now. It isn't just rage. It's fear. It's the image of her breaking. It's the sound of her voice when she thought she was alone. It's the realization that I let this happen to her.

I'm out for blood, and Julien's will do. I want him to feel even a fraction of what we did to her. I want it to writhe under his skin the way it is under mine. My fist is already moving before I register the decision. I don't shove him; and don't warn him. I drive my knuckles straight into his face. The impact cracks through my hand, pain jolting up my arm, but it's nothing compared to the satisfaction of watching his head snap back. His balance falters. He stumbles, barely catching himself before he hits the ground.

He stays down, swallowing his pride. "You're going to tell her everything, Julien. No more secrets."

He slowly raises his head, his eye already swelling shut. "She'll hate me more than she already does."

I shrug, and Zander steps up next to me. "Then you'd better be ready to grovel for forgiveness."

THIRTY-TWO

RILEY

After the last few days, the guys have forced me to stay home from classes. I'm not sure how much that's going to hurt me later, but I'm too exhausted to give it too much thought. I haven't left the house since, but I'm okay with that. Now I have some clothes, my computer, and personal items here, and for the past few days I've spent rotating from Wesley's and Zander's rooms.

The first morning I noticed Julien's eye swollen and bruised, and Wesley was nursing his hand, but I didn't ask questions. Asking questions has gotten me here in the first place. If they want me to know, I'll know. I'm sitting at the breakfast table with Wesley when Julien walks in. Their phone's buzz at the same time, and both look at it, before all eyes fall on me.

My gaze flits between them. This can't be a good thing. "What?" I ask, putting my mug of coffee down. Zander steps into the kitchen and his eyes lock on me too. Three hungry wolves and I'm the sheep that was stupid enough to be grazing.

247

"Luna, mind telling me why you've been emailing a friend information about Pointebreak?"

My stomach drops and my fingers shake as I slide them off the table and into my lap. I knew it was a matter of time until this came out, with how much they have been watching me and listening. My mind races as I think about what to tell them. Do I lie? Do I tell them the truth? What is the truth now, anyway? I had already decided my idea was crap, and I haven't sent Leah anything in almost two weeks. Once I started falling for the Kings, I knew I couldn't. I will never do anything to hurt them—any of them.

"We were planning on writing an exposé. She's a journalism major at Northeastern University." When no one says anything, I continue. "We came up with the plan when my dad forced Pointebreak on me. I didn't want to come and thought if we could expose Pointebreak for what it really is, then we could help shut it down, or change it."

I close my eyes, listening to my hammering heart as I gather my wits to say the next part. "I changed my mind about it a few weeks ago. When I decided I couldn't do anything that would hurt you. *Any* of you." I say the last part staring directly at Julien. Willing him to understand that he is part of the package deal. His safety matters to me just as much as Wesley's and Zander's.

"I think we need a little chat with your friend, Hellcat."

An hour and a half later, we are pulling up to a local coffee shop that's close to the university. Their house is technically off-property, but even if it wasn't, they are third-years and can leave campus. I snuggled in the back with Wesley as Zander and Julien assumed their usual spots. I texted Leah on the way, and while she was confused, she agreed to meet me. I omitted the part about me bringing an entourage with me.

We climb out, and Wesley and Zander take their spots on either side of me, while Julien walks behind. Not that I'm worried about a threat out there, but it's reassuring to know I'm covered. Leah sits at a small table, and when I walk in, her mouth drops.

"Maaaybe let's get a booth," she says, dragging out the first word as I get closer. She stands, and the two of us fall into a familiar hug. Tears sting my eyes. I've missed my best friend and her hugs a lot; especially the past few weeks with everything going on.

"I miss you," I say into her hair as I squeeze her a little tighter. We must look like fools standing here in the middle of a small coffee shop, hugging as if we haven't been together in years. On top of that, I walked in with three large, extremely handsome men and they always attract attention. I glance around at the other patrons and realize I'm not wrong. Several people look up mid conversation and whispers fill the small space. Wesley puts his hand on my shoulder and I step back, allowing her to lead us to the back.

"I'll get us some drinks," Julien offers. We give him our orders, and he leaves the four of us at the small booth, partially hidden.

"So, you must be Wesley," she looks at the handsome man to my right, "and Zander," looking to the man on my left. Both men nod, and Wesley slides into a charming smile. He reaches his hand across the table and she places hers in his.

"It is a pleasure to finally meet you, Leah."

She eyes him up and down before responding, "You too. You three are hard to crack." Zander narrows his eyes a fraction at her as she continues. "Riley's told me a bit about you, and naturally, I've taken to the internet to fill in some gaps. Except there isn't a lot of there. More about Wesley; but from what Riley has told me, that's just a playboy image."

Wesley pushes a quiet snort through his nose. I mean, she's not wrong; but I feel my face heat as she keeps talking. Julien returns with our drinks, and I pull the paper cup close to my face, using it as a shield.

"Okay, Leah, I think they get it. You're an internet sleuth."

I notice Julien takes a seat next to Zander, and I don't know if that's because then his back isn't toward the door, or because it's the furthest he can be from Wesley. I still don't know exactly what happened there, but Julien hasn't been his asshole self to me; so I'll take it as a win.

"Julien, I presume?" Leah locks eyes with him, and he nods, not offering more. "Hmm."

"How much do you know?" Julien asks, getting straight to the point.

She shrugs, taking a sip of her coffee. "Not much. Riley sent me information about her classes, the type of students who attend, and her attempted kidnapping. We haven't gotten into the nitty-gritty." She turns to face me; the Kings having no immediate effect on her whatsoever. "You getting a spanking for this, girlfriend?"

Please let a hole open and swallow me up. "Yes," Zander says without pause, "she'll be punished later."

"Oh, kinky," she winks at him.

Wesley barks out a laugh next to me, drawing a few eyes in our direction. I groan and close my eyes, shielding my face. Yup, please let me die. "Focus, please," I say through my fingers. "We can't go through with the exposé. There's too much at risk if we do. I've wanted to tell you for a while; I don't feel comfortable about it anymore. Not with what I've learned. Plus, I don't think it will get far." I'm learning there are many people in power at the top who would kill to keep this information buried. The last thing I need or want is any sort of target on Leah's back.

She shrugs as if it's not a big deal, and maybe it isn't. It's not for me, and I'm the one who is at Pointebreak. "Okay. Well, I'm glad I got some answers. But that's fine with me. I'll find my breakout story somewhere else."

I release my breath in a slow exhale. I knew she wouldn't fight us on this, but it is still reassuring to know I can trust her wholeheartedly. The three men seem appeased with her answer.

"Anything you know, you keep to yourself. If that gets out, there's going to be a lot of people looking for the source, and it won't end in a talk," Julien warns.

She salutes him with two fingers and gives him the biggest grin. I know he hates it when he stares her down. I'm not sure he knows what to make of Leah, but I love her all the more for it.

"How long have you got before you have to get back?"

I look at Zander, who I know has everything planned down to a tee. "An hour, and then we have to get back."

"Great! I need a few minutes with my girl, alone."

Wesley sits straighter in his seat, his muscles tensing as if she's an immediate threat. I place my hand on his leg, and he looks down at me, his eyes warming as he drinks me in. Yeah, I'm getting fucked good when we get back tonight.

"I'll be fine. You three can sit here, and the two of us will sit a few tables down to talk and finish our coffees. I'd really like to spend a little time with her." I still don't know if I'll be home for Thanksgiving, or Christmas, or anything. That's still yet to be determined. I don't know if they would trust my dad not to keep me from coming back. We move a few tables down, enough to be out of direct earshot. While they don't directly stare at us, I feel their gaze on me.

"Girl, they're intense. And hot. So damn hot. No one at Northeastern looks like *that*. I'm wicked jealous."

"Yeah, they are something."

"What's the sex like? I bet it's mind-blowing."

I smile wide and hide it behind my cup, and I know I must be as red as a tomato. "It's mind-blowing. I'm really happy with them. Well, with Wesley and Zander. Julien and I are on the outs. Oh, I haven't told you. He used me as blackmail to get his dad out of jail. Forced my dad to pull some strings."

"What?" she says a little too loudly, and the guys' heads whip in our direction.

I give them an apologetic look before focusing on Leah again. "Keep it down, will ya? I think he hates me because of my dad. Like I'm guilty by association." I still haven't figured out the real reason he doesn't like me. The guys won't say anything, and he refuses to talk to me, so I'm stuck feeling like I'm in limbo. I never know which side of Julien I'll get.

She turns to the side for a better view of the guys' table and stares at them for a minute. "He doesn't hate you, Riley. He hates that he's not with you."

I furrow my brow and shake my head quickly. "No. Definitely not it. He's been a pain in my ass since I arrived at Pointebreak. Constantly threatening me and forcing me to do what he wants."

"Foreplay."

I sit back in my seat and blink at her a few times. There's absolutely no way. I mean, I know he's been turned on around me; I've felt it. After a chase and he has me pinned, he is rock hard; but that has more to do with the chase than me. Right? He's always so cold, the complete opposite of Zander and Wesley. While they were mean to me when I arrived, they've done nothing like Julien has.

"I'm telling you, that man gazes at you as if you're a feast and he's been starved for months."

Is it possible I've been wrong about Julien?

Chapter 34 Riley-

I relax in the backseat next to Wesley as he plays with the long strands of hair that cover my shoulders. I didn't realize how much I needed to see Leah today. The weight of everything has been crushing me and she was the release I needed. I wish I had more time with her than we did; but I appreciate it all the same. The guys talk amongst themselves, but I tune the conversation out, replaying what Leah was saying to me about Julien. I haven't been able to shake the feeling that she knows something more than she's letting on.

"I liked Leah," Wesley says when we pull into the garage. I sit up to look at his face. "She's good for you. I think we'll get along great."

Smiling warmly, I say, "Thanks. She's been there through everything with me. I don't know where I'd be if I didn't have her."

I stretch my arms over my head when we walk inside and stifle a yawn when it comes out of nowhere. Julien darts off, leaving me alone with Wes and Zan, and my body flushes when I remember what Zander said about punishment. As if he knows what I'm thinking, he holds his hand out to me. I stare at it before ultimately deciding to place mine in his. He pulls me flush to him and lowers his face to mine, kissing me with fervor. He devours me. You'd think he hasn't seen me in days. I grab at his shirt, not sure if I want to pull him closer or push him away to tear it off. I've never wanted him so much.

Wesley stands behind me, pressing himself against my back, and I moan into the kiss. Zander wraps his hand around my throat and squeezes hard enough that I pop my mouth open into an O shape. "You're going to take your punishment like a good little girl, and then Wes and I are going to fuck you until you see stars."

I inhale on a shaky breath and blink up at him, suddenly at a loss for words. He stares me down, and that's when I realize what he's waiting for.

"Yes, Daddy."

I thought we were going to go up to one of their rooms, but they lead me to the basement instead. I've been down here a few times to use the gym space, but there was some sort of construction going on. I didn't ask, but I have been curious. So imagine my surprise when there is a large room surrounded by frosted glass for privacy.

Zander picks up a remote, and with a quiet hum the glass wall shifts from opaque to crystal clear, revealing the room beyond. My breath catches. He slides the doors open with ease and gestures for me to step inside. The moment I cross the threshold, the vibe feels different. Thicker, more charged.

The smell of new leather clings to the air, and my teeth sink into my bottom lip as I stare. Shelves line one wall, each one meticulously arranged. Whips coiled like snakes; leather paddles and floggers lay in neat rows. Below them sit rows of toys. Sleek metal and silicone plugs in various sizes, vibrators, ball gags with glossy straps that gleam under the soft lighting.

A cushioned chair sits in one corner, inviting a voyeur to sit and enjoy the show. A bench sits against the far wall, dark wood and black leather. I recognize it instantly—a spanking bench. The torture class had something similar, but something tells me Zander's imagination goes far beyond anything the professors teach. Then my gaze drifts to the center of the room. A massive king-sized bed dominates the space, draped in blood-red sheets and a black comforter. Leather restraints rest in the middle, the cuffs spread wide like an invitation. My pulse kicks harder as I slowly turn in a circle, taking it all in. This isn't just a room. It's a playground built for control—and Zander looks far too comfortable in it.

"You deserve more than that classroom, Luna. I want you to be comfortable being as loud or dirty as you want to be."

The first sting of tears burns behind my eyes, but I drop my gaze and swipe at the traitorous moisture. I clear my throat. "Thank you, Zan. I love it." *I love you.* But those words don't come out. They settle deep in my chest, making it hard to breathe.

"Strip," he commands.

I catch movement out of the corner of my eye as Wesley sits in the seat, spreading his legs wide. The outline of his bulge is prominent through his jeans. He grins at me and nods in encouragement. I do as Zander asks, pulling my shirt over my head, dropping the material at my feet. Next, I slide my jeans down my legs and kick them off, until I'm standing there in only my bra and panties. I look at Zander, waiting for more instructions, but he raises his eyebrow at me as if to say, "I want it all off." With deft fingers, I undo the clasp of my bra, letting it fall to the floor, and bend over, pulling my undies all the way down, kicking them to Zander, who pockets them straight away. I smile, hoping he was going to do that.

"How's the collection coming along?" I tease.

"Not great. I'm thinking of raiding your drawer."

I smile wide and shake my head in disbelief. Zander steps into my space and pulls me flush against him, lowering his face to mine for a kiss. It's chaste, a simple tease, meant to leave me wanting more. He wraps his hand around my hair, tugging my head up to look into his lust-hazed eyes.

"I'm going to spank your ass until it's stinging, and a beautiful shade of red for keeping the emails a secret. Then, Wesley and I are going to play with you."

I cross my legs and exhale a shaky breath. My nipples are taut not only from the cool air drifting over them but also from Zander's words. I turn my head, looking at the spanking bench, expecting to be placed there, but he shakes his head at my unspoken question.

"You're going to be a good girl and choke on Wes's cock as I spank you." He walks to the wall of toys and holds out the open mouth gag for me to see. Oh God, why is this so hot? I'm more turned on than I have ever been, and he's not even touching me.

"Hmm, sounds good to me," Wes says as he lifts his hips to unbutton and unzip his jeans. He pulls the opening wide, giving me a view of his dark boxers and the tip of his dick pokes out. On instinct, I lick my lips.

"Open," Zander says.

He gives me time to decide if I want this. I know he won't push it if I'm not ready; but he won't hurt me. I swallow and open my mouth, accepting the gag. He places it behind my teeth and secures the leather behind my head. It's not entirely comfortable, but I suppose that's the point. Taking a few deep breaths through my nose, I calm my nerves before bending at the waist in front of Wesley.

"Hands on the armrests. Do not move from this position. Understood?" I nod. "Tap once for yes." I tap once. "Good girl. One tap for yellow, two taps for red." I tap once again.

"Suck it, Hellcat," Wes says as he pulls his cock free. He guides me where he needs me and holds my head in place. The salty tang of his precum hits my tongue and I moan, wishing I could close my lips around him.

Wesley wraps his large hands behind my head and holds me in place as he lifts his hips in a gentle rhythm. I breathe deeply through my nose, listening for Zander behind me, waiting for the first crack of his hand against my skin. Moisture drips down my leg in anticipation, so when the soft leather rubs against my skin, I jerk in response. I barely have enough time to register what's happening when the leather paddle comes down hard on my left cheek. Heat radiates upward, and the sting on the spank makes me cry out. Zander spanks me again, and this time Wesley shoves his cock down my throat, making me choke on him.

"Breathe through your nose, Hellcat. I love when you choke on me. Do it again, Zan."

Zander spanks me again, but this time with his hand. The difference in feeling has me squirming in this position. I wish I could stand, or kneel, do anything but be stuck in this tortuous position.

"Deep breath, Luna," Zander warns.

I take one as Wesley shoves my head all the way down on him and Zander spanks me hard twice in succession. I struggle, trying to pull off him, but he thrusts up into my mouth, making a choked sound tear from my throat as drool spills past my lips. Without warning, he drags me back by my hair. He's panting, chest heaving as he catches his breath, his cock twitching where it bounces against his stomach. My own breathing turns ragged, matching the frantic rise and fall of his.

"Damn girl. I should get you into this gag more often," he laughs.

I blink past tear-filled eyes at him. I need more. Zander's behind me again. He unbuckles the gag, and pulls it out of my mouth, letting it fall to the floor. Then drags his nails down my ass cheek as I hiss in a breath. Without seeing it, I know my cheeks are red and possibly bruised. He hums behind me before gathering my hands behind my back and securing them in the leather restraints that were on the bed.

Zander pushes me forward, and I stick my tongue out, waiting for Wesley to place his dick back in my mouth. He chuckles and taps it against my tongue, but I wrap my lips around the head before he can pull away. The cool drizzle of lube against my rim has me breathless once again. Zan rubs his fingers over the tight bud before pressing the cold metal tip against it. I groan, releasing Wes as I press back onto it, welcoming the blunt toy into me. This one is different, bigger.

Zander walks me to the edge of the bed and presses me back, my arms pinned under me as he lifts my legs and positions himself at my entrance, then with a man in complete control, slowly presses into my soaked cunt.

"Mmm, such a good fucking girl," he praises. "You're gonna come on my cock."

Wesley crawls down the bed and leans over me, swallowing my moans with deep kisses. I'm theirs. There is nothing I can do to stop the sweetest torture they're giving me. I moan loudly into Wes's mouth when Zander hits the sweet spot within me over and over with precision. I don't know how much longer I'll be able to hold out, but that's the point. He wants me to come. So instead of fighting to hold out longer, I let go. I clamp around him so hard and struggle to breathe with Wesley sucking the air out of my lungs.

"That's it, Luna. Milk my cock," he says through gritted teeth, and I know Zander's getting close. "Wes, play with yourself."

Wes goes up on his knees and jerks his dick over my face, his eyes never leaving mine. The muscles in his forearm bunch and his abs contract as he does what he's told. Zander reaches forward, covering my mouth and pinching my nose. My body jerks in response as I fight to breathe. I wasn't expecting it and didn't prepare for it. I widen my eyes in pure panic as fight mode sets in—every cell in my body electrifies.

"Riley," he says my name like an answered prayer as he releases me. He allows me to breathe again, and I arch up off the bed, inhaling deeply into my lungs and shuddering into a mini orgasm. My arms ache from being pinned under me, and I wish I could reach out to touch them. My handsome knights.

"Move Zan. My turn."

Wesley climbs off the bed, and grabs my hips before lining himself up and slowly sinking in. The mixture of mine and Zander's come, making it easy to slide in.

"Forget about that plug you gave her?" he asks, tugging at the bulbous toy. I close my eyes and moan when he pops the toy out.

"Nope, just wanted her to feel good tonight."

I flutter my eyes open to see Zander watching us from the chair set up in the corner. He smirks at me, and I know I must look a mess; but I don't have it in me to care. I'm too far gone now.

"Come Wes. Come in me," I moan.

And he does. He thrusts a few more times, the corded muscles in his neck strain before his face goes slack and he empties inside of me. We all breathe as a collective unit, letting our heart rates settle down again. Before I can mention my arms to Zander, he helps me sit and unfastens the cuffs. He takes my hands in his and examines them. When he's satisfied with them, he places a kiss on each wrist and then wraps his large hand into my hair at the nape of my neck, pulling me in for a loving kiss. It's so gentle, completely different from what we just did.

He drops his forehead to mine and on a whispered breath says, "I love you."

I smile, unable to help myself as I repeat the words, "I love you, too."

THIRTY-THREE

RILEY

I haven't seen Julien since we got back from Boston. He's probably in his room planning on how to annoy me in more ways. I can't get what Leah said out of my head though. The thought of asking him what I can do to help him hate me less has floated through my mind so many times, but each time I work up the courage to offer, something else happens and he pushes me away.

I sit at the dining table, sipping the last of my large glass of water Zander made me drink. I've asked the guys before about Julien, but I've never gotten straight answers. Maybe now's the time to ask. His dad is out of prison, which is what he wanted, based on the lovely call he had with my dad. Am I useful to him anymore, or is he dropping me like yesterday's trash?

Or is Leah actually right, and he's hiding true feelings? Could all of this be some form of foreplay? I shake my head at the thought.

"Whatcha thinking about?" Wes asks.

I look over at him and wrinkle my nose as I smile at him. "Nothing. Just something stupid Leah said."

Another thing that has been weighing on me is what exactly happened to Julien? I know my thought was if they want me to know, they will tell me; but they have said nothing and I really want to know. "Hey, I didn't ask, but how did Julien get a black eye? Did he have a fight I didn't know about?"

Wesley flexes his hand, as if he's remembering. "I punched him."

My brows raise in surprise. Okay, so that's not exactly the answer I was expecting.

"We were supposed to be there for fright night, but his dad was getting released and we needed to be with him. The guards released him later than they were supposed to, so we were delayed in getting back to campus. Derek never should have been able to get to you." He clenches his hand into a fist as his nostrils flare.

I nod, knowing it's best to leave that bit of information alone. "Why does he need me? What's the endgame to all of this?"

They exchange glances before looking at me again. Zander shakes his head, and I sigh, my shoulders slumping.

"Ask him, Hellcat."

That's the one thing I didn't want him to say. Things between us are rocky. I'm not sure how to navigate these waters we're in. There's something that keeps drawing me to him. Some unexplained thing. My brain can't make heads or tails of it. And the secrets are only creating a bigger void.

I nod, deciding I'm going to do just that. My stomach flips with anxiety as the guys stay behind in the kitchen and I make my way upstairs. I take the steps slower than usual, working through the words I want to say to him. I want answers, but he's never been straightforward with me. So why would he be now? I reach the landing. My heart beats quicker with each step I take toward his door.

My hand shakes as I close my fingers into a fist and give three quiet knocks. I hold my breath, waiting for any sign that he has heard me. I purse my lips when he doesn't answer and I knock a little louder. Maybe he's in the shower? My fingers close around the knob, and it twists with ease. Holding my head up high, I push the door open…and freeze.

Well, he's not in the shower, but now I wish he was. No, he's relaxed against the headboard, AirPods in, sweats down around his hips, and his hand is working overtime on his very hard cock. His eyes are closed, he doesn't even know I've walked in. I could walk out, close the door and pretend I've seen nothing. Yeah, that's the best thing to do.

"Riley," he groans as he speeds up. My eyes shoot up to his face, panic rooting me to the spot, but his eyes are still closed.

"Fuck, that feels so good." He licks his lips and rocks his hips up, working himself over. He's got to be close; his chest rises and falls in a sporadic rhythm. The corded muscles in his neck strain with the building pleasure. "Suck it, Princess."

"Come for me," I whisper, unable to help it. I'm enraptured watching this beautiful man pleasure himself as he's thinking of me. That thought hits me hard. He's thinking of *me*. And he has no idea I'm watching him. My belly twists in desire as my eyes remain glued to his perfect form. I wonder what he's listening to. The urge to crawl to him, to breathe him in consumes my thoughts; but the fear of him stopping, or becoming angry keeps me rooted to the spot.

He clenches his teeth and breathes hard as spurts of come cover his abdomen and chest. Holy. Shit. Why did I stay and watch that? I could have easily closed the door and left, pretended not to see anything, and he would be none the wiser.

I lick my lips, taking shallow breaths as my body catches

up with what my mind knows was wrong. Julien opens his eyes and they lock with mine. He says nothing, doesn't move. He stays exactly where he is, almost as if he were expecting me. My face flames at the attention.

"You said my name."

His lips quirk at the corner, and he huffs out a laugh. He grabs a t-shirt that is lying next to him on the bed and cleans himself up; then he pulls his sweats back into place. He walks toward me, stalking me like prey. But I'm not afraid of him anymore. So much of Julien is for show. He acts tough, menacing, but I know that's not all of him; that's only a part.

He closes the door next to me, flipping the lock, trapping us here together. He's so close the heat radiating off him seeps into my skin, warming me further. Resting his forearm on the wall above my head, he leans closer, a hairsbreadth from my face.

"I said your name," he repeats my words back to me.

I bite my lip, forcing myself to stay calm. Julien tucks a strand of hair behind my ear and leans closer still. His breath fans over my face as I part my lips, unsure if I want to say something else or press up and kiss him. We remain frozen in this bubble of our own creation, breathing each other in.

"Why?" I finally gasp.

"Because you're the only one I ever think of."

My heart thrums wildly at his admission. I blink up at him, words escaping me. I'm the only one he ever thinks of. This is news to me. Why has he been so cruel? It's more than my father. I understand there are ties there, even if I don't know Alec personally, but my father is not me. I've tried more times than I can count to put our differences aside, and each time he shoots the olive branch down.

I'm vaguely aware of shaking my head before his plush lips crash down on mine. He presses me against the wall, which is a good thing because my entire body hums to life under his touch. Julien is willingly kissing me. Not out of anger, not out of some game. And he feels so familiar; almost as if I've shared this same kiss with him before. Something pricks at the back of my mind, but it's gone the moment he deepens the kiss. I wrap my arms around his shoulders as he hauls me up, wrapping my legs around his waist.

An annoying voice in the back of my mind sends warning flares up, and the lust haze fades away. My body tenses in his hold, and I know the moment he realizes it because he drops me and takes a much-needed step away. He pushes his fingers through his dark locks and drops his head, looking at the ground.

"What do you want, Riley?"

Riley. Not Princess. The atmosphere in the room grows heavy with an unspoken tension, the air itself seeming to thicken. He's shutting out the glimmer of vulnerability he was showing me only moments ago.

"What part am I playing in this game of yours?" If I don't ask about it now, I won't get the chance.

"Checkmate."

My phone pings with a new Evite message for Julien's birthday party this weekend. Students around campus pull their phones out, and from where I'm sitting bundled up at an outdoor table in the sun, I would assume a handful of them received an invitation. I wonder if this is going to be as big as the bonfire, but somehow I doubt that. Ava plops down next to me, smiling.

"Finally make up with Nick?" I ask.

"Something like that," she adds, a grin spreading across her face.

"Oh my God! Did you…?" I trail off, not wanting to draw attention.

She nods as her cheeks turn pink. "He was the one chasing us, and that's why he let me get away and into the house. Which, now I think of it, makes perfect sense. I know I'm not that fast of a runner."

I hold up my phone and shake it. "Tell me you got an invitation to Julien's birthday?" She nods. Well, at least I'll have someone to hang out with. I'm sure the guys will be busy running the party. "So my next question is, what the heck do we get him?" We both laugh and walk into the cafeteria to get some lunch. Lucas has been my shadow again today; so I invite him to sit down and eat with us. He's growing on me. I like him.

"What are you getting for Julien?" I ask him as I take a bite of my chicken parmesan sandwich. I've got to say, this cafeteria makes some killer meals; but this might be my favorite. The chicken is so crispy and juicy, and I swear the whole thing melts in your mouth. I do a little happy dance in my seat as Ava laughs at me.

He shrugs. "I don't know. A card, if he's lucky. This isn't exactly a gift-giving event. Most of us go to hang out, play pool, and drink. Their house is nicer than the dorms."

Yeah, he's not lying about that, but I have enjoyed having a private room. Lucas has his own too. "How many people show up?"

"Only about twenty of us, or so. It's a chill night. You'll have fun."

I wish I knew more about him so that I could get something he would truly love. Maybe the guys could help me.

We arrive at the house, and the party already seems to be in full swing. The music vibrates through the walls, and shadows of bodies are visible through the drawn blinds. Wesley and Zander agreed to let me come with Ava and Nick, so they could finish setting everything up. I push open the door, and Wesley beams at me.

"Hey, beautiful." He rushes over to me and scoops me up into a big hug, burying his nose in my hair. "Glad you made it. Let me get you something to drink."

"No jungle juice." I tried some of that at the bonfire, and couldn't drink it; it was too strong, and I don't need to be drunk. He smiles widely and helps me out of my jacket. I hold up an envelope. "Where should I put his gift?" The guys were no help, so I had to get some help from Leah, who somehow dug up a picture of Julien and his parents when he was young. I don't recall seeing personal pictures in his room, so I thought it might be nice to have.

He kisses my cheek. "I'll take it upstairs. Zan should be in the kitchen. Have him make you something."

We walk into the kitchen, and Zander is deep in the middle of a conversation with someone. When he sees me enter the room, he excuses himself and comes over, kissing me deeply. Nick whispers something to Ava, and then I hear him grunt. When I look at him, he's rubbing his side. Yeah, there's probably too much to explain right now about our dynamic, anyway. And not everyone is going to understand it.

"Can you get me something to drink?" He nods and gets me a bottle of beer from the fridge, and pops the top off before handing it to me. He then extends the same offer to Nick, completely disregarding Ava's frustrated growl when she is ignored. Nick hands her his and takes another from the fridge, smiling at Zander. It's a pure power move, and when

Ava kisses him, Zander looks like he wants to tear him apart limb from limb.

"Where's the birthday boy?" I ask, looking around at the familiar faces.

Zander glances around the room briefly and looks back at me. "Not sure. He was here a few minutes ago."

"I'm going to go find him. I'll be back in a few."

I give Zander one more kiss before excusing myself. All week long I've avoided Julien the best I could. Even in survival class, I stayed close to Chloe. She should be here somewhere, too. It was nice of them to invite her. I haven't spent a lot of time with Chloe, but she's a good person. We've studied together once in the library, and I've had a few meals with her, but that's about it. I feel like things are calming down now since Julien's dad has been released.

I decide to start from the ground up and open the basement door, closing it tightly behind me. I'm sure they don't want other partygoers down here; especially with the room Zander designed. As soon as I close the door, I hear voices from below. I stop breifly, but when I hear Julien's voice, I decide to keep going. With my heels, there's no way they haven't heard me. I reach the bottom of the stairs and freeze. An older version of Julien stares at me—the same vibrant green eyes piercing into my soul. Their conversation dies mid-sentence.

Julien slowly turns around.

"Sorry, I'll, um, I'll go back up. I just wanted to say happy birthday."

Alec smiles first. Not exactly a warm one, but it at least reaches his eyes. "Hello, Riley."

I look at Julien, and then back to his father, unsure if I should be anywhere near him. I get the feeling he's not a safe man if you're on his bad side. Clearing my throat, I say, "Hello."

The door opens and a set of footfalls creeps closer. I turn on my heel to see who it is, and my entire world turns. I step away, an involuntary response to the familiar face standing in front of me. Blood rushes quickly past my ears, as my heart pounds and sweat coats my palms. It all happens so fast.

"Uncle James, I believe you know Riley."

He offers a sad smile. "Hi."

I spin on my heel, my eyes locked on Julien's, and that's when I see him—truly see him. The summer boy who stole my heart and my virginity years ago. The one I haven't been able to forget about, no matter how hard I try. "Rhys?"

LEAVE A REVIEW

If you enjoyed this book, please consider leaving a review on your favorite platform so others can find me too!

THANK YOU!

Wow! I can't believe I wrote this book, and dare I say it's better than the first one. But none of that would be possible without the help of my amazing family, alpha readers, and beta readers. I appreciate all the time and energy you all have put into helping me create this series. And it makes me so happy you love it just as much as I do!

Amy Crull- I'm so glad we met (online anyway), you have been so incredibly helpful through every aspect of this story and have truly helped me shape it into something amazing! Thank you for being my alpha reader and giving me feedback that made me squeal in delight!

Jamie Buck- You and I have been on this ride for 8 years and I am so glad I have you in my corner. Thank you for always giving me your honest thoughts even when they sting!

Jenn Dean- Thank you for taking a chance on me, and for continuing to chat with me on the daily! I appreciate all your words of encouragement and daily morning messages.

Amie Ambers- I feel this book is like fate in bringing us together! You have been amazing to chat with and I love how invested you are, just like me! Thank you for taking my story on and helping me make it that much better! I appreciate you so so much, and I am so glad we connected though the book world!

Linda Tenda- Southern NH ladies for the win. I am forever grateful that you sent me a list of issues in my first book and trusted me enough to send you the second and taking a chance on it. Thank you so much for all your help to make this book even better!

Vicci Hine- One of my OG's. I love you, girlfriend. You are a gem and I look forward to when I get to see you (the few times a year I can). Thank you for listening to me, and for always putting a smile on my face when I read your feedback.

ABOUT THE AUTHOR

Cara Wade is a daydreamer and a lifelong teenybopper. Boy bands forever! She would love to spend the day in the kitchen baking up sweet treats but hates doing the dishes after. When she is not writing (or suffering writer's block) you can find her reading, hiking, or relaxing by the water. She lives in southern New Hampshire with her husband and children!

ALSO BY CARA WADE

Sugar and Spice

The Publicist (Hollywood Lust #1)

The Playboy (Hollywood Lust #2)

The Starlet (Hollywood Lust #3)

Ever After: A Dark Suspenseful Romance

Infatuated (Black Stallion Ranch #1)

Enamored (Black Stallion Ranch #2)

RISE: A Sin and Secrets Novella

High Rise Secrets (Sin and Secrets #3)

My New Forever (Falls Village Collection)

Darkened Truths (Kings of Pointebreak #1)

Darkened Desires (Kings of Pointebreak #2)

COMING SOON

Darkened Hearts (Kings of Pointebreak #3) - End of 2026

www.ingramcontent.com/pod-product-compliance
Lightning Source LLC
Chambersburg PA
CBHW010937140726
47988CB00010B/3499